PAIN
SLUT

THE **SUBS** CLUB
BOOK II

J.A. ROCK

RIPTIDE
PUBLISHING

Riptide Publishing
PO Box 1537
Burnsville, NC 28714
www.riptidepublishing.com

Pain Slut

Cover art: Kanaxa, kanaxa.com
Editor: Delphine Dryden, delphinedryden.com/editing
Layout: L.C. Chase, lcchase.com/design.htm

ISBN: 978-1-62649-346-9

First edition
February, 2016

Also available in ebook:
ISBN: 978-1-62649-345-2

PAIN
SLUT

THE **SUBS** CLUB
BOOK II

J.A. ROCK

RIPTIDE
PUBLISHING

TABLE
OF
CONTENTS

CHAPTER ONE

I was lying in dishabille on a steel exam table, my feet in a pair of stirrups, a hypodermic needle on a stand beside me—when my phone buzzed.

And kept buzzing.

My wrists were cuffed to the table, so I called to Bowser, who was sterilizing a scalpel over by the sink. "Can you hand me my phone?"

Bowser turned. Under his white lab coat, he wore a *THE DOCTOR IS IN* tee I'd given him years ago. "Now?"

"I'm expecting an important call." Mind fogged. Wrists sore. Rubber tubing tied tight around my balls. How I thought I'd be able to carry on a phone conversation in this state, *je ne savais pas*.

Bowser crossed the room and retrieved the phone from my messenger bag. Glanced at the screen as he approached me. "Not a call. Texts."

A moment of prodigious disappointment. Not the Beacon Center, then.

"Could you show me, please?" My voice was brusque, demanding. I felt slightly guilty about it.

He tried to swipe with a gloved finger, but the latex caught on the screen. He peeled off the glove with a snap that made my balls tighten. Then he swiped again and showed me the screen.

The texts were all from Kamen.

Dude were hangin at Dave's to talk Hal's b-day.

Hey do u still have my windbreaker?

Also, do you ever think about what if Barack Obama was clones?

I sighed and looked away, focusing on the jacaranda-blue wall of Bowser's office. The sharps container mounted on it. I stared at the biohazard symbol. "You can put it back." If my hands had been free, I'd have given a dismissive wave. To the manor born, my mother always said.

And she was one to talk.

Out of the corner of my eye I watched Bowser take my phone back and set it on my bag. He returned to the counter and pulled on a new glove. Placed the scalpel on a plastic tray with other medical tools, then took the tray to a minifridge in the corner and popped it inside. Went back to the counter, where he began warming a bag of saline solution with a hot plate. "Not what you were expecting?" he asked.

I studied the wall again. I'd first set foot in this room seven years ago. I'd been so nervous that I'd focused on figuring out what color the wall was. Not royal blue. Not blue-violet. "Just my friends. Who *know* I'm busy this afternoon."

I turned my gaze to the ceiling, trying to revert to the correct headspace. But now my mind was racing. The Beacon Center should have called by now. And Hal's birthday—really? Why were we celebrating a dead man's birthday?

"I liked that speech your friend Dave made a while back. At the roundtable."

"Ah, yes."

Bowser and I didn't usually make small talk when we played together. It was still strange to think we'd once been fairly close. Back when I was twenty-one and endlessly enthused about kink. The past seven years had lent no small measure of tedium to deviance.

He brought the clear bag of saline solution over to the exam table and hooked it to an IV stand near my left shoulder. "I actually think it's cool—the Subs Club. Even the review thing. I don't know why so many people were upset about it."

I tensed, trying not to recall that the last top who had brought up the Subs Club while I was tied down had held a knife to my face. And not in a fun way.

The Subs Club was an organization my friends Dave, Kamen, and Gould and I had started a couple of months ago. What had begun as an attempt to give submissives a private place to discuss safety concerns in the kink community had spiraled out of control when subs started posting reviews of individual doms on the Subs Club blog. In theory, this was advantageous—it let members call out "doms" who had abused or raped them in the past, and warn other members to stay away. And it let doms who were truly outstanding have their positive traits held up as paradigms.

We'd actually had a great deal of support. But our detractors had grown vocal, perhaps understandably so. In a way, the review blog had been a gross violation of privacy, despite the care we'd taken to only use doms' scene names. Eventually we'd reached a compromise with the community leaders—we would remove the review portion of the blog and focus instead on leading community roundtable discussions once a month at Riddle, a local dungeon. So far, it was working out fairly well.

I pulled against the cuffs again, enjoying the feel. "Are you just saying that because you had such good reviews?"

"Did I?" Bowser shook the tubing to unkink it.

I almost rolled my eyes at his attempt to be casual. Despite the Subs Club blog having a log-in system that prevented nonmembers—i.e., *doms*—from viewing it, plenty of doms had seen or at least heard about their reviews. "You know you did. Everyone loves you."

He grinned. "Just wanted to hear you say it."

Ah, but he was a filthy sweetheart. Dave always said he looked like a Viking, with his stout body, ginger beard, and wide nose. And it was Kamen who'd first pointed out that his laugh sounded exactly like Bowser's in *Super Mario 64*. Now pretty much everyone in the scene called him Bowser, and he was a good sport about it.

He picked up the prepackaged IV needle from the stand. "You sure you want to go through with this? If you're expecting an important call?"

"Of course." I flexed my fingers and pulled against the restraints until the cuffs bit into my wrists. My cock rose at the sight of the needle. My tied-off balls were slightly numb.

He unwrapped the needle. "And you're sure you're okay with at least twenty-four hours of this?"

Once the saline was in, it would be a day, maybe two before the swelling went down. "I've got nowhere to be."

"All right. Lookin' forward to seeing how you do with the infusion as opposed to the injection."

"Me too." I settled back against the table.

Last time we'd done a saline infusion, Bowser had injected the solution into me. The results had been a general lumpiness to my scrotum that had faded fast. This time we were going to try an IV drip, which we hoped would create a more symmetrical and sustainable swelling. He'd tied off my balls to prevent the solution from getting absorbed too quickly into the rest of my body.

Bowser attached the needle to the tubing and let the solution flow for a few seconds to get all the air out of the tube. With his other hand, he flipped open a bottle of Betadine and pressed a cotton ball to the opening. Tipped the bottle, dousing the cotton ball, then quickly swabbed the center of my scrotum. He let that dry, then used an alcohol pad to swab the area again. I tried not to flinch. No matter how many times I played with needles, there was always something disconcerting about them.

I was the only pain slut in my group of friends. I'd met a couple of others at Riddle, but I remained the most masochistic person I knew. I wanted it all—burning, cutting, piercing, choking, you name it. I wanted to scream, to bleed, and come out the other side feeling shaken and unsure and powerful all at once. I wanted someone to take me to that place, push me beyond what I thought I could endure.

And yet, perhaps foolishly, I wanted it done with love.

"Hold still." Bowser lifted my balls and deftly inserted the needle under the skin. I breathed through the sting, which was somehow harder to take than many of the worst whippings I'd ever received.

At first I didn't feel much of anything. But slowly the warm liquid spread, and my sac tightened. The tip of my cock smeared pre-cum over my belly, and my hands balled into fists.

Suddenly, a wave of guilt washed over me.

I wasn't supposed to be doing this. I was supposed to have given up kink weeks ago. *Months* ago. And yet here I was, playing doctor with Bowser.

"How's that feel?" He stroked my swelling balls with one finger.

I trembled, my jaw clenching. I was so sensitive I could have come just from that gentle touch.

What kind of father are you going to make?

"Miles?" Bowser looked concerned.

I nodded, reminding myself to breathe deeply. I shifted as the weight of my balls increased. My legs weren't cuffed, and I had to struggle to keep my feet in the stirrups. I wanted to press my legs together, do *something* to lessen the discomfort of being here, completely exposed, with my balls gradually expanding.

Fifteen minutes went by.

Bowser kept stroking. He slid his finger into my ass crack and circled my hole. The rubber tube around my balls was biting into the flesh now, and the IV bag was about two-thirds empty.

"I'm gonna untie this." Bowser undid the rubber tubing. I watched my massive balls wobble against my groin. Swallowed at the prickling sensation as blood rushed back into the area. It looked like I had a balloon between my legs—the sac taut, every vein visible beneath the skin. The discomfort turned to something closer to pain as I was stretched further.

I hissed. "It feels so weird."

What the hell kind of father? Seriously, Miles.

Cheryl Callahan from the Beacon Center was going to call any day now to schedule my first home visit, and here I was definitely proving that I had no business being a parent.

"It looks amazing." Bowser lifted my balls. "Hurt?"

I shook my head. "Not— Ah!" I closed my eyes briefly as Bowser continued to heft. He flicked lightly, and I dragged air through my teeth.

I looked at the wall again. Bowser had a pleasant, quiet house. It was one of the reasons I continued to play with him. That and his formidable knowledge of erotic medical torture.

He poked my balls again. "Just sensitive, huh?"

"Yes."

This was always how Bowser and I played—he didn't do any of the hard-ass–dom posturing, and I didn't do any of the submissive *yes sir, please sir.* I was here for pain, and he was here to give it to me.

He moved to his minifridge. Opened it and took out the tray of metal tools. *Oh fuck. Yes.*

He picked up a scalpel, which gleamed in the dim light. My dick throbbed, and my throat tightened.

"Oh God," I whispered, as the saline stretched my balls further. The bag was nearly empty now, but my sac was still swelling. I'd worn loose sweatpants, but I was nervous about putting even those on when we were done. And underwear was simply not an option.

Bowser held the scalpel a few inches above my balls. I got a flash of fear that made my lungs seize, my ears ring, the inside of my skull ache. I caught the words between my teeth and crushed them: *Don't, please, please, don't. God, no* . . .

"I know you know this," he said quietly, "but *don't move.*"

"No shit." I took a deep breath and let it out as he pressed the side of the scalpel flat against my balls. It was cold, but I didn't let myself jump. I moaned, feeling all of the stress over Beacon Center and my iniquity vanish as I gave myself over to the thrill of this moment. If I moved, even a little bit, he could slit my skin. Blood would pour over my balls, a hot rush over cold metal, and . . . *Shit, shit, shit,* just the idea made me want to squirm.

I kept my breathing steady and even. Closed my eyes for a second so I could concentrate on the chill of the metal. The way it both numbed my nerves and roused them. I opened my eyes again so I could watch. Bowser dragged the flat of the scalpel lightly over my scrotum. Tilted it just slightly, for a fraction of an instant. Almost immediately, a thin line of blood appeared. I watched in fascination. Bowser put down the scalpel, unwrapped another alcohol pad, and wiped the blood away. The sting of the alcohol made me arch against the table. He held the pad against the wound until the bleeding stopped.

He gave me another small cut with the scalpel, and I closed my eyes, hoping to feel the blood run a little before he wiped it away. I sighed, all at once deeply peaceful.

"There you go," Bowser whispered, keeping a light pressure on the cut.

I smiled.

"You look really good."

I opened my eyes. "You don't have to say things like that."

He leaned over and sucked my left nipple. It surprised me—he was rarely sexual with me. But it felt *so* damn good. Warm and wet, his beard scraping my pecs, his teeth catching my nipple for the barest sliver of a moment, making me gasp. He walked around the table and sucked the other one too, until I was almost sore, until my cock was tapping my belly every few seconds, leaving a damp spot on the skin.

He threw the alcohol pad away, wrapped the scalpel for sterilization, and applied a clear dressing on the cuts before bandaging them. He changed his gloves and picked up a genital whip. My stomach constricted. That thing hurt even when my balls weren't five times their normal size. It looked like a miniature flogger—about the length of my hand. But the falls were strands of plastic beads.

He brushed the plastic falls down my chest, over my stomach. Whacked each nipple, making me jump as the tiny beads stung the swollen peaks. He stopped just under my navel to lightly flog the area above my groin. Since my dick was still pressed against my belly, the falls struck the head a couple of times, and I gulped, tears of sheer pain streaming from my eyes.

He raised the whip and brought it down hard on my balls.

I screamed.

He struck me again, this time on the underside of my taut scrotum.

I clenched and released my hands, pulling against the cuffs. My legs trembled with the effort of keeping them in the stirrups.

He grabbed the alcohol pad and used it to clean off one of the plastic strands. Then he drizzled a bit of lube on that strand. It took me a second to realize what he was up to. Then he began to feed the thin, beaded fall into the slit of my dick.

I choked, beyond screaming. The tears came faster now, and my whole body started to shake. He pushed the fall a little deeper. I bucked, hauling against the wrist cuffs. I had to piss, had to come, had to get enough breath to shout. Deeper. I could feel the tiny beads rub the inside of my dick, and a sort of slippery queasiness formed in my core, followed by a rush of heat and something almost like panic—but wonderful. Bowser slapped my inflated balls with his free hand. I kicked against the stirrups, my back arching. He wiggled the genital whip so the falls whapped against my cock. The one inside me quivered, increasing my agony and ecstasy until I was gritting my teeth to keep from begging for release.

Then Bowser did something surprising. He stroked my shoulder gently with his free hand, then wrapped his arm around me and guided my head against his broad chest. Held me and leaned down to press his lips to my temple. His Viking beard was coarse against my skin. I felt so *comforted* in that moment, so astonished by a flood of emotion I couldn't identify, that I barely noticed when he started moving the whip again. Softly at first, then harder and harder until I couldn't ignore the pain as the strands caught my hypersensitive balls. Until I was curling and uncurling my fingers, my legs shaking so hard they didn't seem under my control anymore. The gauze over my cuts deflected a couple of the blows, but it didn't help much.

Two sensations collided—physical agony and a desperate *need* for him to keep holding me. I nearly pressed my face against his shirt and cried. Instead, I clamped my jaw, took a breath, and held perfectly still.

He released me. Pulled the fall out of my dick and gave me two lashes across my balls. Pressure welled inside me, and I felt a warmth inside my shaft, as though I were coming. But nothing happened. I was still right there on the edge, desperate, and I couldn't go over.

He gripped my cock and started pumping.

"You wanna come?" he asked.

I didn't know if I could. Each time he pumped, his fist hit my engorged balls and knocked the air out of me.

"Go on," he whispered. "I wanna see you come with your balls the size of a fucking melon."

I panted, groaning softly. He held the whip in his other hand and started striking my balls full force. I inhaled with a choked cry, my face contorting. It was like someone was punching me just below the belly button, but from the inside. My bladder felt like it was going to fucking burst.

He paused, and I struggled for a second against the tension in my throat before my breath rushed out. "Yeah," I whispered. "Fuck yeah."

"Spread those legs."

My feet were still in the stirrups, but my knees were dropping toward each other in an involuntary effort to shield my groin. I spread as wide as I could. He lashed the whip upward, striking my asshole and the skin behind my balls, and I whimpered, my stomach spasming. He kept his hand moving on my cock, and everything was discord and brilliance. Mismatched rhythm and different levels of sickness and pleasure.

"I can't. I really can't." It was too much—sensitized skin, the fear that if this went on any longer, I'd be sick on his table.

He stroked my shoulder. Brushed his lips over the edge of my ear, flicked my balls. His whisper was nearly drowned out by my grunt of determination. "Try."

He went back to stroking my balls, and I closed my eyes, concentrating on his touch, on the feel of the needle under my skin when I moved a certain way. He placed his thumb on the scar from my PA piercing, and a memory flashed through me of him playing with the ring, back when I still wore it.

I imagined he was my partner. Not just for this afternoon, but forever. And I was so embarrassed by the fantasy that I dashed it out of existence, like swiping at a drawing I'd made in the sand. I didn't want that illusion to be part of what made me come. I wanted the pain to do it. I wanted to be able to leave Bowser's with a friendly handshake.

He was staring at my balls, his own breathing harsh, one hand hovering at the front of his pants. I wanted to invite him to touch himself.

When I did come, it was sort of a pathetic drizzle. I lay back against the steel table, relieved.

He drew the needle out of my balls and disposed of it in the sharps container. Removed his gloves, then undid the wrist cuffs. I slid my feet from the stirrups and let them dangle off the sides of the table.

"Do you wanna . . .?" I tipped my head toward his crotch. "Or want me to . . .?"

He shook his head. "It's okay."

He tried to help me clean up the needle entry site, but I took the alcohol pad and did it myself. I felt awkward now that we were finished.

He took the pad from me and tossed it in the trash. "So how'd that stack up to the injection?"

"Better." I glanced down at my balls. "They look a lot more even. I don't know how I'm supposed to stand up, though."

"You can hang out here as long as you want." He paused. "But I know you like to bolt as soon as we're done."

"You know me too well."

"You need anything? Tylenol? Water? A hug?"

Part of me wanted to accept. And part of me shut down the idea immediately. "I'm good. I think I'll just head home."

There was something forced about his smile. "Some things don't change."

I laughed. "We really have been doing this a long time."

"Uh-huh."

I folded my hands over my belly. "Sometimes it just feels so comfortable that I wish I didn't have to . . ."

"What?"

"Seek out new partners. Explain myself to them."

He pulled a rolling chair over to the exam table and sat.

I looked at him. "Do you ever feel like that?"

"Commitment's not really for me. Sorry."

"Oh no. No, no, I didn't mean that I want to—" I stopped before I could say something truly insensitive. "Not that you're not . . . I just wasn't thinking about that. I prefer that things remain casual."

But every once in a while I wanted something passionate with someone who was just mine.

Bowser flicked my balls affectionately. "Well, anytime you wanna get off, you know you can *come* here."

I snorted. "I appreciate that. And will most likely take you up on that. Many times."

He opened his mouth, hesitated, and then closed it again.

"What?" I asked.

"We've been playin' for years. I guess I always hoped one of these days, you'd actually submit to me."

I raised my brows. "I was just tied to a table while you stuck a needle in my balls and cut my scrotum."

He offered a hint of the *Mario* laugh. "I know. You do a real good job takin' what I give you. You're just a little clinical about it. Even when you're cryin' from the pain, you feel kinda removed from *me*."

That actually hurt. But I forced a grin. "Yeah, well. You can't have it both ways. You want to keep it casual, you can't expect me to cry in your arms and sleep in your bed."

"I know. I oughta shut up."

"I've never felt like much of a submissive. A bottom and a pain pig, more like."

"Well, hey. That's—"

My phone buzzed. I sat up and tried, not quite successfully, to move my lower body. "Could you . . . ?"

Bowser walked over to my bag and retrieved the phone. Handed it to me.

Texts from Jason, one of my employees at A2A Wear. Frantic and past the point of coherency.

Problem with the rush order I don't know what to do please come in shirts are wrong too late to do anything its team funeral they'll freak out omg omg.

Jason must have been sincerely distressed to forego punctuation. My heart started pounding as I realized there was no way I could go into the shop when my balls were the size of a melon.

"I'm sorry," I told Bowser. "I have to make a call."

And so I sat naked on the exam table with my balloon balls resting on my thighs and called Jason. His story was even less coherent over the phone. Apparently a very large and important shipment of T-shirts had a spelling error. I started to ask if he could text me pictures of the disaster, but his voice got half an octave higher, and I said, "Forget it. I'm coming in."

"Trouble?" Bowser asked when I hung up.

"A work emergency." I put down the phone. "Fuck. I'm so sorry. I need to be there." I glanced at my balls again. "But . . ."

"You wanna borrow a T-shirt? XXL?"

The only thing worse than going to work with an inflated scrotum would be going into work in sweatpants and a T-shirt. But I had little choice.

I sighed and struggled to my feet. "All right. Show me what you've got."

CHAPTER
TWO

I parked in A2A's side lot, facing away from the street. Slid carefully from behind the wheel, attempting to subtly support my balls with my hand. I'd borrowed XL sweatpants from Bowser because my own had been too tight, as well as his baggiest T-shirt and a hoodie that matched the pants, but there was no way the clothes were going to fully hide my condition. Whatever this T-shirt crisis was, I should have told Jason he had to solve it himself.

Except I was A2A's owner, and I was a control freak, and I needed to know what was going on. I shuffled toward the door.

As soon as Jason saw me, he started flapping his arms. "Miles—"

"Jason? Take a breath."

He paused momentarily in his fluttering as I approached. "Why are you wearing a sweat suit?"

"Long story. What's the problem?"

Jason looked horrified. Jason always looked vaguely horrified.

"Jason, don't look so horrified."

"I can't help it. They're going to *freak*."

"Who?"

"It's the Team Funeral shirts."

Oh God.

Team Funeral. The Segers, who had placed a rush order by phone last week for twelve matching T-shirts to be worn at a relative's funeral. Why a family would wear matching T-shirts to a funeral was beyond me, but they had added a generous tip on top of the rush price, and I'd promised we would have the shirts done in time for the service.

I ignored the discomfort as my swollen, welted balls rubbed against the front of my pants. "What happened to the shirts?"

Jason pulled a seafoam T-shirt out of the box. Shook it out. I read the purple airbrushed letters: *UNCLE MATT, REST NOW WITH THE ANGLES.*

"Oh dear."

Jason's head popped out from behind the shirt. "I looked for the original order to see if it was their mistake or ours. And it was theirs; they definitely spelled it 'angles' on their form. But—"

"But we should have caught it," I finished. We prided ourselves in checking submissions carefully. We'd been able to stop an "Andesron" soccer jersey from happening, as well as a *Will Work for Foot* hoodie and an order of five hundred *My Other Cat Is the Millennium Falcon* bumper stickers.

"And their funeral is tomorrow!" Jason sounded dangerously close to hyperventilating. My friends all thought *I* was wound too tight. I really, *really* wanted to introduce them to Jason. Except that anytime one of them stopped by the store, Jason was always charming and serene as a Constable painting. "I mean, not *their* funeral, but . . ."

I nodded. "And perhaps our funeral too. I'll give them a call."

I got on the computer and pulled up the Segers' order. Gave the number a call.

"Hello?" The voice that answered was soft and calm.

"Hi, Mr. Seger? This is Miles Loucks from A2A Wear. Your—"

"Hi, Miles."

I paused at the interruption. "Yes, hi. Your order's ready for pickup, but we've just noticed a problem."

"Oh?" He didn't sound ready to kill, so that was something.

I explained the situation to him. There was silence when I finished. Then he said, without the slightest change in tone, "I'm in the neighborhood. I'll stop by and see how bad it is."

"It's pretty bad," I admitted. "I mean, the shirts all say that your uncle is resting with the angles."

He laughed. "It's all right, Miles." The way he said my name was quite beautiful. And God, what was with that voice? It had an otherworldly quality, like he was narrating the prologue to some epic fantasy movie. "I'll be over in a few minutes."

No. No. Terrible. I did not want to meet the man whose order I had failed to proofread while I was wearing a sweat suit three sizes too large and my testicles were the size of regulation softballs. "Listen . . ."

But he'd already hung up.

"You'll have to deal with him," I told Jason. "I need to get out of sight."

"What? No! You're the one who knows how to talk to people."

"Jason, I'm wearing a sweat suit. I can't possibly interact with him."

"What do I say?"

"Apologize. Offer him a refund—fifty percent, since technically it was their mistake. Offer to reprint the shirts, even though the new ones won't be ready in time for the funeral. I'm going to the back to take inventory."

I left Jason standing there stammering and took refuge in the back room. There I didn't have to worry about keeping my crotch sheltered. The air was warm and held the vinegary smell of new shirts. I took out my tablet and pulled up the inventory list.

I'd opened A2A three years ago. My friends had thought a T-shirt design company was a bit of an odd choice for me, since I struck them as neither particularly creative nor fashion-conscious. My cardigan-heavy wardrobe contained, as Dave was fond of saying, Mr. Rogers's rejects, and I tended to judge harshly anyone over sixteen who wore graphic tees. But the demand was high, and I had a good head for business and a great creative team. Even Jason, who practically burst into tears if the cash register drawer was slow to open, had surprisingly viable ideas.

My friends had all been very supportive. Kamen had been adamant that I name the shop No Shirt, Sherlock, but had eventually come around to the idea of Arm 2 Arm Wear—A2A for short. Dave and Gould had helped me decorate. Our tech-support friend, Ricky, had done the website. A2A currently had a four point six on Yelp, and the store was probably the accomplishment I was most proud of.

Which made "resting with the angles" all the harder to deal with.

After a few minutes, I realized I needed a couple of boxes that were under the register counter. I hobbled cautiously into the front. No sign of Mr. Seger. Jason was out on the floor, organizing the clearance racks.

I went around the counter and soon discovered that crouching was not an option. Keeping my legs stiff, I bent at the waist and lifted one of the boxes out. Set it on the counter. As I lifted the second box, someone slapped a sheet of paper on the counter and left his hand on it. White dude. No wedding ring. Overgrown cuticles. Nice nails. Faint knuckle hair.

I looked up. And up. Until I got to his face, which was closer to the ceiling than I was accustomed to faces being.

La beauté.

I would estimate that eighty percent of the people I encountered were acceptable looking. Twelve percent were captivatingly ugly. Five percent were celebrities and had help. And three percent were outlandishly beautiful.

Mr. Seger was probably close to six foot seven. Lean, and long-limbed. He wore an odd overcoat—knee-length, black, with a belt and a Sherlockian turned-up collar. Long, dark-gold hair gathered into a ponytail, and his eyes—were they *purple*?

"Miles?" That same low, gentle voice from the phone.

I straightened partway, but kept my knees bent enough that my crotch was hidden behind the counter. "Yes?"

When I met his gaze, he smiled.

"I'm Mr. Seger."

I caught Jason's frozen expression from over by the racks. Looked back at Mr. Seger, who appeared too young to be a "mister." "Hello, Mr. Seger. I'm Miles Loucks. I'm the owner. And I can't tell you how sorry I am about—"

"May I see the shirts?"

He didn't sound demanding in the least. Just cheerful and amused.

I had to reach sideways for the box to avoid leaving the shelter of the counter. I removed one shirt and shook it out, as Jason had done. Mr. Seger took it from me, and our fingers brushed. I might as well have been in high school again, jolting when Tyson Ellis handed me his Jell-O at lunch. My face heated, and I waited for the implosion.

But Mr. Seger laughed. And laughed some more.

Rich sound. White teeth. Absurdly sharp canines. My cock, despite being weighed down by a balloon filled with sand, was more than a bit interested in Mr. Seger's laugh.

He wiped under his eye with one finger. "Oh. Oh, oh. Uncle Matt would have *loved* this."

"I'm so sorry," I said again. I didn't really feel *guilty* per se—I have a hard time sympathizing with other people's grammatical errors, or with the idea of wearing matching shirts to a funeral—but I was sorry about the potential negative Yelp review. "We can offer you a partial refund—"

"No, no. It's all right." He folded the shirt and set it back on the box. "I've looked at the order form. It was my mistake."

"We usually proofread carefully, and check with the customer if there's any confusion about spelling. I can't believe I didn't catch this."

He was looking at me with his head tilted, a half smile still on his face. Those pointed teeth were really throwing me. "Please don't feel guilty."

"I understand how much stress you must be dealing with. You didn't need this on top of it." I winced as I shifted and my balls rolled along the side of my thigh.

He leaned forward slightly, gazing into my eyes as though—well, as though he were about to kiss me. "I suppose there is one way you could make it up to me."

I was startled. My apologies were really just a formality, given that *I* hadn't been the one to misspell angels. "Yes?"

"Could I take you to dinner?"

What?

I mean truly, *what?*

At what point had I given him *any* indication that I . . .

But when I opened my mouth to refuse, politely but with enough of an edge to let him know that his offer was entirely inappropriate, the words "All right" came out.

"Friday night?" Mr. Seger smiled softly at me. The sort of smile you gave someone you'd known far longer than five minutes.

No. No, no. This was not happening. I was not standing here in a sweat suit trying to hide my engorged balls behind a counter while a towering, ponytailed stranger asked me to dinner.

And yet, I said, "Okay."

He straightened. "I'd like to get my full name out of the way now. Feel free to laugh."

Who was *this joker?*

"How bad can it be?"

"Hendrix Seger."

I hesitated. "Like . . ."

"Like my last name is Seger, as in Bob, and my parents liked Jimi Hendrix."

A bark of laughter escaped. "I'm so sorry."

He grinned. "I'm pretty used to it. I go by Drix, which makes me sound like a douche bag action hero. But 'Hend' wasn't really an option."

I tried a movie preview voice. "Drix Seger stars in . . . *Shirtsaster!*" What was wrong with me? This was a grieving stranger. And his funeral shirts were ruined. I flushed. "I'm so sorry. Again."

"I won't require any more apologies." He spoke quietly, sounded amused.

I studied him a moment. Decided I liked something about him. His certainty, his oddness, his teeth. His *voice.*

He took out his phone. "What's your number?"

I gave it to him.

"I'll text you closer to Friday."

And just like that, I had a dinner date.

I drove toward Dave and Gould's, feeling floaty, distant. The pressure of my balls against the steering wheel kept bringing me back to reality every few seconds.

A date. I had a date.

And I hadn't even had to do anything except fuck up the guy's order and wear a baggy sweat suit. Which made me suspicious. *Why* was Hendrix Seger interested in me?

I turned onto Wayne Street. I'd been friends with Dave, Gould, and Kamen for going on seven years now. We'd met when I was twenty-two and they were twenty, and we'd gotten along right away, despite some notable disparities in personality. Kamen was as laid-back as they came. Dave was more volatile, but in such an earnest and cheerful way that most people forgave his overexcited moments. Gould was so quiet that he tended to appear chill—though I suspected he dealt with more anxiety than the rest of us put together.

And then there was me: humorless Miles, with his Fred Rogers cardigans and the stick up his ass. I preferred to see myself as the mature one. The intellectual. The stoic voice of reason. But apparently this was not a universal perception.

We were an odd crew. Dave thought of us as a family; I thought of us as profoundly codependent. I was particularly confounded by how we'd ended up in this exclusive little queer-man cluster, with nary a straight or female friend in sight. I'd tried to have other friends of other genders and orientations over the years, but it seemed like those relationships faded quickly, leaving me once more in the company of my nonheterosexual male brethren.

We'd had a fifth member in our group—Hal. Reckless, fun-loving. An absolute cad, but as charismatic as they came. He'd died nearly two years ago during a bondage scene. It had been, to put it mildly, a blow to our group. Especially when Bill Henson, the dom who'd left Hal tied up alone with a cord around his neck, had been found innocent of second-degree murder.

I parked on the street in between a minivan and a stubby smart car. Headed to the front porch of the duplex, keeping my hand in front of my balls. Before I reached the door, my phone buzzed.

Cheryl Callahan was calling.

"Miles, hi!" Cheryl sounded cheerful, as usual. She'd probably sound exuberant even as she told me my dreams of adopting a child were dead. "I have some good news."

I gripped the phone tighter. "Oh?"

"Yes. Your interviews and background check all went great. So how would you feel about us beginning your home study?"

Oh God. Oh God oh God oh God. Breathe.

"That's wonderful," I managed.

"So what I'd like to do now is set up a time in the next couple of weeks for us to meet at your house. The visit shouldn't last more than three hours, and it's just a chance for me to get to know you and your environment better. We'll talk about your family, your routines, your neighborhood . . ."

My family. Oh God. "No problem."

"It's really not that scary, I promise. So if you'll email me what your schedule looks like, we'll set up a time and get rolling on this."

I wanted to ask what I could do to make sure I aced this. Like it was a test—which, in a way, it was. And yet I didn't want to give away that I was nervous. I wanted her to show up to my house and see that it was naturally a wonderful environment for a child. That everything I did and owned and enjoyed fell right in line with what the Beacon Center wanted to see.

"My schedule is fairly flexible," I said. "I'm self-employed, so really, I can make almost any time work. The sooner the better."

"Okay. How do you feel about next Monday, then? Three o'clock?"

"Perfect." I was still gripping the phone so hard my fingers hurt. "Um, can I ask you something?"

"Of course."

"Did you do interviews with my parents and my sister?"

"I did."

"And they were . . . They went fine?"

"Absolutely."

Interesting. Cheryl and I said good-bye and hung up.

I stood staring at the duplex door for a moment.

I'd been putting off telling my friends that I was trying to adopt. I wasn't sure why exactly, other than the fact that I was afraid of screwing this up. Afraid the Beacon Center wouldn't approve me, and that I'd then have to explain my failure to the group.

But now . . .

Why not? Why not tell them?

The door was unlocked. It was always unlocked, no matter how often I lectured Dave and Gould about locking it. I was too excited to care. I couldn't determine how much of my excitement was actually blind terror, but for the first time in weeks, I felt . . .

Really fucking hopeful.

The others were at the kitchen table, as usual. Years ago, Dave's father had built this giant, lacquered dining table, and Dave and Gould had found a fairly nice set of chairs at a garage sale, and we'd all started hanging out around the table. Dave and Gould's kitchen was open and roomy, and they kept it well stocked with food and beer. Kamen even had a spare guitar here just so he could entertain us during hang-out sessions and Subs Club meetings.

I had a nice house—bigger but less homey than the duplex. My pantry contained a few sad-looking cans of beans and vegetables, and about twelve boxes of cracked-pepper thin crisps. This was something I intended to work on before my home study. I needed to make my place seem lived-in. Kid-friendly. A place where one could eat things besides thin crisps.

"Miles!" Kamen threw an M&M at me as I entered. "What kind of cake would Hal want?"

"Since we never really celebrated his birthday when he was alive, it's hard to say." I pulled out a chair and sat. *Very* carefully.

Kamen was staring at me. "Dude, do you have to poop or something?"

"What?" I glanced up.

"You're sitting like you're trying not to shit your pants."

Kamen. Doofus extraordinaire. Lovable, clueless, and still experiencing eight-year-old levels of amusement at anything stool-related. "My back just hurts from work."

Dave and Gould, who had been talking to each other, turned at that. Dave grinned. "Miles probably got laid."

"Nope."

Dave scooted his chair in. "We were thinking about vanilla cake. Because, you know, irony. Plus Gould can't sleep when he has chocolate."

I shot Gould a questioning look. He shrugged.

I adjusted my shirt over my crotch, but now that I was sitting, it was difficult to cover the situation. "Can someone tell me why we're throwing Hal a birthday party?"

Dave cleared his throat. "We were talking about it last month, but you were too busy freaking out about a work email to listen. We thought it would be a good way to remember Hal."

Kamen nodded. "Mostly we just haven't had cake in a while."

I tried to grab the M&M bowl without jostling my balls. All I could think about was the home study on Monday.

"Dude," Kamen said to me. "I don't wanna be the one who points this out, but are you hard?"

Suddenly Dave was leaning across the table to see me. "Oh my God. Miles. What is going *on* down there? Is the alien from *Alien* about to explode from your balls? Are you gonna have a crotchburster?"

Now even Gould leaned over. Quiet, compassionate Gould. Surely I could count on him not to interrogate me. He looked up and met my gaze questioningly. "Saline?"

I nodded.

"Wait, what?" Kamen asked.

Gould turned to him. "You can inject saline solution into parts of the body to make them swell."

Kamen glanced at my crotch again. Then up at me. Then down. "But . . . but . . ." Up at me. His jaw dropped. "Did you do that to your *balls*?"

I sighed. "You know, I did actually want to talk to you guys about something serious. But if all you can focus on—"

Dave sat back. "Is that your balls look like they could be manacled to prisoners' ankles to keep them from escaping? Forgive us."

"Oh my God," Kamen said. "That's why you're wearing a matching sweat suit instead of your Mr. Rogers sweaters."

I sighed again and looked up at the ceiling.

Gould shifted. "What's your serious thing, Miles?"

"No. I'm not telling you now."

"Come on," they chorused.

I bestowed a withering glare on each of them. Then I took a deep breath. "I just got some news."

They were all staring at me. It was now or never.

"So for the past few months, I've been in contact with the Beacon Center."

Dave nodded. "Is that the retirement home you're moving in to?"

I ignored him. "It's an adoption agency."

Dead silence.

"Are you adopted too?" Kamen asked. "Like your sister?"

"No, I'm not adopted." Did I really have to spell it out for them? "I'm *adopting*."

They just stared.

Dave's brow furrowed. "Adopting what?"

"A child," I said.

More staring.

"But you put electricity up your ass." Dave said it calmly, slowly, as though there were some very simple aspect of this situation I'd failed to grasp.

"What does that have to do with—"

"If you have a kid, how are you going to explain your TENS unit? 'Oh, don't mind this, kiddo, that's just for when your old pop needs to electrocute his own rectum . . .'"

I shook my head at him, stunned. "What are you *talking* about?"

"Are you saying you don't have any qualms about the fact that you're a huge masochist and you want to adopt a kid?"

"What, you think I'd be a bad father?"

"No, no. I just . . . wow."

"You're, like, not much older than us," Kamen said. "And you want *kids*?"

"I'm twenty-eight. Lots of people have kids by my age. By *your* age too."

"But don't you want to wait until you have a partner or something?"

Oh my God. My friends thought I wasn't ready to be a father. *Me*. The only one of us who had his own business. Who lived in a *house*, not an apartment. Who knew how to do taxes without software.

I shook my head again, irritated. "I'm not going to wait around for my dream man to show up." I looked to see if any of them planned to give me any support.

"We don't have any money," Dave said, as though the four of us were collectively adopting my theoretical child.

"*You* don't have any money," I pointed out, my anger growing. "I've been saving for a long time. You guys act like I haven't thought this through. I've been planning to do this for *years*."

"You never told us!"

"How many times have I told you I want children?" I demanded.

Dave stammered. "I just thought you meant when you were, like, thirty-five."

Kamen gave his guitar string a tentative pluck. "Do they even let single dudes adopt?"

"Of course they do."

Dave glanced at Kamen. "Yeah, buddy. Think about *Annie*."

"But single gay men . . ." Gould spoke for the first time since I'd made the announcement.

"Single gay men are allowed to adopt," I snapped impatiently. "It's not an issue."

Gould flushed slightly. "You just caught us by surprise is all. This is good. Really good news."

"Yeah, man." Kamen nodded. "We're really happy for you."

I was practically shaking with anger. This was not how I'd expected my announcement to go. I'd thought they'd be surprised, sure, but that they'd all acknowledge that if anyone in our group would make a great father, it'd be me.

"Well, you don't act like it. This is big news for me. I've been working on this for over a year, and we're just now getting ready—the caseworker and I—to start on my home study."

"What's a home study?" Kamen asked.

"They're gonna look at my house and make sure it's a good environment for a child." I shot Dave a deadly look. "I'll be sure to hide my electric butt plugs."

"Okay." Dave nodded, but he looked shell-shocked. "Okay. Cool."

I stood. Didn't give a shit if they saw my bulging sweatpants. "I thought you'd all be happy for me. I thought I could count on you."

"I just don't understand how you could plan all this without saying anything to us," Dave said as I headed for the door.

"Jesus Christ, I'm not *married* to you guys. I have my own life!" I left them all to their birthday planning for a dead man. Who apparently warranted more support than a living friend.

CHAPTER
THREE

The next day, my balls were back to normal, so I drove to my mother's house in the suburbs. I was still furious about my friends' reactions. I'd already ignored several apology texts this morning.

I sat in the car for a few minutes with the engine running. I was itching to throw the car in reverse, back out of here, and speed away. I wasn't sure if I could handle any more loved ones weighing in on my life choices. But eventually I shut off the car and got out.

I could hear music blaring as I stood on the front porch. I knocked. Tried the knob. Pounded for a few minutes. Finally the door swung open.

My twenty-two-year-old sister, Malina, stood there. Her blond-streaked black hair was gelled flat to her scalp and gathered into a high ponytail. She was wearing black yoga pants and a red-and-white-striped T-shirt. No bra. Mascara was clumped in her eyelashes, and her nails were painted tangerine. She had a container of yogurt in one hand and a plastic spoon dangling from her mouth.

She let the spoon drop to the floor. "Heeeeyaaa, *babi*!" She threw her arms around me and pulled me inside. Off-balance, I stepped on the spoon and cracked it.

She let me go. I glanced over my shoulder and saw that I had a smear of yogurt on my jacket.

"How're you?" I asked, wiping at the spot.

"Good, good." She led me through the house to the kitchen, where she stabbed at her phone with one finger until the music stopped. "Sit. You want juice?" She pronounced it *yuice*.

My parents had adopted Malina from Honduras when she was a baby. And though she'd grown up not speaking a lick of Spanish, she had, over the past four years or so, developed a random, quasi-Spanish accent. Last fall, she'd decided she needed to get in touch with her culture, so she'd started hanging out with a group of Honduran women she'd met at Hymland College—aka Hymen College, to the local youth. As far as I could tell these women did nothing but compete to see who could wear the croppedest crop top, have the highest ponytail, and look the most nonchalant while she stared at her nails and chomped gum. Every now and then they'd break out in snarling fits of rapid-fire Spanish. But when they spoke in English they had the lowest, most languid voices.

Malina still didn't *speak* Spanish, except for a few random words she'd picked up from the group, but the accent fascinated me. It was like she was a non-Hispanic actor studying to play a Hispanic role and presenting the most botched, ridiculous stereotype imaginable.

"Sure."

She got out a carton of orange juice and poured two large glasses. She brought the glasses to the table one at a time so she could continue to clutch the yogurt in her other hand.

"Where's mom?" I asked.

"She went to the mall." *She wen to de mall.*

"How's living with her?" Malina had moved back in with Mom after she'd graduated from college last year. A choice I found interesting, since she and Mom had never gotten along particularly well.

"It's fine. She's like always."

Regal. Despotic. Cruel and glorious. Dave called her Lady Bracknell. When she spoke, she had a way of making you feel like you were interviewing for a job she was never going to offer you. She'd spent years with a whiskey in hand, and now she still walked around with one arm slightly out, fingers curled around an invisible glass. She snapped a rubber band around her wrist whenever she wanted a drink, and her wrist was always crisscrossed with red marks. "Not drinking, though?"

"No." Malina was scraping yogurt out of the carton with her finger. She looked up and caught my gaze. "Miles! I'm watching her."

"Just checking. You know I can't afford to have her slip now."

"Yeah, yeah." She sipped her *yuice*, then started humming with the glass still pressed to her lips. She put the glass down. "I had an audition."

"For what?" Malina had majored in musical theater. Her dream, for some unknown reason, was to be cast as Katherine Plumber in the touring company of *Newsies*. But according to Malina, she needed to build her résumé first.

"*The Last Five Years*. I won't get it. They'll cast a white bitch."

"Don't say 'bitch.'"

"I am a bitch. I can say 'bitch.'" She got up and went to the silverware drawer to get another spoon. "Just like you can use the N-word."

"I don't want to use the N-word."

She shrugged and took a bite of yogurt, slurping it into her mouth. "*Babi*. It wouldn't kill you to learn your culture, you know?" She had recently taken to calling me "*babi*"—which, as far as I knew, was the Spanish word for a baby's bib.

"My culture is minivans and caramel macchiatos." The last thing I needed today was a lecture from my sister on not being black enough. "Listen. I want to hear about your interview with the social worker."

She took a big bite of yogurt. "It was good, you know?"

"No, I don't know. How good?"

"Very good."

I could tell she was hiding something. I waited.

Eventually her gaze flicked up before returning to her yogurt container, which she was scraping with a Shawshank level of thoroughness. "She asked me a lot of questions. About you. About me. About our growing up." She stared dramatically out the sliding glass door. "Then she asked if I'd ever been arrested."

Shit. "She did? She asked about that?"

Malina threw herself back in her seat. Pulled her legs up onto the chair and continued to scrape. "You told her Mama and I were going to help with the parenting. So she said we needed background checks too."

But Cheryl had also told me the phone interviews with my family had gone fine. What the hell?

"So how did you answer?"

"I just told her no."

"Malina!"

"What? Why is it her business?"

"Because if they do an official background check, they'll find out the truth. And they'll know you lied, and they might think *I* told you to!"

"I was seventeen!"

"It's still on your record." I rubbed my temples. "Malina. You have to talk to Cheryl again and tell her what happened."

Her look was somewhat hostile. "Sorry I'm such a potential problem for you."

"That's not what I'm saying. But the truth *is* important here." I hesitated. "Did Mom say anything about how her interview went?"

Malina slammed the yogurt carton onto the table. "No."

"Do you know if she talked to them about religion?"

"Why are you so worried about us embarrassing you?" she snapped. "I don't get it, *babi*. We are not bad people." She sounded like a drunk Sofía Vergara.

"It's not a matter of embarrassing me. It's about us showing that we as a family would provide a stable environment for a child. Are you telling me you'd give a baby to someone if he admitted his mother pays to have her thetan audited?"

Mom had converted to Scientology last year. It had come as a shock to Malina and me. I'd thought Scientology was the province of celebrities and criminals. Dad was the only one who hadn't seemed terribly alarmed. Apparently anything that kept Mom's mind off alcohol was to be supported. He treated Scientology like her hobby. Like she'd taken up quilting instead of holding cans and journeying through her past lives.

Malina stirred the contents of her glass with the yogurt spoon. I tried not to make a face as little white chunks floated through the juice. She took a sip. "I wouldn't judge you for what your family does."

God, let the Beacon Center feel the same way.

Really, it could have been worse. Kamen's mother was into BDSM. They'd had to start going to separate clubs because Kamen couldn't deal with the idea of doing scenes on the same furniture his mom had played on. I sighed. "It's just that Mom's—"

Right on cue, I heard the garage door open, and a minute later, Mom walked in. She was wearing a low-cut, bright-yellow dress, and her black-framed glasses that looked—I realized suddenly—way too much like mine. Her forehead was covered in beads of sweat, and there were dark patches on the fabric under her arms.

She paused when she saw me, then set her shopping bags down by the door. Went to the refrigerator and opened it. "Malina." She spoke before the fridge door was even fully open. "You use the *last* of the juice, put it on the *list*."

Malina draped her arms over her knees and rolled her eyes. "I am not ten anymore, Mama."

"Wonderful." Mom grabbed a can of diet caffeine-free Pepsi. "Are you old enough to get a job and a place of your own? Help me out. I forget."

Malina mashed her face in her knees. "Mamaaa . . ."

"Then put OJ on the list if you use it up." Mom let the fridge fall shut. "Miles." Her voice was loud, authoritative, and in some strange way comfortingly familiar. "I haven't seen you in weeks."

"I know. Been busy. I dropped by to talk about the Beacon Center interviews."

My mother looked at me suspiciously. "Just *where* did you find an adoption agency with such an *extensive* application process?" She lumbered over to the table and sat. "When I agreed to take Malina, the orphanage gave me twenty-five percent off the adoption fee and a coupon for a free Dairy Queen Blizzard."

Malina raised her head with an exaggerated glare. "*Eres mala.*"

"'Eres mala' right back at you, little girl. Throw your yogurt cup away."

Malina got up and threw the container away.

Mom watched, then turned to me again. "The interview went just fine."

"Did you tell them you're a Scientologist?"

She folded her hands. She had long, gold acrylic nails. Bangles. A gauzy leopard-print scarf wrapped around her shaved head. She smelled like she'd been sampling perfume at the JCPenney counter. "I did not."

"Thank you," I said sincerely. "I really appreciate that."

"So wait!" Malina stormed back to the table, jabbing a finger at me. "You're mad at me for not telling the truth, and happy at her for lying?"

"The Scientology thing isn't something they can prove if Mom doesn't tell them. They *can* check your criminal record."

My mother coughed into her hand. "When do they start the home assessment?" Her voice sounded papery after the cough. It gave me a sudden flash forward to what she might sound like when she was old. And then suddenly I was worrying about a future where I'd have to care for her, or put her in a nursing home. I was imagining myself accidentally picking one of those horrible places where the staff abuses the residents, and not finding out about it until the damage was done.

I refocused. "Monday. I'm about to have a nervous breakdown."

"Don't be dramatic." Said the woman with the lemon muumuu and the body thetans. The trick was to know when Mom was joking. Her humor was so dry it was hard not to be stung, if only for a second, by nearly everything she said.

"Fine. I'm just nervous."

She softened slightly. "They're gonna give you a baby. They'd be insane not to."

Malina came closer. "I think so too." She put a hand tentatively on my shoulder.

I felt a rush of warmth toward both of them, which dissipated when Mom asked, "Do you have a crib yet?"

"Mom. We haven't even done the home study yet. I don't know what baby I'm adopting."

"You've *got* to start thinking about it."

I gritted my teeth for a second. "I have thought about it. A lot. I have a lot of ideas for furniture and decorating. I'm just waiting."

She shrugged. "Don't wait too long."

My whole childhood. A science fair project for which I'd custom-ordered materials the day I'd picked my topic. The materials took two days to ship. During the interim, she'd reminded me to not *"wait too long to get started."*

Eight college applications filled out. I was just waiting to take the ACT a third time to try for a perfect score instead of a high one. *"You're going to miss the boat if you don't get on those applications."*

Her assumption was always that I was falling short in some way. That I was never doing enough or doing it soon enough. And I was deeply bored with my own efforts to psychoanalyze her. Was it because she thought if she hadn't waited so long to start a family, she could have locked Dad down, guided him away from a job where he was always in transit? That if she'd spent her junior year of high school researching colleges instead of drinking, she'd have had her pick of any school in the country instead of getting shuffled into Hymland? Who fucking knew.

I was cool toward her for the rest of the visit, and I left wondering how talking to my mother could make me feel worse about myself than standing in front of Hendrix Seger in sweatpants, trying to hide my cantaloupe balls.

By the time Friday arrived, I was wound so tight that just sitting still hurt. So I put in as many hours at the shop as I could. Used my lunch break to take a walk. At 7 p.m., Mr. Hendrix Seger and I went to Opal, a Thai restaurant with water fountains all along the front windows. I tried not to think about the home study on Monday.

I focused on Hendrix instead. He was so tall. His shoulders drooped forward as he studied the menu. His long hair gleamed under the gold lights. His black coat was draped over the chair back, and if I glanced under the table, I could see thick-soled black boots with spikes on the heels. He looked up at me and caught me watching. Were his eyes seriously purple? I couldn't tell.

"Did you find something you can eat?" God, why was I like this? Dave made fun of me whenever we ate out, because I always asked Gould, who was gluten intolerant, if he could find something on the menu to eat. And then pointed out options I thought were possibilities. I'd just used the same brusque, parental tone with Hendrix.

Hendrix—Drix—smiled at me. "Well, I did pick the restaurant. So yes."

"Sorry." I adjusted my napkin on my lap. "I can be overbearing, I'm told."

"Maybe I kinda like it."

"Oh. Well . . ." Was this flirting? Flirting made me deeply uncomfortable. I took a gulp of water. "This might be a bad conversation topic. But how was the funeral?"

His grin broadened. Sharp teeth. I wanted him to put them against my skin. I wanted to feel their damp points anchored in my lips, my throat. My shoulder. "It was great, actually. My family really enjoyed the shirts."

"Are you serious? They didn't mind the angles?"

"Aunt Rhonda's a math teacher, so she loved it."

"Oh. What grade?"

"Seventh. Right when kids are turning into terrors."

"Yes, of course." In seventh grade, I'd been taking high-school-level courses. I'd never so much as spoken out of turn in class. "So did she help you with your homework when you were younger?"

"No. She lived in Milwaukee."

Conversation with Drix proved easy. He was refreshingly normal, aside from the teeth and the eyes and the fact that his family wore matching T-shirts to a funeral like it was a trip to Disney World.

To confirm my status as this wearying world's ultimate definition of pathetic, I indulged in a couple of fleeting domestic fantasies. This man and me. Living in my house, turning it into a home. Basking in Cheryl Callahan's approval. Our kid, running through the rooms, laughing.

Yes, Drix was most likely vanilla. But that would be good for me. I'd learn to live without kink. I *had* to. As David had pointed out, I couldn't break out my TENS unit when I had a kid sleeping in the next room. And anyway, I wasn't getting the same satisfaction from the scene that I used to.

Pointy motherfucking teeth.

Dragging along the edge of my ear. Sinking into my throat.

My face got warm. A buzz traveled from the base of my spine up the back of my neck as I watched the way he toyed with the napkin wrapped around his silverware. I imagined those long fingers gripping my dick. Or holding a knife and pushing the cool flat of it against my ribs. Imagined kissing him. His lips were full enough, but not outlandishly pouty—a deep rose that contrasted with the pallor of his face. Long, straight nose that would bump against mine, and . . .

"Are your eyes purple?" I asked finally.

"Oh, uh . . ." He half put his hand up to his face, as though to say, *These eyes?* "Yes. Somewhat."

"What does 'somewhat' mean?"

"My eyes are dark blue, but I enhance the color with contacts."

"Ah." I looked at the cocktail menu to discourage my imminent erection. "I find people's cosmetic choices fascinating."

"Hmm." He nodded, taking a sip of jasmine tea. "I suppose I do too."

I wanted to make some flip comment about my own social maladroitness, but I didn't do self-deprecation. And I really should have, because there was so much to deprecate. But I was always afraid of having someone agree with my negative assessment of myself. *Uptight. Controlling. Thinks he has all the answers.* As though if I didn't say those things aloud, no one else would think them.

"So, Hendrix Seger," I said.

One side of his mouth twisted upward. "I hate my parents."

"Ah. But Hendrix and Seger are both fine artists."

"I like Jimi. Bob not so much."

"My friend Kamen sings and plays guitar. We hang out a lot at our other friends' house, which is on Wayne Street. So Kamen always sings 'Down on Main Street,' but changes 'Main' to 'Wayne.'"

I was generally the hardest to amuse in our group, but I'd laughed the loudest the night Kamen had introduced that song. It had been one of those perfect nights, back when Hal was still alive and none of us was fazed by the uncertainty of our futures. Including me. The duplex was lit with Christmas lights. We were all a little buzzed, and we'd just eaten our combined weight in burritos, and then Kamen had picked up the guitar and started singing. I'd had one of those flashes of youthful optimism where I'd thought we were all going to be together forever. That we'd have endless nights like this, nights we could pit the strength of our friendship against all the sorrows of the world and win.

Shit. I needed to put things right with my friends.

I took out my phone and sent a group text under the table. *I'm sorry too. See you all for Hal's party.*

Drix and I talked awhile about A2A.

"How'd you come up with the name?" he asked.

"I don't know. It's not that great, but I wanted something short and catchy." I didn't tell him about the list I'd made of more than fifty possible names. About the way I'd agonized over the choice. Stayed up nights going back and forth. Polled my friends until I felt fairly confident about a certain choice—and then changed my mind as soon as I was alone again.

We moved on to discussing the difference between red and green curry, the city's traffic patterns, a handsome dog that passed by outside. And then I asked what he did for a living.

He looked up from his shrimp curry. Fixed me with those violet eyes. "You wouldn't believe me if I told you."

"Go for it."

"I'm a private investigator."

"No way."

He stabbed a shrimp with his fork. "See?"

"Do you have the frosted glass door with your name on it?"

"No. I was shocked to find that being a private eye involves very few pipes, cigarettes, secretaries with beautiful gams, or trench coats."

"What does it involve?"

He chewed the shrimp. "Mostly computers. I keep an eye on social media accounts, if it's like an I-think-my-husband-is-cheating case. I do some pay-per-view stuff too, where I basically just go to bars and check whether they're showing pay-per-view events without a license."

"That sounds action-packed."

He laughed. "It's so boring. Especially since what I like to do is interact with people, not spy on them."

"Well, it's still an intriguing job." I tried to relax my shoulders. I could hear a very Dave-like voice in my head making Mr. Rogers jokes. I adjusted my cardigan self-consciously.

Whatever Drix said next washed over me as I studied him.

What if I invited him back to my place and fucked him? Just *did it* with a stranger, no kinky context at all? Sure, I'd *played* with strangers over the past few months. But there'd been no kissing and no penetration in almost a year. I'd even noticed lately that some of the solo activities I'd once enjoyed—using plugs or dildos—were now actually painful. I was, quite literally, becoming a tight ass. And as much as I loved pain, it was only fun when I was with someone who enjoyed inflicting it.

". . . bodies and stuff," Drix was saying.

"Oh?" I raised my brows, trying to pretend like I'd been listening. He smiled slowly. "You weren't listening at all, were you?"

"I'm sorry," I admitted. "I was . . . You're just so . . ."

Unexpected.

"Boring?"

"No," I said immediately. "You're . . . beautiful."

I ducked and scraped up the last of my curry, wishing I could disappear. When I finally looked up, he was still smiling at me. "You're not bad yourself."

I glanced around for some sort of distraction, but my food was gone and my water glass was empty and I'd already made a tiny crane out of my straw wrapper. So I forced my gaze back to him. "Thanks."

"You're looking at me like you want to come back to my place."

"I don't . . ."

Let's go back to mine instead so I can shower and go to sleep in my own bed immediately after we have sex.

Miles. Don't be an idiot. Go back to his place and fuck all night.

"Yes," I amended firmly. "Yes, let's do the thing you said. Yes."

He had a house. An actual house. Not an apartment or an extended stay motel room or a hovel in one of the neighborhoods where you can't go outside after 7 p.m. He also had a very large, red SUV. And a birdbath in his front yard.

The inside was lived-in, but clean. Abstract art on the walls. Massive flat-screen TV. Carved wooden bowl filled with fresh fruit on the kitchen island.

He slipped his jacket off and hung it on a kitchen chair, then turned to help with mine. One hand slid over my rigid shoulders.

He breathed gently on my neck, still holding my jacket. I shivered. He didn't move. "You're so tense."

"I know. I think I just need to . . ." I knew what I was going to do a second before I did it. I'd never done anything like it before. I had just a fraction of an instant to wonder if I would regret it, but I couldn't have stopped myself even if I'd wanted to.

I turned around and kissed him. Hard.

He dropped my jacket and wrapped his arms around me, and we staggered through his kitchen, kissing furiously and moaning like we were already in midfuck. A pile of mail fell from his counter as he put a hand out to brace us. We turned, and my head banged against a cabinet. Turned again, and this time I had him pinned against the counter edge. I plunged my hand down the back of his pants and grabbed his ass. He made a sharp, frantic sound and rubbed his groin against mine.

He picked me up and practically threw me onto the island. The wooden fruit bowl plummeted. A banana splatted on the tile, and plums rolled everywhere. He tugged my fly down. I managed to get two of his shirt buttons undone before I just started yanking on the shirt. It didn't rip open quite as elegantly as I would have liked. He had to help me, and together we tore it off his body. His chest was pale and already slick with sweat. Light hair between his pecs; a tattoo of a bird on his right biceps. I kissed down his torso and then up again. Pulled his head down so I could reach his lips.

He tugged my pants off while I tossed my cardigan aside. I sat there for a moment with my cock poking out of my boxers, staring at the lines of his chest, his almost delicate collarbones. I wanted to make him *scream*.

I slid off the counter. We started kissing again. We hit the fridge, and magnets clattered to the floor. He reached for my cock, making this deep, satisfied noise, like he'd been waiting all night just to feel my dick. He jerked my boxers down to my thighs and turned me around, kneading and rubbing my bare ass as he bent me over the counter.

Oh God. Yes. Please.

I let my boxers fall and then stepped out of them. Spread my legs and let him touch anywhere he wanted.

I heard him start to take his pants off, and I spun to help him. Once he was naked, I made him take a step back so I could look.

God *damn*.

He had the longest pale thighs, lean and muscular. His cock was long too, and rising steadily. His balls were large and pink, the right one hanging heavier than the left. There was a dusting of gold hair on his inner thighs and around the base of his shaft. His hips were narrow, but his ass was round and taut.

"Fuck," I whispered.

"Good 'fuck'?" He sounded shy.

I stepped forward. Dug my fingers into his shoulders and kissed him, searching with my tongue for the points of his teeth. I grinned when I found them—pushed so hard against them they almost drew blood. He seemed surprised for a moment, and then he raked his nails down my back, and I let out a hiss of utter pleasure.

"You like that?" he murmured against my lips.

I nodded.

His hand cracked hard across my ass, and I jolted onto my toes. His hair was coming loose from the ponytail, strands of it sticking to the sweat on both our faces. He pulled back, gasping and gulping. "Condoms . . . in the bathroom."

We tried to keep kissing as we headed toward the bathroom, but we tripped and ended up on the floor in a heap. After that it was a Crawl of Champions down the front hall, both of us on all fours, stopping occasionally to grab each other and kiss or scratch or bite. When we reached the bathroom, he grabbed the condoms from under the sink. "You or me?"

"You."

He put the condom on.

I slammed the toilet lid down and climbed on it, on my knees. Braced myself on the tank and pushed my hips back until my ass was spread. I felt filthy, in a way I hadn't in years—maybe ever.

"Go for it," I whispered. "Hard as you can."

His breath was in my ear, his teeth skimming my jaw. "Don't say it if you don't mean it."

"I mean it."

I heard the click of the lube bottle opening. I clutched the tank. Tried to spread myself wider.

He smacked my hole, then stuck his slick fingers in. I moaned and rocked the toilet tank and tried not to clench as he finger-fucked me fast and hard.

"Oh God," I said between gasps. "Okay, okay. Oh God."

He withdrew his fingers and then tried to push his cock in. I closed my eyes, my breath catching as he made another unsuccessful attempt. He stopped trying to get it in and ran it up and down my crack a few times.

What happened to 'hard as you can'?

"I'm too tall," he whispered with a laugh. "Over the sink."

I laughed too and stood, stumbling over to the sink. He caught me and bent me over with one hand between my shoulders. The other hand guided his cock in. He stretched me, creating a hundred frissons of pain. I was so tight, and the edge of the counter dug into my stomach, a constant ache. He started to thrust, slowly at first, and then faster, so that I cried out with each stab of his cock.

My knees bashed the doors of the cabinets under the sink, and the crack of his hand on my thigh was like a gunshot in the small room. Some of his thrusts lifted my feet off the floor, made me kick and grunt. I flattened my spine and pushed back against him, sticking my ass as far out as it would go. I let my socked feet slip farther and farther apart on the tile until I was spread so wide my thighs hurt. He had to bend his knees to stay inside me. He started his thrusts down in a half crouch and lifted me up with each one, impaling me on his dick.

All the while his teeth were on my neck, teasing the damp skin there with gentle nips. He licked a bead of sweat that was rolling between my shoulder blades, and I trembled with pleasure.

"Hurt me," I whispered. "Please."

I almost never said that to vanillas—it tended to stress them out. But Drix immediately buried his nails in one shoulder and his teeth in the other, like he was trying to rip me apart. His cock hit some place so deep inside me that I nearly screamed, and he grabbed my chin and pulled my head back toward him so he could bite my jawbone. His teeth sank deeper and deeper until I cried out. He let me go and grabbed my wrists, forcing my arms out in front of me, until my hands touched the mirror. He was tall enough that he could lean over me, his chest against my back, keeping my wrists in that iron grip.

Bang, bang, bang, bang...

My knees hit the cabinets. My ass felt ready to split in two. He reached around and jacked my cock until I came in his hand.

Then he kept fucking me.

I didn't know if he had amazing self-control or if he just wasn't getting there. But no matter how many times I clenched around his cock, he stayed hard, and he continued thrusting. Until I was limp and every breath was an effort. I watched through the mirror as he slammed his hips against my ass, arched his neck, and shuddered. That alone almost got me hard again.

He fell forward slowly, running his lips along my spine while I panted into the sink. He traced my hips with his thumbs and slowly pulled out. I heard the condom drop into the trash. He helped me up and tugged me against him. I glanced in the mirror. We stood there back to front, our chests heaving, his long, pale arms wrapped around me. My ass and knees still throbbed, and my wrists were bruised, but my mind was quiet.

Slowly he rested his chin on the top of my head. He closed his eyes, a slight smile on his face.

I felt like I'd slipped into the skin of a younger me. Like there was something I wanted out of sex that went beyond pain, beyond orgasm. And if I just stayed here, with this man, maybe I'd understand what it was.

Later, we lay in his bedroom in the dark. He'd said I looked too tired to drive home, and as much as I preferred my bed to a stranger's, I hadn't protested.

"I haven't done it like that in a while," I said softly. My head was on his shoulder, and I was having a hard time concentrating on anything beyond that point of contact.

"That rough?" he asked.

"Well . . . I often do it in ways that hurt." I couldn't believe I was telling him this.

He glanced down at me. Stroked my cheek with one finger. "Yeah?"

I looked up. "I'm pretty kinky."

In my experience, when dealing with a vanilla I was hoping to have sex with multiple times, it was best to get this confession out of the way pretty early. Then reassure the guy that I could still have "normal sex," but that if he wanted to try anything wild, I was amenable.

He continued stroking my cheek, fingers moving lower until they brushed the sore spots his teeth had left along my jaw. I closed my eyes. Nothing but this moment and that touch.

"Really?" he said at last.

I opened my eyes. "I mean, like, a real masochist." I waited for the horror, but it never came.

"Interesting. So you're into—into S&M?"

"BDSM, yes. Or I guess I prefer the term 'kink.'"

He nodded. "Because . . .?"

"Because it's broader." I paused, sitting up. "You're not freaked out? You know I mean, like—whipping and knives and blood . . ."

Stop there. Why would you say that? Why?

He shook his head, smiling. "I guess, then, I should make a confession too."

What?

I waited, irrationally hoping his confession was that he was a professional dominant who specialized in knife play. He opened his mouth, but he didn't speak. His gaze flicked away.

"It's all right," I urged him. "Unless you've killed somebody, it can't be worse than my 'I like knives in my sex.'"

He nodded as though considering this. Then he took a deep breath. "I'm a vampire."

CHAPTER
FOUR

"What?" I assumed I had misheard.

"I mean, not a real one, of course. They don't exist. But I'm a part of the vampire subculture. So I'm a vampyre with a *y*."

He kept saying the word "vampire," and it was troubling me. "I don't understand."

"Well, ah . . ." He propped up on one elbow. The sheet fell away from his body, and my gaze traveled immediately to the tattoo of the bird. "There are people in the world who believe they share traits with vampires—the mythological creatures. We call ourselves vampyres. With a *y*," he clarified again.

This was *not* happening.

Everything started falling into place. "The . . . the teeth?"

"I got them filed last year."

Of course. He got them filed. As you do.

When you're *batshit crazy.*

"And the tattoo?"

"It's the mark of my coven, the Dark Ravens."

I gaped for a moment. "As opposed to all those albino ravens?" I said it more sardonically than I'd intended.

He laughed. "I know, right?"

I'd just had sex with a vampire.

Vampyre.

No. Don't indulge him.

I needed to get out of here.

"And it's funny you should mention masochism," he went on. "I'm not a—whatever the BDSM term for it is. A dominant. But I am known in the vampyre community for . . . Well, I like to see blood. And I like the ways people react to pain. Like causing the pain."

I froze. "You're a sadist?"

He smiled with one side of his mouth, revealing a pointed tooth. "You could say that."

Be still my beating, motherfucking heart. A sadist.

For the most part, doms who identified as sadists weren't true sadists. Just as most masochists weren't true masochists. Because sadism and masochism were technically disorders. I had played once, years ago, with a man whose sadism had been incredibly real—and incredibly pervasive. Inflicting pain was what he thought about when he got up in the morning, while he brushed his teeth, while he stocked shelves at the One Stop Mart. Our affair had been exciting. Terrifying. Short-lived.

Drix nudged my leg with his under the covers. "You look a little shocked."

"This is just . . . a surprise. So what do you do as a vampyre? Drink blood?"

"I don't *need* blood. I enjoy blood play, but I actually get my nourishment by feeding directly on a person's prana, or life force."

"Oh." I tried to nod.

Sadist, sadist, sadist, went my brain.

But also: *Adult man pretending to be a vampire.*

"It sounds really parasitic, but it's not. In return, I give them some of my own prana. And I only feed on beings with really powerful life forces."

It was useless to try to respond to that. I rubbed my temples. "Can we just take a step back for a minute?"

"Sure."

"How did you get into all this?"

"I suppose I always knew, to an extent. I'm a *klavasi*, though. I wasn't awakened until after puberty." He grinned, sinking back against the pillow. "I know it all sounds weird. I don't tell many people, but I figure since you also live an alternative lifestyle, you'd understand."

No. I understood people using pain to help them get off. I did not understand grown men pretending to feed on people's life forces.

He ran a finger over my shoulder. In spite of myself, heat rushed to my groin, and I had to shift so he wouldn't feel my cock rising again.

I tried to banish an image of him piercing me with his teeth, drawing blood, making me cry out as I came . . .

Nope. Nope, nope. Nope.

End it now. Go home. There will be other sadists, and they will not be vampyres.

"You okay?" he asked.

"I should go," I told him, getting up.

"Hey. Miles?"

"I'm sorry, I just . . . sleep better in my own bed."

He was sitting up now, but I didn't look at him.

I went downstairs to get my clothes. Dressed in his dark kitchen among the spilled plums and splattered banana.

Then I left.

A few years ago, my friends and I had been at the mall, in the bookstore. And on an impulse we'd each bought a copy of some About Me journal that asked dozens of extremely personal questions. We'd agreed to fill them out, and then I'd agreed to be the one who would keep them all— *"I won't read them; I promise"*—for ten years, so that we could read them a decade later and see how we'd changed.

We'd filled them out together one evening, sitting around Dave's kitchen table, drinking beer and laughing at the questions.

I'd gotten stuck on *What's your darkest secret?*

I'd thought about it for a while. Started to write: *I don't have dark secrets.*

Then I considered writing something about my masochism, like *I don't always know if my thing for pain is healthy.*

Finally I'd written about this awful game I'd played once with Malina when I was nine and she was almost four. She and I were walking to the park down the street. She had trouble keeping up. I walked faster and faster, until she asked me to slow down. Then I'd told her I was going to leave her there. That our parents didn't want her anymore, and that I was going to leave her too.

I'd wanted to make her cry, and when she did, I immediately went to her and comforted her. Told her that everyone loved her and that I was never going to leave her.

I didn't understand at the time what I'd been trying to do. But when I look back now, I think I just really wanted to comfort someone. But I needed them to need my comfort. I liked that exchange—bringing someone to the point where they thought the world was ending, and then telling them everything would be all right. Cruel, I know. And I'd felt guilty about it for years afterward, even though Malina said she didn't remember it at all.

I'd even talked to the guidance counselor about it in high school. Ms. Warren told me it was totally normal for siblings to do rotten things to each other. She said she'd once duct-taped her little sister to the side of the house. But I couldn't stop feeling guilty. The older I got, the harder it hit me how especially unforgivable it was to tell an adopted kid her family didn't want her. And even now, I worried that streak of cruelty was still in me, and that it would make me a bad parent, a bad friend, a bad person.

So that was my dark secret. Worse than the TENS unit in the closet.

I'd read the others' answers. I had a terrible nosy streak, but I wasn't like Dave, who was very open about his inability to keep other people's secrets or to stop himself from snooping. People trusted me because I was the mature one, the one who seemed to have willpower. And I hated myself a little for not actually being that trustworthy.

Kamen's darkest secret had been that he'd once put a cucumber up his butt. David's had read: *I shot a man in Reno just to watch him die. Ha-ha, Miles, I know you're reading this.* Okay, so maybe people didn't actually trust me. Gould's was that he'd once played the police sergeant in a Hebrew school production of *The Pirates of Penzance.* Did any of them even know what a dark secret was? I'd been hoping for secrets worse than mine. I'd been hoping each of them had hurt somebody, but that they'd all been forgiven and had moved on with their lives. And that would be permission for me to move on with mine.

Hal's About Me journal was the only one I never read. I'd gotten a call while I was reading them, and I'd shoved them all in my keepsake box. By the time I was done on the phone, I hadn't wanted to keep reading. I'd felt too guilty about having snooped in the first place.

On Hal's birthday, I arrived on Dave and Gould's doorstep half an hour after the festivities had started. I stood there with my chips and dip, surprisingly nervous. We'd had no few fights in our years together. But this one had really hurt my feelings.

The door was unlocked, so I wandered in, and within seconds was accosted by a very cheerful, somewhat drunk Dave. "Miles! The man of the hour. Wait until you see what we got you!" I was immediately suspicious, since I was *not* the man of the hour. That honor belonged to a dead man.

Dave led me through the living room and into the kitchen. There were already three bowls of chips and about six different dips on the table. Plus a giant bakery cake with a picture of . . .

"Who's on that cake?" I asked.

"It's you," Dave replied.

The man on the cake was approximately twenty years older than I was and at least forty pounds heavier. Plus he had a mustache.

Kamen, who was dunking potato chips in sour cream, nodded. "Yeah. We got you a face cake."

I stared at both of them. "What's going on? Who is that? Why do you have a cake with someone else's picture on it for Hal's birthday?"

Dave and Kamen exchanged glances. Gould, over at the refrigerator pulling out beers, sighed loudly. "I told them not to do it."

Dave made a face. "We sort of . . . turned Hal's birthday into a 'We're sorry, Miles,' party."

"You what?"

Gould approached. "That wasn't the part I told them not to do."

Kamen clapped me on the shoulder. "Yeah, dude. We're sorry we acted weird about you wanting to adopt a kid. We think it's really cool."

Gould started opening beer bottles on the edge of the table. "Explain the cake."

Dave shrugged. "I went to the bakery. And they'd made this cake for a guy's birthday party, and the party ended up not happening because I guess the guy's wife found out he was cheating on her. So they just had this photo cake with this adulterer's face on it, and they offered to sell it to me at a discount. And since it looked a little like Miles . . ."

"It looks *nothing* like me."

Kamen half shut his eyes. "If you squint."

I shook my head. "You're just saying that because he's black."

Everyone turned away guiltily, except Gould, who offered me a beer. "It was *not* my idea."

"Well, anyway." Dave slung an arm around me. "We got a cake, and there's plenty of chips, so sit down and enjoy yourself. And please, please forgive us? We support anything you want to do. We promise."

"We're really excited about having your kid," Kamen added. "I mean, not, like, *we're* having it, but—"

"I absolutely forgive you," I said to all of them. "And I'm sorry too. I shouldn't have kept it from you."

We group-hugged, because Dave was incapable of resolving anything without a five-minute embrace.

Gould and Kamen went to Gould's bedroom to look at a wall Kamen was going to help repair. Which left Dave and me alone. I worked on my beer and cut a hunk out of the cake stranger's face.

"I'll have some too." David sat gingerly and rose almost at once. He caught me watching and gave me a tentative smile.

"I won't ask." I cut him a slice.

He accepted the plate. "I told D what I said to you when you gave us the news. So, if it makes you feel any better, I'm not in any hurry to be an asshole again. And not just because I got caned," he added quickly. "I felt bad way before that."

Dave had recently initiated a domestic discipline relationship with his partner, D. One of the things Dave had asked D to hold him accountable for was his tendency to speak without thinking.

He must have felt *really* bad, to have confessed to D. He hated being caned more than anything. And now *I* felt guilty because I knew he hadn't meant to hurt me. Dave cared about the rest of us to an extent that made me almost uncomfortable at times, because

I worried I didn't experience our group's friendship at quite the intensity he did.

"It makes me feel a little better." I held my arms out.

He came around the table and gave me a massive hug. "I'm so sorry, man," he said into my shoulder. "I'm really fucking proud of you, and you're gonna be an awesome dad."

Just for fun, I slid a hand down and squeezed his ass.

He yelped and jumped straight up. "Ow! Not cool!"

I grinned. "Now we're even."

In the back room, the stereo started blasting Lil Wayne.

"Can you guys hear that from out there?" Kamen called.

"Yes, and we don't want to!" Dave yelled back. He waited a few minutes, but the music remained at the same volume.

I raised my voice to be heard over the music. "I'm still impressed you're making this discipline thing work."

Dave collapsed in his seat, wincing. "Getting caned is the worst thing that can happen to a human. But my ability to communicate nicely with people has improved a ton already." Kamen danced into the kitchen, bumping and grinding his way past the table. Dave looked up in time to see him hit the table edge with his hip, sending a bowl of chips sliding toward the edge. "Watch the chip bowl, ass!"

I smirked. "A ton?"

Dave turned back to me. "I'm still a work in progress."

"I see."

"Someone's gotta dance, or it's not a party!" Kamen snagged another handful of chips, stacked them carefully on his palm in a neat little tower, then danced back to the spare room.

"Let's go somewhere quieter," Dave suggested to me.

We took our cake to the living room, which wasn't much quieter.

He sat on the couch, stuffing a throw cushion under him. "So how old is your kid gonna be?"

"I'm not sure. The next step is to look at some profiles and get an idea of which kids I feel a connection with. The Beacon Center will send me some potential matches."

"God, that sounds awful. I mean, think about all the ones you won't be able to take."

"I know." I'd thought about that every day for the past year. If I couldn't even make decisions about what furniture I wanted in the nursery, how was I going to choose a *child*?

"Girl or boy?"

"Not sure."

He studied me for a moment. "This must have been, like, a crazy-big decision."

"Yeah."

His voice softened. "You really could've told us, you know?"

I could have.

And yet I so rarely told them the whole story about anything.

Dave frowned. "I mean, I know you told me a few months ago you were taking a break from BDSM because of some life-choice things. But I had no idea this was what you meant."

"I know. I was so scared it wouldn't work out."

After the incident a couple of months ago with the dom who'd threatened me with a knife, I'd gone to them immediately. Had called Kamen to pick me up and let him take me over to Dave's. But they hadn't known I was meeting the guy in the first place. In the weeks that followed, they'd sometimes asked me if I was okay. And I'd always said yes, even when I wasn't.

Dave had finally said, *"You know, sometimes it's hard for us to help you out. You don't always tell us things."*

I guess what I needed to realize was that any major event in my life had an impact on them. I'd just never been able to see us as a family quite the way the others seemed to. To me, family members were the people you were stuck with through some genetic crapshoot. Friends were different. You supported them, but you weren't obligated to save them. You could shed them if they weren't working for you. You loved them deeply, but when you lost them, you . . .

You moved on. You recovered.

But in Dave's eyes, I'm pretty sure we were bound together for eternity.

I didn't really know what to do with that kind of friendship. Didn't know how to share my life so completely. Sometimes I thought I had an ally in Gould, whose habitual silence might have indicated a certain level of detachment. But I got the sense that even he was more invested in the group than I was.

"I'm sorry." I took a bite of the stranger's face.

"No, no. This is our apology party to you. Don't steal our thunder. And after how we acted, I totally get why you didn't tell us."

"It's okay."

Dave was silent for a moment. "So are you really giving up the scene? Because you came in here the other day with saline balls, and I'm just saying . . ."

"Yes, I'm giving it up." I thought about Drix, and a sharp ache went through my body.

"You just haven't yet?" Dave said quietly.

"Starting tomorrow."

"Does that mean tonight you—"

"What're you guys doing?" Kamen asked, as he and Gould entered with cake. Actually, Gould's plate just had a pile of frosting on it, in deference to the gluten intolerance.

"Having a serious conversation." Dave waved him away. "Go back to your dance party."

I suddenly felt ridiculous. Hopeless. I wanted Drix beside me in bed again. I wanted to burn from the thrust of his cock, wanted his sharp teeth buried in my skin. And I wanted to teach him how to make me come utterly undone.

But not as much as I wanted to be the world's best father.

Gould wiped frosting off his mouth with the back of his hand. "Is the serious conversation about Miles's kid?"

"Hold on." Kamen ran to Gould's room and turned off Lil Wayne. Then he raced back to the living room. "I'm ready."

"It's been stressful," I admitted. "Like, the whole adoption process is exhausting. Interviews and letting them scrutinize every detail of my life. It's taken months, and the home study will take more months. And it doesn't help that I . . ."

They all waited. God, I was an asshole. Such an asshole. But they were the people who could help.

"I sort of . . . met someone."

"Ohh?" Dave looked ready to leap on me.

"But it didn't work out," I said quickly. "And I think I didn't do a very good job letting him down. I know I didn't."

I expected merciless teasing from David on the subject of my social awkwardness. But he only said, "Aww, Miles."

"So I wanted to ask you guys . . ." I pursed my lips. "Should I apologize to someone I never intend to see again?"

"Sure, dude," Kamen said. "If you weren't nice to him."

"Not to pry—" Dave shifted on the cushion "—but what was he like?"

"He was . . ." I couldn't come clean about the whole vampyre Gordian knot. Just couldn't. "There was nothing really wrong with him. He was polite. Fun, I suppose. If you're into that sort of thing."

Dave furrowed his brow. "What, fun?"

"He was even a sadist," I offered reluctantly.

"Holy shit, dude!" Kamen said. "That's your dream."

"So what exactly was the problem?" Dave asked.

I spread my hands on my thighs. "The problem is, I'm giving up kink until I've figured this adoption thing out. That's my final answer."

Dave shook his head. "But you're always talking about how good sadists are hard to find."

"This is no longer of importance."

Dave wouldn't let up. "And this guy is *fun*. You need someone who's fun. To force *you* to be fun. Miles, keep fucking the fun man!"

"I will have fun being a father."

"Yeah, but even dads have sex."

"Just tell me how to apologize."

Kamen shrugged. "Makeup fucking, dude."

I sighed. "I shouldn't have bothe—"

"Miles," Gould interrupted, "I think you're missing an important opportunity."

I turned slowly to him. "What?"

Gould glanced around at all of us, looking uncertain but a little mischievous. "The home study's gonna go on for months. So there's no chance you'll have a kid before the year's out, right?"

"Very unlikely."

Gould rested one hand on the arm of the sofa. "What are some things you've always wanted to do? Kink-wise?"

"What does that have to do w—"

"Just answer the question."

"Vacbeds," I said.

"And branding," David added.

"Yeah. Uh . . ." I couldn't think. "Urethral torture."

Dave and Gould exchanged a look. Dave turned back to me. "The things that you think are things just . . . it blows my mind. What else?"

"Um . . . piercing . . . bullwhips . . . I'm sure I could think of other things."

Gould nodded. "Welcome to your pain-slut bucket list."

"Huh?"

He gave me a half smile. "You have six months or whatever to do all the masochistic things you've always wanted to do."

"Oh my God." Dave turned to Gould. "You're a genius." He whirled back to me. "And as long as the adoption people never find out you're into that shit, you'll have it all out of your system by the time Fred Rogers Jr. arrives."

Gould was not a genius. All of my friends were fools. Absolute fools. And this idea made no sense—especially coming from Dave and Gould, both of whom had reacted to Hal's death by becoming convinced that kink was dangerous and that they couldn't trust doms.

"I support this," Kamen volunteered.

"Come onnnn!" David tugged my hand. "You apologize to him. You explain the situation. You set up the expectations. He's a sadist; you're a masochist. You're not looking for a relationship. But you want to try all kinds of kinky shit together. Until you get sick of each other, or the baby comes along. Whichever happens first."

"This sounds like a terrible idea."

"How. How is it terrible?"

They all waited for me to tell them how it was terrible.

"Because it just is."

They did not find that argument compelling.

"Because Drix hates me," I tried instead.

Dave slapped my shoulder hard. "Then fix that, douche bag."

CHAPTER
FIVE

I had an email draft open. The cursor blinked. But I couldn't figure out what to say to Drix. I'd grabbed the email address off his order form, which was completely unprofessional and could backfire if it turned out not to be his account. But since the name "Hendrix" was in the address, I figured I was at least safe on that front.

Riddle's monthly newsletter arrived in my inbox. I pounced on it, eager for the distraction.

Information about the roundtables. About the dungeon's extended spring hours.

A headline toward the bottom caught my eye: *COME PLAY WITH OUR NEWEST TOY.*

The accompanying image was of a narrow, upright chamber. The door to the chamber was open, and inside were colorful projections. I squinted. It looked almost like . . .

MEET THE DILDO IRON MAIDEN! read the subhead.

Riddle's newest piece of equipment is sure to heat you up in time for summer. This chamber is seven feet tall, and the inside has over three dozen mounting pegs for toys of your choice. Just put your bottom boy or girl inside—not for the claustrophobic!—and make them impale themselves in as many holes as you choose, with whatever wicked dildos suit your fancy. Then close the door and listen to your bottom whimper as s/he is impaled in every orifice! We're very proud of our latest addition, and we can't wait for you to come try it out.

Please note: The dildo iron maiden is BYOD—Bring Your Own Dildos. No dildos will be provided.

My phone buzzed. A text from Dave. *You see the iron maiden?*
Yep.

See, you really don't want to quit the scene now, do you?

Damn it, I did want to try that iron maiden.

I texted back: *I'll add it to the bucket list.*

Atta boy!

I shook my head and set the phone down. Touched the marks on my jaw left by Drix's teeth. They were barely visible, but I still felt self-conscious every time I went out in public. Yet at home I couldn't stop admiring them.

Desperate for further distraction, I logged into the Subs Club site and checked the message center. We'd received a new application for membership. Someone named Ryan W. I glanced over his application. It all looked good, so I added him to our members list. A few minutes later, I had a message from Ryan W himself.

HEY. REALLY INTERESTED IN WHAT YOU GUYS DO. WOULD LIKE TO MEET SOMETIME. DRINKS? POOL? MY TREAT. —RYAN W

Ugh, I did not want to deal with that request right now. Humbling myself to Drix seemed infinitely preferable. I went back to my email draft.

I typed a brief apology. Frowned at it. It sounded so . . . terse. But how to sound sincere without risking utter humiliation if he blew me off?

Hi Drix,

I understand if receiving this email does not exactly fill you with delight. But it is imperative that I apologize for what I said the other night. I really enjoyed my evening with you; you were extraordinarily accepting when I told you about my masochism, and I regret that I didn't show you the same courtesy when you told me of your—

I closed my eyes for a second and forced myself to keep typing.

—vampyrism.

It just came as a surprise to me. I don't know much about that subculture, and I got a little overwhelmed. If you think you can see past my inexcusable rudeness, I would like a chance to get to . . .

To . . .?

To apologize in person and start again.

Preferably from the point where we'd knocked over the fruit bowl.
If not, then just know that I am sincerely sorry.
All the best,
Miles

I half expected never to hear from him again. But he wrote back a day later with an unembellished *apology accepted* and a question about tote bag pricing at A2A.

We chatted online several times over the next week. The chats got progressively dirtier. On Friday we went to dinner again. Once more, I was impressed with how easily our conversation flowed and how impossible it was not to imagine him contorted in all sorts of strange positions while I fucked him and he fucked me and we mutually fellated and he whipped me bloody. And so forth.

We went back to his place, where we sat across from each other at his kitchen island with some plums and discussed what had gone so wrong last week. I told him again that I was a jerk; he told me again that it was fine.

"The sex was incredible." He took a bite of his plum. A stream of juice rolled down his chin, and it was beguilingly gross.

"Yes," I agreed. "I don't often make love that . . . passionately. Is it hard to chew with your pointy teeth?"

"No. It's especially easy to eat corn and steak. Also, watch this." He held the unbitten side of the plum to his lips and put the tip of one fang to the skin. Pressed down slowly. The fruit's skin stretched, buckled, and then finally punctured in a tiny spray as his fang sank in.

I blinked several times in rapid succession, wondering why I'd found that so arousing.

He used the fang to tear a hunk of fruit off. I watched him chew, glancing briefly at my own untouched plum.

"Your teeth really are exciting." My voice sounded slightly unsteady.

He swallowed and grinned. "Miles, I really am prepared to try to learn about what you want. How to, like, do pain in a way that's more BDSM, less vampyre. I would do that for you. You'd just have to teach me."

"Most excellent. I'm certainly open to learning how you inflict pain in a way that's more vampyre."

"That would mostly involve the teeth. And vampire gloves."

My balls pulled tight. "You have vampire gloves?" I loved vampire gloves. I'd once known a dom who made his own—stuck thumbtacks through a pair of plush gloves and ran those tacks all over my body.

"I made some last year. They're great for sensation play at the coven meetings."

"So you guys . . . play?"

"It's more about getting familiar with our bodies and less about sex, if that makes sense. We do massage, touch therapy, a lot of stuff with blindfolds. We have a few rituals that involve pain or permanent marking. But mostly our goal is to pay attention to others' energy and to awaken one another to new methods of touch, communication, and being present."

Sounded like a lot of bunkum. But not altogether unappealing. "So it's not giant vampyre orgies."

He scraped the last of the flesh off his plum. "I won't say orgies have never happened."

"I've just never thought about vampyres before. At all."

He nodded. "I'm actually really involved in the physical stuff that goes on. Not the orgies that may or may not exist, but just—this is gonna make me sound like the kind of person everyone wants to punch in the face—I really love helping people get in tune with their bodies. I like making people happier."

And if I were Dave, I'd have made some lascivious joke about how he could get in tune with my body—but I wasn't Dave, and the moment passed me by. "I think that's really neat."

Neat. That was a grandpa word. What the fuck was wrong with me?

He grinned. "You know, I really would like to invite you to a Dark Ravens gathering."

"And what would I do at the gathering?"

"Just observe. Be present. Participate in the giant vampyric circle jerk."

I dropped my plum on the floor. Scrambled to retrieve it.

He laughed. "Kidding, kidding. Honestly, most gatherings are pretty laid-back. We just talk and eat."

"Eat life forces, or . . . ?"

"String cheese and Milanos."

"Okay."

"But the next gathering will involve an initiation ritual. Which I think you might like."

"Why?" I asked suspiciously.

He shrugged, smirking. "It involves a little pain."

"For whom?"

"Someone newly awakened."

I reached for reserves of nonchalance I didn't know I had. I could do this. I could accept Drix's . . . vampyre thing. Support him, maybe. If it meant we could have sex again.

"Maybe we could do an exchange," I suggested.

"Oh?"

"Yes. You come to Riddle with me for a night. We don't have to engage in sportive activities. But you could see what a BDSM club looks like. And I could go with you to a, uh, gathering."

"That actually sounds awesome."

"Really? Should we take bets on what's gonna be weirder—my club or your coven?"

He laughed. "I think there will be equal strangeness."

My plum was covered in floor grit, so I went to the sink and washed it. He caught me before I could go back to my seat, and kissed me.

I was alarmed by the way my body responded. Even as a teenager, when I was supposed to be a walking agglomeration of hormones, I'd never gotten this turned on this fast. I kissed him back and then pulled away. "How did you get into the coven?" I asked.

He was watching me like he didn't think that kiss was finished. "I had a friend who was a member. And I was a little lost at that time in my life, but I'd always felt like a . . . like something more than human. I attended a gathering with my friend, and I was really impressed with what the Dark Ravens had to offer."

That unsettled me a bit. It sounded too much like religion. "So you felt like a vampyre your whole life?"

"Lives." He grinned mischievously. "For us, time is a construct with little meaning. Dark Ravens have been walking this earth for millennia."

"Oh."

"So we live in the moment, because the moment has no beginning and no end. We savor it. And we are never slaves to the clock."

"Of course not. Why—why would you be?"

He grinned. "You're having such a hard time with this."

"I'm not." I was.

"I know it sounds strange. But I promise I'm not, you know, crazy. I love getting to play a role that feels so real to me. But I understand that it is a role. It's entwined with who I am, but it doesn't define me."

This did sound oddly like how I viewed kink. "So tell me about your . . . lives."

"So, um, my vampyre name is Diaemus. I've been around for just over six hundred years. And in that time, I've fed on sexual and spiritual energies of countless people."

"If time is a meaningless construct, how come you have ages?"

"It's easier to explain things to black swans if we mark our lives somehow."

"Black swans?"

"That's what you are. That's someone who's a non-vampyre but is a supporter of vampyres."

"Ah, so now I'm your ally, huh?"

He looked a little pink in the cheeks. "Are you?"

"As long as you promise you won't convert me by making me drink your blood or biting me or anything. I mean, you can bite me, just . . ." It was my turn to flush.

He gave me a damn wicked grin. "You know we don't really drink blood, right?"

"I was kind of hoping not."

Though I wouldn't mind you making me bleed.

He set his plum pit on the counter. "I live my life according to the tenets of my coven. But those tenets are, like: slow down. Be aware of the spiritual connection between all living things. Allow a silence at the end of each breath. Not, like: drink blood, or sleep only during daylight."

"I think it sounds interesting."

"Really? Because you look like you think we're a creepy cult that will steal your firstborn child."

I jolted at the mention of a firstborn child.

I shook my head slowly. "My mom . . ." I wasn't sure this was a second-date revelation ". . . recently converted to Scientology. I do see that as a cult. I worry about people who go looking for answers as a group, because I think 'answers' are specific to individuals. As soon as someone says you can find your code of conduct, your reason for *existing*, in a book—I get suspicious. So as long as you can assure me that you don't let the coven make decisions for you, I have no problem."

It was more than I should have said, and part of me expected him to be offended. But part of me already knew him well enough to figure he wouldn't be.

He smiled. Took my hand, which prompted an immediate and formidable erection. "I promise. Think of it as a very elaborate LARP."

"I prefer never to think of anything as a LARP." I squeezed his hand. "But okay."

After a moment where I wasn't sure whether to kiss him, he said, "I want to hear more about your Scientologist mother."

"No, you don't."

"I do."

I gazed into his eyes, feeling about fifteen—terrified and horny and enraptured. "I want to engage in all manner of osculation with you."

"I don't know what that means."

"Let's make out."

We did, and it was way, way better than talking about my Scientologist mother.

I'd met Cheryl Callahan once for coffee back before we'd started my interviews. But I'd forgotten most of the details of her appearance. She had dark curly hair that she wore loose. No makeup, flawless brown skin, and bushy eyebrows. I let her in and bit back a request that she take her shoes off and leave them in the boot tray by the door. Instead I offered her a drink.

"You have a beautiful house," she remarked as I poured us both some water.

"Thank you." I glanced self-consciously at my black-and-white minimalist wall art.

She drained her water glass in one go. Set it on the counter. It suddenly occurred to me to offer her a seat at the table, but before I could she said, "I promise, this is just a casual visit. Since you live alone, there's not as much for me to keep track of. Some households have large families, pets, smokers . . . lots to consider."

"My house is pretty straightforward. And I have a fenced-in yard." I immediately cringed. Like this was great because I could let my kid out back to play like a dog?

I took her on a tour of the house. Stood tense as she studied the purple-walled room that would become the nursery. "I haven't done anything in here yet," I said. "But I . . . I mean obviously when I know who I'm adopting, there'll be some decorating, and . . ."

She was making notes. I wanted to see her notes. I wondered if I should show her my folder full of nursery ideas. No. That would definitely make me seem weirder. I forced myself to finish the tour, and then we sat in the living room to talk.

First I was asked about my reasons for wanting to adopt. "I know you covered this in your initial interview," Cheryl said. "But is there anything you want to add?"

"I feel ready," I told her. "I've always wanted kids. I'm good with them. I've never felt like I was in a better place in my life. My business is doing well; I've accomplished a lot of my personal and professional goals. I—I want to—to keep growing up." Amazing how I could have the best, most eloquent answers in my head, and yet when I opened my mouth, I sounded ridiculous.

We talked about my home and my neighborhood. My upbringing. My mother and sister. That was where I started to get really nervous.

"Well, you talked to them." I forced a laugh. "I know they can come off a little intense, but they're really good people."

"They came off just fine," Cheryl assured me.

"My mother is religious. I'm not, but we've discussed how—how she'll keep her faith private until . . . I mean, not private. It's not like she can't ever mention it or let my child ask questions. But I'd like to raise my son or daughter without religion until they're old enough to make an informed decision."

"That's fine." Cheryl made more notes.

"There's something I should tell you." I waited until Cheryl looked up. "My sister didn't mention this in her interview, but she was arrested at seventeen for stealing. I think she worried that by telling you, she'd hurt my chances of getting to adopt. It was a one-time thing when she was young. She's grown up a lot since then. I just didn't want you to find out during a background check and think we were lying."

Cheryl set her clipboard aside. "You're really worried, aren't you?"

I nodded.

"Don't be. We *want* this adoption to work, Miles. We're on your side."

"Do you adopt to many single men?" I blurted. "Does Beacon Center question their—their motives more?"

Cheryl smiled. "It is almost always harder for a single parent to adopt than for a couple. Especially an LGBTQ single parent. But I know you told us one of the reasons you went with Beacon Center is our reputation for helping nontraditional families adopt."

"Yes."

"It works in your favor that you have a strong support system— that your mother is going to help raise the child, and that your parents have experience with adoption."

Of course. How could my thetan-auditing, recovering-alcoholic mother *not* work in my favor?

"It seems unfair, I'm sure. But the demands of single parenting are rigorous. Add to that the concerns specific to raising an adopted child . . ."

"I understand."

"Many mothers who choose Beacon Center to help find a home for their child do so for the same reason you chose us—because they're open to diverse definitions of 'family.'"

I almost made a face.

We carried on with the chat. It was unnerving to be asked so many questions about my childhood. Did I consider my mother a good parent? Aside from the drinking and the scathing commentary on my life choices, yes. What about my father? He wasn't around a lot—but no, not in an absent-father way. Just that he had to travel a lot for work. Did Malina and I get along? Fairly well. How much time did I expect my future son or daughter to spend in the care of my parents or Malina? Ummm . . .

Finally we discussed my daily routines. My plan for balancing my business with parenthood. Everything seemed to be going well.

"This may sound like an odd question." Cheryl had her pen poised above her clipboard. "But we do ask everyone: are you sexually active?"

My stomach clenched. "Excuse me?"

She smiled. "I know, it's personal. But believe me, we have reasons for asking."

I tried frantically to decide how she wanted me to answer. Obviously I didn't have to share what kind of sex I had. But was it okay for me to tell her I occasionally had sex?

Crazy fang-fetish vampyre sex?

"I, um . . ." My mind went completely blank. "I . . . Yes. I do sometimes have . . . partners."

"That's fine." Cheryl made a note. "I'm just curious as to whether you've considered how you'll navigate relationships once you're a father."

"Well, of course, I . . . I've thought about it." Dave's voice popped into my head: *You have a TENS unit . . .* "And my plan is to put my child first. If the opportunity for a romantic relationship arises, I'll consider the impact it might have on my son or daughter, and I'll—"

"We don't expect you to stop being intimate. It's just something we ask our single parents to think about. Sometimes a parent's frequent change of partners can be confusing to a child."

"Well, I'm definitely not frequent," I assured her.

The visit finally wrapped up with Cheryl saying, "We'll use the results from your surveys to find some matches we think would be ideal, and we'll pass those along to you. And we'll make sure in advance that the matches we send you have birth mothers who are open to the idea of a single parent. Does that sound good?"

"Yes. Yes, very good." I couldn't believe this was really happening. I'd expected something in the home study to bring this whole process to a halt.

"I know you've said your budget won't allow for you to pay a birth mother's medical expenses. That may limit your options somewhat, but shouldn't be a huge problem."

"I wish I could," I said.

Cheryl gathered her things. "We'll have one more visit in the next two months, this time at your workplace."

God, I hoped I could tranquilize Jason for that.

"Beacon Center asks that you take a four-week educational class with other potential adoptive families. The next class starts at the end of the month at the Gardner Center in town—Thursday nights from seven to nine. Does that sound doable?"

"Absolutely."

Cheryl stood. "But really, Miles, everything looks great. I'm very happy to be working with you."

"You too." I shook her hand numbly. I'd promised myself I'd remember every moment of the adoption process, but this felt too surreal for me to hold on to.

I sat on my spotless couch for a long time after Cheryl was gone and tried to imagine my floor covered in toys. My carpet with grape juice stains. Tried to imagine a house that didn't feel so lonely, that felt warm and noisy and ... perfect.

I wanted everything to be perfect.

CHAPTER
SIX

D rix was in my living room, checking out my bookshelf, when I brought over a—for lack of a better word—dossier.

He was crouched, trying to get the books on the third shelf to stay upright. The third shelf had a massive gap where I'd removed all my parenting books—*Single Mothers, Single Parenting That Works, Tales from a Single Father, Adoption Nation, Dear Birthmother, In Their Own Words: Transracial Adoptees Tell Their Stories*—and hidden them in my bedroom closet.

I put a hand on his shoulder.

He jumped and turned, giving me a sheepish grin. "Sorry. I'm putting my hands all over your stuff." He stood slowly, towering over me, and glanced back at the shelf. "It's just, the rest of your house is so perfect, and then you had this shelf where the books were falling down."

I puffed up a bit at the acknowledgment of my perfect house. "I wanted to show you something."

We went to the couch and sat.

"I have some supplementary documents to get you started on understanding what I like and why." I offered him the dossier. "Now, I don't want to overwhelm you, but I've put my preferred activities in order starting with what I feel would be the easiest for a beginner to learn."

He opened the folder and began to browse. "Wow. This is . . . thorough."

I was such an idiot. But I had learned over the years that, especially with edge play, it was best to be honest and specific. "You must view your continued liaison with me as a regrettable life choice," I said softly.

He was scanning page one: Simple Impact Play and Light CBT. "Au contraire," he murmured. "I've never been with a masochist before. 'Rough body play: body punching.' Hmm."

I flushed. "I debated placing that with the intermediate activities, since it is a form of edge play. And yet, safe punching technique is fairly simple to master."

He nodded, still reading.

I grew increasingly nervous. "What kind of pain do you like causing?"

"I like whips. I have a leather single tail. I learned to use it when I was a teenager."

"What brought that on?"

He turned the page. "Indiana Jones, mostly. But I guess, just a general fascination with blood and welts and the way people try to keep control when they're being whipped. The sounds the whip makes. The sounds the person makes."

"Interesting. So you don't think it's odd that I sometimes like to bleed?"

He glanced up. "Would you relax? You haven't scared me off."

I gave you a dossier. You should be scared.

"How do you disinfect your whip?" This was an important question, if we were going to be seeing more of each other.

He shifted the folder on his lap. "Vinegar. And antiseptic mouthwash."

I nodded my approval. Leaned back against the cushions and tried to relax. "If you have supplementary documents detailing your affiliation with your coven, I would be happy to read those."

Not making the situation any better.

He grinned. "We do have an ancient tome, untouched by the hands of the unawakened and written in the blood of our founders."

"Okay."

"I'm kidding. We do have a book. But it's mostly a history of the group and a description of how to treat people with compassion." He flipped the page. Raised a brow. "Barebacking?"

Shit. "Oh. Uh. Not really a kink, I know. But I do have a strong preference for lack of barriers."

"We have that in common."

My heart thudded. No point in putting this conversation off. It was part of the reason I'd included barebacking in the dossier. "I'm on Healthvana."

He looked confused. "What?"

"The app that lets you, um—share your STI test results with partners."

I caught the brief upward jerk of his brows, but in true Hendrix Seger form, he took it in stride. "There's an app for that?"

"There is. I was skeptical at first, but it is quite useful. My verified results are on there. I'm clean. I can show you."

"So it's, like . . .?"

"Your doctor can send your results to your phone. The results are stored in the app. The app even helps you find nearby testing clinics if you've just had sex with someone and weren't sure if they were clean."

"What will they think of next?"

I snorted. "I don't know how important this is to you. But if you are interested, you might consider getting the app."

He ran a long, pale finger along the edge of the dossier. "I'm clean too. And I've been tested fairly recently." He looked slightly embarrassed. "Dark Ravens believe that physical contact—no barriers—is the best way to exchange energy."

"Well, uh. Good."

"I'll get that app."

"Yeah, I mean—" I tensed as he set down the dossier and scooted closer to me "—it's really easy to download."

"Relax. I'm not going to bite. Yet." He traced my cheekbone with one finger.

All the gods of all the ages, he made me want to *fuck*. Every time he touched me. Every time he looked at me. For all my kinkiness, I had always been careful to fuck at appropriate times and in appropriate places. When it was safe and private and emotionally manageable. He made me want to fuck at Windsor Castle during the Garter and Thistle services. He made me want to fuck loudly and messily, while I was crying or scared or delirious with joy.

I kissed him. I must have been kissing in a way that suggested I wanted to fuck forever, because after a minute he moaned and drew back and stared at me with—I mean, just crazy eyes. Like he was about to consume my prana.

Then he was on me again, using his teeth, his tongue, running his hands over my shoulders.

"Whatever you want," he murmured. "I'll learn it."

"Just fuck me," I said between gasps. "Right now."

He had to run to the bathroom and get a condom. But then he got back on the couch, and he did fuck me.

Right on top of my dossier.

Later, we were lying in bed, his head on my chest. "What if I can't learn?" he asked softly.

I ran my fingers through his long hair. I felt half-asleep. "Learn what?"

"All the stuff you like to do."

"You only learn what you want to learn. I'm happy with what we're doing right now."

"But I *want* to learn."

I hesitated. "Do you wanna see my gear bag?"

"Huh?"

"That's kind of how kinky people flirt. You look at each other's gear bags."

"Is that . . . a metaphor?"

"Literally the bags where we keep our equipment."

He sat up. "Okay. Where's your gear bag?"

"Uhh." I rolled and swung my legs over the edge of the bed. Went to my closet. Beside my actual laundry hamper was another wicker hamper filled with folded blankets. And under the blankets was my gear bag.

I let him go through the contents and ask questions. There was nothing too scary in there except for a couple of imposing dildos, some talon clamps, and a rather medieval-looking cock cage. The rest of the toys were pretty standard.

"What's this?" He held up an implement I hadn't used in a while.

"That is a carpet beater made of steel cable."

"You let people *hit* you with this?"

I grinned. "I thought you were a sadist?"

"Yeah, but . . ." He whacked it lightly against his hand. "No way."

I laughed. "It hurts a *lot*. And leaves bruises for weeks. But not as bad as those." He'd pulled out a trio of Delrin canes.

"I can't even imagine. I mean, I can take pain, but, like, do you let people hit you full force with these?" He swung one of the canes through the air. The swish made me cringe. Made me wish I were bent over the bed, hearing that sound behind me.

"Sometimes."

He found a small glass vial of amber liquid. "What's this?"

"Cinnamon oil. My archnemesis."

"Do you put it . . . in secret places?"

"Uh-huh."

He grinned. "Miles. You are full of surprises."

"It's the cardigans," I said. "And the glasses. Nobody ever suspects."

"This?" He held up a black-and-red wand.

"Like a cattle prod. But designed for humans."

He ran his thumb over the switch, but didn't turn it on. "So what do you like best?"

I tried to savor the moment: this incredibly tall, beautiful man, kneeling on my floor, surrounded by canes and carpet beaters and cages and clamps, asking me what I liked best.

"I like a lot of things. Knives are amazing. But that's not a beginner thing."

"People cut you?"

"Sometimes. Not deep or anything. And it's more about the fear. I can—can get off on just a blade running over my skin. No cuts at all."

"Wow."

I knelt beside him. "What I like depends on the moment and the person. But there's not a lot I won't try."

"I really think this is amazing." He swished the cane again. "I'm just worried I won't ever live up to, you know. This."

"Nobody learns to dom in a day. Most people have a mentor. That mentorship can last years." An idea started to take shape in my head. I wasn't sure Drix would be interested. But he'd *said* he liked exchanging energy with other people. And he'd *said* he wanted to learn. "I actually know somebody who's an excellent teacher. If you really do want to get a handle on some of this stuff."

He tilted his head, a soft smile on his face. "Someone could teach me?"

"If you want. I wouldn't ask you to do anything that makes you uncomfortable. He knows me well. And he's not an ex, so there wouldn't be that weirdness."

"Who is he, then?"

"He was my mentor, for a while." I shrugged. "I taught him a few things too."

Drix nodded. "If he's willing to accept that I might be a disaster, I would love to become his apprentice."

"I highly doubt you'll be a disaster." I couldn't stop looking at him. It wasn't just that he made me want to fuck. He made me feel quieter too. Tender. There was a sweetness to him, a gawkiness and an elegance that coexisted peacefully. I smiled—a smile as broad and genuine as any I'd managed over the past few months of stress and confusion and uncertainty. "I *know* you won't be."

He reached out and poked me with the cane. "For you? I'll make sure I get it right."

I wrote to Bowser when I got home the next day.

Do you have any interest in mentoring a very pleasant man who is not a dom but would like to learn to inflict pain on me in a dominant manner?

Bowser replied ten minutes later. *Interested. Who?*

I'll introduce you. He's a sadist. Just not into the BDSM scene.

Two days later, the three of us had a coffee date. I tried not to think about how out of control this was getting. *Pain-slut bucket list. Remember?*

Drix and I walked to the coffee shop. He walked very close to me, and I wondered if I ought to try taking his hand. High school was the last time I'd done the sort of dating where you held hands; I wasn't even sure public hand-holding was a thing with which adults bothered. And if it was, I didn't know if Drix and I were at that point yet.

We passed the Lutheran Church of Christ the King. The billboard read: *Let's meet at my house Sunday before the game. —God.*

I saw Drix notice it, but he didn't comment. I appreciated that, in some odd way. I was no defender of organized religion, but sometimes it got tiresome when Dave, for instance, went off on a tirade each time we saw a church.

I searched for something to say. "Which of these passersby would you most like to investigate?" I asked at last.

He looked at me quizzically. "Investigate?"

"Yes. As a PI, who looks the most promising in terms of dark secrets?"

"Well, there's only one person here whose secrets I'm interested in knowing." He smiled, half-sly, half-embarrassed, and bumped me with his hip.

At first I was too startled to reply. Then I managed, "Oh, please."

"It's true." He was silent for a moment. "Spying on people when they're at their worst isn't something I really enjoy. I'd rather let people keep their secrets. Unless they want to tell me."

"So why become a PI?"

"I don't know. I didn't have another plan at the time."

We walked by a small park—unnaturally green grass, a couple of benches, a kids' playground. In the playground was a wooden sunflower with the center cut out. "Miles!" He turned to me again. "Be a sunflower."

"*What?*"

He was fishing his phone out of his pocket. "I want to take a picture."

I opened my mouth to tell him I would *never* be a sunflower. "We're going to be late."

"Please?"

I looked at him. All six foot seven of him, with his blond ponytail and long-sleeved burgundy and white baseball tee and his goddamn stupid-splendid eyes . . .

I walked stiffly past a group of tag-playing children and a gaggle of adults who were engaged in private conversations instead of watching their children every second to make sure no one tripped and split their head open on the slide. I cautiously put my face through the cutout.

Drix grinned and positioned the camera. "Smile."

I managed an approximation. I didn't fare well in photos. He took the picture, and I quickly got out from behind the sunflower.

He was shielding his screen from the sunlight so he could look at the picture. "Oh, that's perfect." He showed me.

I was surprised by how genuine my smile looked. I glanced away quickly. "We'd better get going."

"I didn't have another plan at the time." I tried to imagine a life without multiple plans. What confused me was that Drix didn't seem disorganized or unreliable. He simply seemed at peace with spontaneity.

His gentleness, his openness, were admirable, if a bit terrifying. That willingness to let things happen rather than make them happen. I was slightly afraid to submit to someone like that.

But oddly enough, not nearly as nervous as I was to be walking through a park with someone like that.

What do I say?

Nothing. Just take his goddamn hand.

But seconds went by, and I kept not doing it. And pretty soon, we were at the coffee shop.

CHAPTER SEVEN

D rix and Bowser hit it off beautifully. They were both so naturally calm and friendly that even though they seemed to have little in common beyond sadism, they appeared entirely comfortable with each other.

So after a long talk about medical tools and single tails, and an embarrassing moment where they bonded over a mutual appreciation for my ass, we went back to Bowser's place. Drix seemed a little anxious, but was still cheerful as ever. *I* was the one who was sweating. I'd participated in multipartner scenes before. I'd done demos to help others learn. But I'd never been watched by someone whose opinion I cared so much about. Someone who could make me be a sunflower just by saying please.

Bowser took us upstairs to his "office."

Drix had been warned, but he still gave a little excited gasp when he saw the steel exam table. The stirrups. The small counter and sink. "This is like a legit doctor's office."

Bowser grinned. "Well, I'm by no means a 'legit' doctor. But I do play one on TV." He laughed the Bowser laugh. I hid my grin at Drix's startled jolt.

"So medical play's definitely your thing?" Drix wandered over to look at the sharps box.

I set my gear bag down along the wall.

Bowser went to the cabinets and took out some equipment. "Yep. Been doing it almost a decade." He flipped off the main switch so the room was lit only by a set of fluorescent tubes over the counter and a standing lamp in one corner. Enough light that we could see what we were doing, but not the harsh overhead glare of a typical doctor's office. "I got the sink and the hot plate in here a few years ago, so I could do all the sterilizin' right in this room."

"There is nothing more foreboding than watching him sterilize his tools," I told Drix. "If you can imagine, like, he's boiling water, and picking up scalpels and poky things and pliers . . . It's like being in a Saw movie."

Drix's eyes widened. "I already hate going to the real doctor, so yes, I can imagine."

"I don't know what you want to do—" Bowser closed the last cabinet and turned to us "—but I always like to start by having Miles strip."

Drix grinned. "That's one of my favorite ideas ever."

My cheeks grew warm. "Don't doctors usually pull a privacy curtain and leave you alone while you undress? And give you a gown?"

Bowser laughed again. Drix raised his eyebrows at me. I should have warned him about the laugh. I'd warned him about the exam table and the pliers, but not the laugh.

"We do things a little differently here," Bowser said. "My assistant and I want to see you take your clothes off."

Slowly I unbuttoned my fly. Pushed my jeans down and stepped out of them. Removed my socks. I pulled my shirt off and stood there in my boxers, facing them.

"Gorgeous," Drix murmured.

"Get those shorts off," Bowser said.

I took off my boxers. My cock was already hard, and I felt embarrassed in a way I never had in front of either man individually.

Then something occurred to me. *They both think you're hot. They both like hurting you. And Drix wants to learn what* you *enjoy.*

I had an incredible amount of power here. And damned if I wasn't going to use it.

I stepped forward. "All right, you two. I'm going to teach Drix how to handle me. And Bowser, you're gonna help."

They both grinned.

"I kinda like being ordered around," Drix said.

"Then come on over here." I walked to the table.

"Can I kiss you first?" he asked behind me.

I turned and nodded, surprised. And considerably self-conscious at the idea of doing this in front of Bowser.

My awkwardness dissolved as Drix cupped the back of my head and pressed his lips roughly against mine. He ran his hand over the fuzz on my scalp, and I closed my eyes, moaning softly. Then the point of his canine sank into my lip, and my body jerked. I pressed my hips tentatively against his. His other hand went to my ass and pulled me even closer, so that our hardening cocks rubbed together. I dug my fingers in just behind his shoulder blades and gasped softly, wishing he would slam me against a wall, put his arm over my throat, and kiss and bite me while I struggled for breath.

I got the sense there was something *claiming* about this kiss—a sort of unsubtle message to Bowser that I was already pissed-upon territory. It made me feel absurdly wonderful.

Drix pulled back. His gaze was soft as he trailed his fingertips across my forehead. "I want to see you hurt." It was a whisper, and he gave me the slightest grin afterward.

He made the whole idea of being hurt seem new.

I climbed on the exam table with my heart thudding. Bowser adjusted the back so that I was propped up, and pulled the stirrups a little farther apart. Which made me wonder who had been on this table since the last time I was up here. Bowser had said I wasn't his only partner. I wondered who else he played with, and how often. I put my feet in the stirrups. Felt intensely vulnerable, spread like this in front of both of them. I kept my focus on Bowser, but I was aware, always aware, of Drix watching.

What if he thinks I'm a freak for liking this?

He's a vampyre. That's way freakier.

Right?

"You're going to tie me down," I told Bowser. "I have cock cages and rings in my bag. Maybe a ring, so you have more access."

Bowser nodded and picked up one of the wrist cuffs that were chained to the table. "Miles is real good at holding still," he explained to Drix. "But I still like to restrain him."

I swallowed as Bowser fastened the steel cuffs around my wrists. Then he secured the padded neck restraint. I took a deep breath. He didn't always tie my neck down, but when he did it brought about this instant feeling of calm that I loved, because it was so incongruous with the knots of anticipation in my stomach, the racing of my heart. He reached into the drawer of the side table and pulled something out. Showed it to me.

Two small, blunt steel hooks with rawhide laces attached.

I nodded. Lifted my hips slightly, as though that might somehow help me forget how hard my cock was, then settled back down and waited. Bowser showed the device to Drix. "Nose hooks. These little guys go up his nostrils." He slipped the hooks up my nose with a practiced ease, holding the rawhide taut. They didn't go in far—but the effect was immediate—I felt completely powerless and very aware of just how much damage they could do if I moved my head.

Bowser held me like that a moment longer, increasing the tension fractionally until I stopped breathing. He pulled the rawhide laces gently over the top of my head, and I exhaled. "Chin up." He fastened the rawhide to a ring on the back of the table. Now, if I pulled my head forward even a little, I was in danger.

I took a couple of deep breaths.

"That's right," Bowser said quietly. "Breathe."

I nodded slightly, feeling the pull of the hooks. "Cock ring," I said.

"Drix." Bowser reached into a drawer of the stand and took out a skin stapler and a staple remover. Set them on the stand. "Could you go to Miles's bag and find a cock ring, please? There should be a steel one with a little ball on it."

I listened to Drix walk to my bag and rummage in it. I couldn't move my head to see him, and having him out of my sight left me surprisingly unnerved. I caught Bowser's eye and flicked my gaze to the skin stapler. "Good choice," I whispered.

"Is it gonna freak him out?" Bowser asked.

"I think he'll be all right."

Bowser grinned. "I like him."

I smiled back. *Me too. I think.*

Drix returned with the thick steel cock ring. Stood where we could see each other.

Bowser gestured with the stapler. "Go ahead and put it on him."

Panic flickered across Drix's face. "Uh, I've never . . ."

"It unscrews where the ball is," I said. "Turn the ball counterclockwise."

Drix unscrewed the ring.

"Now pull it open a little wider and put it around the base of my cock."

I tried very hard to hold still as Drix obeyed. His fingers kept brushing my dick, making me tense up.

"Rotate it so the ball is at the bottom."

He did.

"Now you screw it tight." I stared at the ceiling, closing my eyes each time his fingers grazed me. "There's a tension knob right by the ball. Turn it counterclockwise to keep tightening it."

Drix hesitated, then turned the knob.

"More," I said softly.

He kept going. I could hear his breathing get shallower. The ball was digging in hard to the underside of my cock.

"A little more," I whispered.

He gave the knob one more turn. My voice stuck in my throat for a moment.

"Good," I finally managed.

"This is gonna make him real sensitive," Bowser said, flicking my cock just above the ring. I jolted. "But it'll keep him from coming while we play with him."

I lay there, my head held back by the nose hooks, the padded restraint taut around my neck. I was trying to decide what to tell them to do next, when Drix's fingers skimmed my stomach. I shivered.

"I like playing with him," Drix whispered. This time his fingertips dragged along the crease between my thigh and groin. Then my inner thigh. My breath shuddered out of me, and my legs tensed.

He put the pad of one finger on the slit of my cock. I tried reflexively to press my legs together. But the stirrups held me wide open.

"With Miles, you can start pretty hard," Bowser said. "Some pain pigs, you gotta build, layer the pain. But Miles, you don't have to."

"Thanks." I rolled my eyes. "Why don't you start with ballbusting? That's something Drix can pick up pretty quickly."

Bowser gave Drix a brief explanation of where to hit. Then he hauled off and slapped my balls. Hard.

My hips jerked, but I didn't cry out. The pain was enormous, spreading quickly into my gut and pooling there.

"Or you can punch," Bowser suggested. "But you can't punch and kick as hard as you slap. Common sense."

His fist connected with my balls, and this time I did shout. It wasn't a brutal punch—he'd pulled it at the last second, but it still hurt like hell. I slowly forced myself to relax back onto the table. I was panting.

"Jesus," Drix said.

"And you can mix that with what you were doing." Bowser stroked my shaft lightly with two fingers. "Keep him turned on. Keep him wonderin.'"

I moaned as Drix took over touching me. He wrapped his fingers tentatively around my throbbing balls. "Pull," I suggested between gasps. "And twist."

He wrenched them. My face contorted, and for several seconds I couldn't breathe. I wanted to come so bad. It was so hot, having Drix here, feeling his uncertainty and his power.

Bowser slapped my abdomen. My hiss changed to a whimper as Drix trailed a finger lightly over the skin behind my balls.

"Good," Bowser said. "Now you slap his balls—don't be afraid. You're just using the flat of your hand, so you can hit hard."

"I don't—" Drix laughed shakily. "This is gonna sound weird, but I don't want to hurt him. Like, really hurt him."

I almost laughed too. "It's okay. You don't have to do anything you don't like. But I promise, I'm fine."

Bowser stepped closer to Drix. "If you want, I'll slap first. You watch my arm position. Watch how hard I hit. Then you try."

I swallowed and waited.

Bowser's slap was sharp and sent bile into my throat. I waited for the queasiness to pass, and when it didn't right away, I forced myself to calm down enough to say, "I need a minute before the next one."

Bowser turned to Drix. "You know how when you get hit in the nuts, it's like you feel sick and you can't move? Because moving or having anything even touch you seems like it would kill you?"

"Yeah," Drix said.

"Okay, so if Miles says he needs a minute, it's best to just back off and let him get the pain under control. I know the impulse might be to touch him, reassure him. But just give him some space, and then when his breathing gets a little more normal, you can touch him."

I steadied my breathing with effort.

Bowser nodded. "There now. See?" He stroked my shoulder. "Miles is doin' a real good job taking this. And he knows his body real good. Knows when he needs a break."

Miles knows his body. Knows how to process pain. Knows the entire BDSM dictionary, from A-frame to zip strip.

And is terrified of anything he doesn't know.

I glanced up at Drix. I swallowed, my Adam's apple pushing against the neck restraint.

Drix's warm palm touched my thigh. He rubbed gently. "You sure you're okay?"

I tried to tilt my head to see him better, but the nose hooks dug in. "I love it. Are *you* okay?"

He laughed that awkward laugh again. "I thought I was a sadist. But I am clearly not the badass I thought I was."

I grinned. He hadn't seen anything yet. "I promise, I love this. But if you don't, we'll stop."

"No, no, no. I just want to make sure you really love it. But I guess that's stupid, since you know what you're doing."

"It ain't stupid," Bowser said. "This is a lot to take in."

Drix shifted. "I think maybe I'd do better with the—the knife play and stuff? Anything with blood and blades. The punching and slapping just seems so—against everything I've been taught."

I snickered. "And cutting isn't?"

He laughed too. "Shut up! Fine. I'm a weirdo."

Bowser's laugh drowned out both of ours. "Well, we can move on to something a little bloodier." He picked up the skin stapler.

"Do I want to know?" Drix asked.

"Skin stapler," I told him.

"Is that exactly what it sounds like?"

"Yes."

"Oooh."

"See, now you sound excited."

Drix came around to stand by my head. "I am. I'll bet you can make all kinds of pretty patterns with that."

Bowser's voice was slightly hoarse when he spoke again. "Miles likes impact play. But he also likes predicament-type stuff." He placed the stapler on my stomach. "It actually doesn't hurt bad to put the staples in. But you can do all kinds of painful things once the person's stapled."

"Will you try it on me?" Drix asked. "Like on my arm or something. So I can see?"

"Sure."

Drix held out his arm. Bowser put the stapler to his skin and squeezed the lever. Drix winced as the staple lodged in the surface of his skin. "Okay, ow. But not as bad as I thought."

Bowser picked up the staple remover and plucked the staple out.

Drix yelped. "Okay, that hurt worse."

Bowser chuckled and set the remover aside. He got out the alcohol pads and disinfected the stapler.

He started with a couple of staples in my belly. They didn't hurt, and Bowser cleaned each tiny wound as it formed.

Then he let Drix try doing one. Drix placed the stapler tentatively against my stomach.

"It's okay," I told him.

"Just squeeze the lever," Bowser said.

Drix's face screwed up in an almost comical look of concentration. He squeezed the lever. I looked up at him. "See? I'm still alive."

He reached out and touched the staple. Pressed on it gently. My breath caught, and I held his gaze. He smiled and bit his lip, raising his eyebrows.

Bowser took the stapler again and moved to my inner thighs. Four staples in each. I was sensitive there, and the staples stung, but I remained still.

Bowser gripped my cock. I could barely tolerate the pressure of his hand—my cock was so swollen, and I had no hope of release. He put the stapler to the ridge under the head.

"Oh God," Drix said. "You're not—"

Click. A sharp, startling bite as the first staple went in, half under the ridge and half buried in the head.

Click. Click.

Bowser made a circle around the ridge. I jerked and sucked in air. He wiped up the blood droplets with an alcohol pad, and the alcohol stung my slit so badly my legs spasmed. Then he put the stapler right over my slit. I flinched.

Click. The pain seared from my dick into my gut. I let out a long groan and squeezed my eyes shut. The pressure in my cock was worse than the pain of the staple. I *needed* to come. But my dick was stapled shut.

I opened my eyes. "Drix," I whispered. "Please. Please?"

What was I begging for?

"What?" he whispered. He was looking down at me, his face flushed, his breathing slightly rough. "What do you need?"

I closed my eyes. "What you did before." I opened my eyes again. Watched it dawn on him.

He ran his finger up my shaft, stopping just before the ring of staples. Then he kept going, touching the staples, pressing them deeper into my skin.

I moaned, my throat tightening, my shoulders shaking. "Harder."

He pressed harder, until my eyes watered with the pain. He stopped abruptly.

"Very nice." Bowser sounded appreciative.

Drix helped Bowser tie thread around each set of staples on my inner thighs.

"Pull his dick down," Bowser said.

Drix obeyed. I yelped as he tugged my cock downward. Bowser looped both threads through the staple in the slit and tied it. This time, the pain didn't stop. The thread kept constant tension on the staples, and the ache filled my body. My dick curved like a vaulting pole. Tears slid from the corners of my eyes.

"Take the ring off," Bowser said softly to Drix.

Drix turned the tension knob. It was a bizarre sensation: the pressure from the ring lessened as a new pressure built in my balls. Drix unscrewed the metal bead and pulled the ring off my shaft.

I lost control immediately, cum leaking out from around the staple and dripping down my shaft. Drix kept his hand on my hip. It had been a long time since I'd had anyone watch so intently while I came. I felt completely helpless as the last spurts drained out of me. Drix took my softening cock and squeezed the base, milking a little more from me. He pushed his thumb down on the slit staple.

I stared at him, gulping unsteadily, as he continued to press the staple deeper into me. Bowser, meanwhile, had grabbed the rawhide laces of the nose hooks. He gave them a couple of tugs, forcing my head all the way back, and I came again. A long, dry orgasm so powerful I had to yank my feet from the stirrups and press my legs together.

When it was over, Bowser and Drix let me go, and none of us moved. I was still shocked, panting. Slowly, Bowser untied the nose hooks and slid them out. Drix unlocked the wrist cuffs and the neck restraint.

I just lay there, dazed, soaring.

Thank you. I wanted to say it. To both of them, but mostly to Drix.

"Oookay," I said when I could speak again. "Well. That's one way to get me off."

Drix smiled, but he looked pale, even for him. He moved his hand slightly, like he wanted to touch me.

Bowser nudged Drix. "And here's where you'd normally start the aftercare. Which is whatever Miles needs to bring him down from the scene."

Drix gazed at me, and the corners of his mouth lifted again. "And what does Miles need to bring him down from a scene?"

I opened my mouth to reply, *nothing*, but was stopped by something in his expression. A hint of awe and uncertainty, like he'd stumbled upon some secret, wild place and wasn't sure if he should stay.

Bowser took a handful of equipment over to the sink. "Miles ain't big on aftercare."

I turned my head toward him. "I'm perfectly capable of bringing myself down from a scene."

Bowser spoke over his shoulder to Drix. "For some bottoms, it's hugging, cuddling. Food, drink, watching a movie. I had one woman, she needed these Wal-Mart-brand chocolate cupcakes—one after every scene."

I addressed Drix again. "In play like this, the combined sensations of pain and pleasure cause the adrenal glands to release epinephrine, as well as endorphins and enkephalins. These are chemicals that produce a—"

"Euphoria," Drix interrupted softly. "A sense of ecstasy and detachment from reality."

I hesitated. "Yes." I rarely played with anyone who had an extensive knowledge of the human body, or the physical effects of BDSM. "Anyway, there are some bottoms who experience a period of incoherence or lack of coordination after a scene. And they require monitoring and careful reintegration into the real world."

Drix's gaze traveled my body. "The person's temperature usually drops too."

All right, I suppose I was shivering a bit. Nothing that putting my clothes back on wouldn't solve.

"I'm guessing there's also an emotional comedown?" Drix went on. "I've known people in the coven for whom touch therapy—or physical pain—dredged up all kinds of somatic memories."

Well, I certainly wasn't experiencing somatic memories. Perhaps, when I was younger, I'd been surprised by the mess of inarticulate-able feelings I often experienced in the wake of a scene. But anymore, I was used to the physical and psychological effects of play, and could handle them with ease.

Drix turned to Bowser, who was watching us. "Can I try?"

Bowser leaned against the counter. "Try what?"

"Aftercare. Just me and him."

What? Had I not just made it clear I didn't need ... And for him to ask Bowser, not me ...

Bowser lifted his eyebrows. There was a slight hesitation—a moment where I couldn't read his face. Then he said, "Be my guest. I'll give you two some privacy."

He left before I could protest.

I wasn't sure I wanted to protest anyway.

Once I was alone with Drix, I felt a thousand times more naked. I stopped shivering, the heat of embarrassment enough to warm me up. "I was being serious when I said I didn't need anything."

He whacked my shoulder lightly. "It isn't all about you. *I* need something."

This was . . . unanticipated. "What do you need?"

He shook his head. "I don't know. That scene was— It did a lot to me. *For* me. Psychologically." He held up his hand. "I'm still shaking a little."

He really was.

I met his gaze again, anxious. "You didn't like it?"

His face held a quiet amusement that managed not to look at all like mockery. "I didn't say that. I just need to process it."

Okay. Well. That was understandable. Topspace existed as well as subspace. Dom-drop as well as sub-drop. I'd just never had to deal with it.

"All right." I patted the table. "Come here. Talk to me."

He sat beside me. The steel creaked. Before I could think too much about it, I took his hand. And then I didn't know what to do with it.

He glanced down at our laced fingers and gave them a tiny smile.

"How did it feel for you?" I asked awkwardly.

"Overwhelming," he replied at once.

"Even for a sadist?"

He snorted. "This is gonna sound crazy, but I've never really gotten sadistic with someone I was—was attracted to, I guess? Like, most of the blood play I've done has been with members of the coven. And I care about them. A lot. But, I mean . . ."

Attracted to. I was fucking blushing. "I'd think it would be more rewarding to hurt someone you found attractive."

"Yeah, but it's not just about being attracted to you."

There was a pinched, warping sensation in my stomach. "So what's the issue?"

He looked at me, patiently exasperated. "It's not an *issue.* I'm just dealing with liking you as a person but also not having a long history with you and not totally understanding the things you want. And wishing— I don't know, that I knew more of the nonhurting things you want."

This conversation was making me deeply uncomfortable. *Liking me as a person? The nonhurting things I want?* I studied the staples glinting in my skin.

He shook his head. "Sorry. I don't mean to make this weird."

"Come here." I pulled him into a hug—fierce, unplanned, but it was what I hoped he needed. And as soon as he was in my arms, *I* felt better. Not exposed and nervous, but calm and like . . . like I had something to give him, something to teach him that went beyond how to use a skin stapler.

He buried his face in my shoulder, and he breathed quietly and shallowly, seeming to press himself closer with each passing second. He was either feasting on my prana or . . .

Or we were both right where we needed to be.

CHAPTER
EIGHT

I showed up for the Subs Club meeting the next day sore but disarmingly happy. I had little bug-bite sized wounds on my thighs, dick, and belly from the stapler, and I was replaying snippets of things Drix had said to me over and over in my head.

"What do you need?"

". . . dealing with liking you as a person."

". . . never really gotten sadistic with someone I was attracted to."

Dave sat at the head of the table, his laptop open in front of him. "I have an announcement. Where's Kamen?"

Nobody knew. We worked our way through a bowl of cherries as we waited. I kept imagining Drix's fingers brushing my cock. Felt his touch across my stomach, the slow bite of him pressing the staple into my skin . . .

Kamen eventually arrived, a lollipop stick jutting from his mouth. "Hey," he said around the sucker. "Sorry I'm late."

Gould motioned to the bowl. "We've got cherries."

Kamen peered into the bowl. "Oh man. Those are sugary, right? I just went to the dentist."

Dave waved him off. "Yeah, buddy. But, like, fruit sugar. That's healthy."

Kamen sat on the side of the table opposite Gould and me. "I'm trying to be better. My mom got me a gift card to the dentist for my birthday, so I finally went."

That yanked me out of my Drix fantasies. "What?"

"I couldn't afford to go otherwise. But I went, and no cavities." He sucked on the lollipop.

"What are you talking about?" Dave asked. "Dentists don't have gift cards."

Kamen leaned back, spreading his legs. "Mine does."

We all stared at him.

I tried to choose my words carefully. "A medical care provider is not an Outback Steakhouse. If your dentist is handing out gift cards, something is wrong."

Kamen shrugged. "He's great. He's always got suckers."

Dave sighed. "Kamen, the suckers are a trap. He's trying to rot your teeth so you'll have to see him more."

I nodded. "Yes, how can you be worried about cherries while you indulge in your complimentary cavity generator?"

"What dentist *is* this?" Gould asked.

Kamen crunched the sucker. "Bobby's Discount Dentist."

The rest of us exchanged glances. I looked back at him. "You're kidding, right?"

"It's on 14th and Addler. Right next to the arcade."

No. Just . . . no. "There's no way there's a place called Bobby's Discount Dentist."

"Yeah-huh. I've been going there forever. There's that commercial that's on all the time." He sang: "'Bobby's Discount Dentiiist . . . Your teeth are safe in our hands!'"

Dave slowly lifted a cherry to his mouth. Bit it off the stem, still staring at Kamen. "That sounds like something a serial killer would say just before he rips out your molars with rusty pliers. 'Your teeth are safe in my hands.' And then he, like, yanks them without anesthesia and cups them in his hands and then feeds them one by one to his imaginary rheumy-eyed rabbit friend who has ten-foot ears made of wilted lettuce leaves."

Kamen shook his head. "Dude, Dave. He's a really nice, affordable dentist who just happens to have a drive-thru and Free Fluoride Fridays."

"A *drive-thru*?" Dave and I said together.

Kamen kept a straight face, then burst out laughing. "You guys totally believed me!"

I put a hand to my chest. "Oh, thank God."

"Does this place really have a drive-thru?" Gould asked quietly.

Kamen shrugged again. "Just a small one where you can pick up floss and stuff."

I closed my eyes briefly and took a deep breath. "Bobby's Discount Dentist doesn't even make any sense. It sounds like Bobby owns a dentist who is available for a reduced price. When in fact, he's offering discounted dental *services*."

"Aw, lay off Bobby." Kamen finished the last of his sucker, then started on the cherries. "If you went to him once, you'd see how cool he is. I'm getting Mexico prices there."

Kamen had once gotten three cavities filled for ninety dollars when he'd stopped at a dentist's office during a trip to Mexico. God only knew what they'd been filled *with*.

"Kamen. Look at me." I waited until he was looking at me. "You need to go to a real dentist."

"Whatever, you guys." He glanced at Dave. "I got your text. What's your announcement?"

"Well, this is a very exciting meeting." Dave lifted his gaze from his laptop. "I have two big pieces of news to share with you all. First—" he turned his computer around so Kamen and I could see it "—is this."

I squinted at the webpage. Adjusted my glasses.

Kamen was already reading aloud: "'50 Grades of Grey: Hymland College starts kinky club.'" He paused. "Hymen has a dungeon?"

"No, buddy," Dave said. "Read the article."

The article was about nearby Hymland College, where students with BDSM interests had formed a group to talk about kink. The article was dated a year and a half ago.

"Right," I said. "I knew they'd started one."

"Yes." Dave was smug. "And now they want to bring in guest speakers."

Kamen rubbed his hands together excitedly. "Can we be the guests?"

"That's the plan." Dave turned the computer back around.

"Wait, what?" I said.

"*Seriously?*" Kamen's jaw dropped.

Dave nodded. "I told them that my friends and I were active in the local community, and that we even had experience leading discussion groups. They'd love to host the Subs Club at the end of the semester."

It took me a few seconds to process this. For years, there was little I'd wanted to do more than educate people about kink. And there was still a part of me that wanted desperately to do that.

"Yes!" Kamen punched the air. "College guys are so fuckin' *ungh*."

Dave winced. "Okay, buddy. Let's maybe make sure we're doing this for the right reasons. Yeah?" He looked at the rest of us. "This is cool. Because they could probably find a billion hetero guest speakers. But we're gonna be their first guests, and we're super queer."

"I'll tell you," Gould said, "back in my day, we did *not* talk about this stuff at college."

"Well, that's probably because you went to Hebrew college. And nothing dirty ever happens at Hebrew college."

"That's . . ." Gould shrugged. "Kind of true."

Dave looked at each of us. "So we're gonna do this, right?"

I couldn't do it. Not with Cheryl Callahan keeping tabs on my life. I straightened my cardigan. "I won't be able to participate due to my pending fatherhood. But you guys will tear it up, I'm sure."

As long as Kamen didn't hit on college kids and Gould didn't stand there silently, acting like he'd rather be anywhere else than in a group of people. And as long as Dave didn't . . . God only knew what Dave might do. I needed to be there. I was the only one in this group who could be trusted to remain professional and represent BDSM accurately. But . . .

Dave stared at me. "Miles, come on. You *want* to mentor college students."

I shook my head. "I really can't."

Dave gave me an *uhhhh*-huh look and glanced at Kamen and Gould. "You guys are in, right?"

Kamen grabbed a fistful of cherries. "Hell yeah." He started arranging the cherries neatly on his palm.

Gould nodded. "As long as you two do most of the talking."

They chatted a few minutes more while I tried to think of any conceivable way to be part of this without jeopardizing my chances with the Beacon Center.

You don't need to give a talk at a college. You're leaving the lifestyle, remember? All that's left is the pain-slut bucket list, and then you'll transition willingly and peacefully into Nillaland.

Right, almost done with the lifestyle. That was why I was training Drix to staple my cock shut and punch me in the balls. *Mon œil.*

Dave drummed the table. "I wonder if Ricky's in this group. Isn't he taking some computer class at Hymen?"

Ricky Chuy was the Subs Club's IT guy. Twenty-two and so sweet and earnest he made Kamen look like a jaded asshole, Ricky was still fairly new to kink and often sought our advice.

"We haven't seen him in forever," I said.

Gould took the last cherry. "I think he's seeing someone."

"Don't be ridiculous." Dave grinned. "He would never date someone without introducing us. We're like his collective dad."

Gould made a face. "That's not weird or anything. But no, his Fetmatch profile says he's in a relationship."

"Whoa. I've gotta do some digging, then."

Kamen spit out a cherry pit. "Hey, what's the second news?"

Dave clapped his hands, then typed on the laptop for a moment. "I don't know if any of you have been on our website today." He tapped the mouse hard, then leaned back. "But Fucktopus has returned."

Kamen gasped. "Fucktopus lives! I thought some old seaman had killed him." He proceeded to laugh at the word "seaman."

"Ohhh, Fucktopus." Gould nodded amiably.

I was drawing a blank. Then I remembered: When we'd first started the Subs Club, we'd had a one-time commenter on the blog called Fucktopus, who had posted a personal ad stating he was a tentacle furry, that he'd built eight robotic arms for use in scenes, and that he longed to do a role-play that involved someone hunting him in the water. Dave, who had an irrational terror of furries, had found the concept of Fucktopus particularly nightmarish.

Dave went on, "He posted this gem in the comments section of our article 'How to Navigate Multiple-Partner Scenes': 'Hi. I am a creature of the deep still looking for my ideal hunter. Am eager to be your Moby Dick. Chase me through the bleak deep waters and when you catch me have no mercy for I will show you none. Chain me up and use me to your pleasure and specifications. Impale yourselfs on my eight homemade tentacles or pull me from my watery debt so I cannot breathe. I have recently billed a harpoon gun for our scene as well as a room that stimulates water. Message me if you are interested in capturing a lonely and sexually skilled sea monster.'"

Gould had gone around the table to read over Dave's shoulder. "'Stimulates water?' I'm hoping he means 'simulates.'"

Dave nodded. "I'm guessing he also meant 'watery depth.' Though 'debt' does have a certain poetry to it. And 'billed' a harpoon gun? Billed it for what? Overhead?"

Gould tilted his head thoughtfully at the screen. "Do you think 'yourselfs' is a misspelling of 'yourself' or of 'yourselves'? Like, does he want eight partners—one for each tentacle?"

Dave blew out a breath. "These are the questions that will plague my dreams."

Kamen raised his eyebrows at me. "Miles? You gonna go for it this time?"

I had made the mistake years ago of telling them that I'd been aroused by a work of tentacle-themed erotica I'd read online. The last time Fucktopus had posted on our site, my friends seemed to think I ought to seize the opportunity. "If he didn't sound batshit crazy, I'd think about it," I admitted.

Dave was looking at me all too knowingly. "But maybe you don't need Fucktopus? Maybe you've kissed and made up with the man you were incredibly rude to?"

"As a matter of fact, yes."

Cue the "oh snaps." It was as if these boys had never left high school.

"Hey, listen." I was desperate to change the subject. "Did you guys see the message we got from someone named Ryan?" They shook their heads. "I just approved his membership. Big fan of our site, and wants to know if we can meet for drinks sometime." I didn't feel any pressing need to meet Ryan, but I figured the others would be glad to know we had a fan.

"Sweet." Dave got back on the laptop. "Oh, yeah, I totally missed this message. I'll write him back and tell him we're in."

While Dave was messaging Ryan, I got a text from Drix.

Thinking about you. And staples.

Immediately my heart started pounding. I pictured the quiet awe on his face yesterday. His earnest desire to learn. Those moments he'd grown confident enough to try something without Bowser's or my guidance. I could think of a thousand things I wanted to do with Drix. I responded with a request that he accompany me to Riddle on Friday.

A moment later, he sent the picture of me as a sunflower.

I sent back a smiling alien emoji, which wasn't dignified, but I wasn't sure what to say.

Shit, I had it bad.

What if, when the time came, I couldn't give up kink?

More specifically, what if I couldn't give up Drix?

That night, I scrutinized thumbnail photos of two cribs. They were almost identical. But one was convertible—it could transform into a toddler bed.

I clicked on the picture of the convertible one. Then X-ed out so I could study the other.

The convertible would be a better investment. But it has scrollwork. What if the baby's clothes get caught in it?

I stared at the photo. That was very unlikely. The scrollwork was minimal, and was at the very top, out of the baby's reach. The crib met the JPMA Certified Safety Rating, so one could assume it had not been responsible for any deaths thus far.

But the nonconvertible, in addition to being free of potentially fatal scrollwork, was cheaper. Which was good for my budget, but made me uncomfortable. If I wasn't willing to give my child the best, then what business did I have being a father?

I glanced at the clock: 3:01 a.m.

It doesn't matter, Miles.

It doesn't matter which crib, because they're both good cribs. The baby isn't going to care about the crib. The baby won't even remember *the crib.*

But if I got the wrong crib, what if something happened to the baby? Not even because the crib was somehow inadequate or dangerous, but just . . . because I'd made the wrong choice. Because the universe was watching me and judging me and planning horrible consequences if I screwed up.

"Life doesn't work that way, Miles," Mom had always told me when I'd come to her with similar worries.

"If I do my book report on The Giver *instead of* Where the Red Fern Grows, *will I get a bad grade?"*

"Only if you do bad work."

"If I pick the wrong college, what if I can't find a job?"

"You'll be able to get a job no matter where you go. Stop being ridiculous."

I refocused on the cribs. *How can I choose a crib when I don't know what color the nursery will be?*

I'd looked at a hundred nursery ideas—in catalogues, on Pinterest, in a book called *Nursery Doctor!* Everything was too cliché, or too colorful, or too muted, or not adequately gender neutral. It had gotten to the point where just the thought of working on the nursery paralyzed me.

Which I hated, because people who were paralyzed by their own fears were useless. There was an easy way past being afraid, and it was to face your fears head-on, and then bowl right over them. That was how I'd started a business. How I'd gotten back into BDSM after Hal's death. After the knife guy.

I called Kamen, of all people. The least likely to judge, or to care about being awoken at 3 a.m.

"What's up, dude?" He sounded groggy, but not pissed.

"I can't stop thinking about the crib."

"What?"

I rested my forehead in my hand. "Don't tell anyone. I'm— I'll be fine tomorrow morning. Just, tonight I can't stop— I'm trying to pick out a crib, and these two cribs are very similar, but . . ."

I stopped. Silence on the other end. What had I been thinking? No way would Kamen understand.

I plunged on. "And I can't decide which one. Because I'm . . . an absolute idiot."

"Dude." I heard him yawn. "Eeny, meeny, miny, moe."

"I'm not going to do that. Everyone knows that if you eeny, meeny, miny, moe with only two items or people, you will land on the first thing you eenied."

"Okay." Kamen sounded more awake now. "Here's what you're going to do. Put pictures of the cribs side by side on your computer. On the count of three, you're gonna close your eyes and put your finger somewhere on the screen. Whatever crib you land on, that's the one you get."

"I can't make a huge life decision that way."

"Yes, you can."

I stared at the pictures of the crib. "I . . ."

"Do you have the pictures up?"

"Yes."

"Close your eyes, Miles."

The screen seemed to blur as I gazed at it. With a slight sigh, I closed my eyes.

"Ready?"

"Mm-hmm."

"Now point to your screen."

I did. I purposely aimed for the side of the screen with the more expensive crib.

"Did you pick one?" Kamen asked.

"Yes."

"Bam. Miles just made a life decision."

"Thanks," I murmured. But I was already on a different website, looking at other cribs. I didn't want the convertible one with scrollwork. And I didn't want the less expensive one. There had to be something perfect out there, and I *would* find it.

I hung up with Kamen and got back to work.

CHAPTER
NINE

Friday night I picked Drix up to go to Riddle. He was wearing his black coat and boots. His long, gold ponytail shone under the porch lights, and on an impulse I reached up and gathered it in my hand, letting the silky strands fall through my fingers. Then I leaned forward and kissed him.

In the car, I asked him about his day, his week, his opinion on the new Burrito in a Bag location opening next month . . . as though if I didn't keep the conversation going, we'd descend into an intolerable laconism and discover we had no reason at all to spend time together, ever.

But eventually I relaxed and let him ask some questions too. Which gave me time to sneak glances at his hands, his hair, his profile. He was so tall he had to hunch slightly to keep his head from brushing the ceiling, and for some reason my cock found this a compelling reason to harden. I wondered how I was going to spend an entire evening with this man in a building full of BDSM equipment without nurturing an extensive and painful erection.

He looked around as we parked. "Where *is* it?"

"Above that creepily papered-over storefront. When we knock on the door, a slot opens and a man's eyes appear, and we're asked for the password."

He reached over and pinched my thigh. "You're a dirty liar."

I jerked back in surprise. Turned to him.

He burst out laughing. "Do you not have any brothers or sisters?"

"I have a sister."

"You just act so startled whenever I tease you."

Please don't talk about teasing me.

Strapped to the exam table, his hand on my cock . . .

I undid my seat belt. "I'm told I'm wound a bit tight."

"Mmm." He grinned. "Well, let's head into this sex dungeon and I'll loosen you up."

"Okay, but we're not—" *Playing. Tonight. Are we?*

He was already out of the car.

I followed him to the papered storefront. We rang the buzzer for the second floor, and after a moment, we were admitted into a narrow, musty stairwell. "Hold on," he said, as I started briskly up the stairs. He glanced around. "This stairwell is spooky. Seems like the sort of place you might get accosted by creatures of the night."

"Oh really?" I struggled to keep my tone dry as my heart rate picked up.

He stepped to where I was, grabbing my wrists and pinning them over my head as he kissed me. It was a rush—he towered over me, and the kiss made me so dizzy I was afraid I'd plummet down the stairs.

"There are cameras," I whispered.

"Ah." He kissed me again. "So there'll be a record of you getting accosted?"

"I just meant people can see us right now."

"Yes, I'm sure the people who run the kinky dungeon have never seen a kiss before."

I laughed as he pushed me harder against the wall. His coat smelled like rain and the outdoors, and he smelled like something dark, raw, and sweet all at once. I sighed as his cock rubbed mine through layers of fabric. He moved against me until I was painfully hard, then he squeezed my groin and said, "Come on."

We pushed open the heavy door at the top of the stairs, and then we were in an exposed-brick lair of dubstep and naked people.

"Whoa." Drix nearly had to duck to get through the door. "So there really is no dress code."

"Nope." It was still early enough that the club wasn't too crowded—hardly anyone was in the lounge. We stopped at the counter. Regina, one of the regular DMs, hooked Drix up with the guest waiver.

"This is like a *tome*," Drix said.

"Yep."

"Do I have to read the whole thing?"

I shrugged. "If I were you, I'd just initial and sign. I can tell you if you're breaking any house rules."

"Ooh," he said, initialing the pages. "Miles is gonna make me follow the rules."

I gave the belt of his coat a yank. "Damn right I will."

He grinned, still looking at the waiver. He signed and dated. Showed Regina his ID. Paid the guest fee. And then we were in.

"So this is Riddle," I said.

"It's very . . ." He moved his arms to the beat of the music. "Thumpy."

"The owners have an inexplicable admiration for Skrillex. Come on, I'll give you the grand tour."

I led him past a trio of clothespin-titted French maids and into the largest of Riddle's three rooms, Chaos.

And stopped dead.

There was a line of people winding through the room. Hell, it even extended into the next room. At the front of the line, I could see the top of a narrow chamber.

The dildo iron maiden.

"Um." I turned to Drix, backing him out of the room. "I forgot they added a new piece of furniture recently. So, we might want to steer clear of Chaos."

"Good life advice. What's the furniture?"

"It's a . . . a dildo iron maiden."

"Sweet. Are we gonna use it?"

"Well, not tonight, since it's nine thirty and the line is already ridiculous. But yes, someday, if you decide you like BDSM, perhaps we will have a dalliance with the DIM."

I led him toward the second room, Refinement, where the music was softer, the furniture more elegant. Drix stopped at the fishbowl full of condoms and grabbed a couple. I pretended not to notice. "So, Chaos is where all the major furniture is. Cages, horses, chain spider webs—"

"Dildo iron maidens."

"Exactly. But this is Refinement. It's a little more boudoir. It has nice suspension bars."

"Suspension bars?"

"For rope play."

He looked around. Pointed. "Those bars?"

"Yep. And note all the hooks in the walls."

"Ooh. Yeah. Lots of hooks. What's that?" He nodded at a piece of furniture by an alcove.

"Spanking bench. You'd get up on your knees here." I patted the knee surface. "Then you'd bend over this taller part."

He raised his eyebrows at me. "*I* would? Or *you* would?"

I grinned and rolled my eyes. "I do not get *spanked*. I have no patience for it. I get whipped. Beaten. Flogged. Spanking is juvenile and ineffective."

"Ooookay, then."

We came to Tranquility next. The smallest of the three playrooms. There was a velvet rope across the doorway, and a sign instructing us not to enter if other players were doing a scene. The bench that Hal had died on stood in one corner. Every time I saw it, I expected it to look less ordinary than it was. I stared at it for a long moment.

"This room's, like, legit pretty," Drix said.

The walls were dark red, the lights were dim. There was erotic art throughout the club, but unlike Chaos's in-your-face images of people plugged and chained and clamped, the photographs here were elegant. Men and women in deep bondage, their eyes closed. I hesitated only a second, then told Drix, "This is a smaller, more private room. Really nice atmosphere. It's, um . . ." *It's where my best friend spent his last moments.* "It's peaceful."

"I'd love to do something in here." Drix gazed around. "It looks sort of like the Room of Shadows. That's where the Dark Ravens have our ceremonies when someone moves up in the ranks."

Comments like that were beginning to faze me less. I led Drix back to the lounge area, where we laid claim to a sofa next to a shelf of kinky books and magazines. I straightened a copy of *Carrie's Story.* "So let's talk."

"About what?" He was too tall for the couch. He looked like a teenager trying to ride a drugstore coin-operated pony.

"I wanna play Ask a Vampyre."

"Can I play Ask a Masochist?"

"Sure." I saw the looks he was getting from others in the club, and I felt a mix of pride and possessiveness.

He seemed oblivious to the stares. "What do you want to know?"

"Where'd you go to school?" I asked. "As a kid?"

"Did you seriously bring me to a dungeon so you could talk to me about my childhood?"

"Maybe."

"I think you're just scared that I might want to put you on that spanking-bench thing and give you a juvenile and ineffective spanking."

I blushed. Pressed my legs together and tried not to squirm. "I just feel there's a lot I don't really know about you. So I wanted to talk."

"I went to Drummond Montessori. Grades one and two. But I got kicked out."

"You got kicked out of *Montessori* school? I thought they let kids do whatever they want there."

"You're still not supposed to throw things."

"You *threw* things?"

"Not at people! I just loved throwing. It was, like, this unstoppable impulse."

I laughed. "I never would have guessed."

"Oh yeah. I was a thrower. My mom signed me up for baseball early, hoping I'd become some major league pitcher. But I sucked at sports."

"Are you close with your mom?"

He nodded. "Yep. Total mama's boy."

I fell silent, not sure where I wanted to take that.

"My turn," he said. "Would you rather sleep on a bed of cow dung, or suck the dick of someone who hadn't showered in two months?"

"What kind of question is that? The dick sucking."

"If I didn't shower for two months, would you suck my dick?"

"No."

"Awww."

"Maybe." I wanted to suck his dick right *now*.

He smirked. "Your turn."

I thought for a moment. "Were you always a vampire for Halloween?"

"Never. I was a dog."

"A dog?"

"Mostly. I loved *101 Dalmatians*. So my mom made me a Dalmatian suit and painted my face so I had a patch over my eye."

I shook my head. "There is nothing hard-core about you at all, is there?"

"I beg to differ." He reached out and took my hand. A casual move that created utter chaos inside me. He held it while he asked, "Who was your childhood best friend?"

I hesitated. "I sometimes played with a kid named Kevin West. But I didn't really have close friends until after college."

"Really?"

"Yes. I was quite the loser."

"I can't believe that." He continued holding my hand, staring at me with a soft smile. "But you have friends now?"

"A very, very close group." Should I tell him about Hal?

"I remember you talked about Kamen. The one who sings Bob Seger."

"Yes. It's pretty much a package deal. You hang out with me, and you end up hanging out with Kamen, Dave, and Gould too."

"Gould?"

"It's his last name. I don't know why he goes by it. I'm not even sure what his first name is. Robert, I think."

"You should ask him sometime."

"It doesn't seem too important. Okay, my turn: Is it hard being that tall?"

"Ha! It's fine, mostly. I think the worst part is I end up feeling guilty. Because, like, women cross the street when they see me. Especially at night."

"Well, you are a ruthless bloodsucker."

"*Prana* sucker," he corrected.

"Yes, see? They can tell you're trying to feed on their energy."

"I think sometimes I let my voice get extra gay when I'm around women, just so they feel more comfortable."

"But it must be awesome sometimes, right? Like, you could beat up anyone."

"Yeah, sometimes it's fun. But it kinda hurts my feelings when people run away from me."

"Aww." I scooted over and put an arm around him. I wasn't as smooth as he was, but he immediately leaned against me, and I was suddenly warm and giddy and afraid to move and ruin it. Why was it that every time I touched him I felt like the luckiest fucker in the world? "I see a children's book: *The Loneliest Vampyre*."

He laughed. "But you probably know what I mean, right? It must be hard for you when people—" He stopped and drew back. Clapped a long, bony hand over his mouth. "Oh my God. I was just gonna say something probably really awful."

I racked my brain for what he could mean. I grinned suddenly. "Were you gonna say—?"

He dropped his hand to his lap, shaking his head. "Nothing. Nope, nope. Dumb moment. Moving on. *Loneliest Vampyre*, what?"

"Were you going to say you think people cross the street when they see me because I'm black?"

He looked so guilty I almost laughed. He straightened and hunched away a little. "I soooo should not have assumed that."

I couldn't hold back the laughter then. "It's totally fine. The cardigans help. People don't typically cross when they see black men in business suits or dressed like Mr. Rogers. But yeah, every now and then I get a crosser."

"A crosser. Nice."

"My dad actually has a big thing about how it's important for black men to be good role models and represent the community positively. I've never felt that way. Like, I don't see black people as a 'community.' Just a diverse group of humans who are under no obligation to like or support one another. *However,* my friend Dave thinks this is funny because technically the kink community is the same way. Yet I talk about that community like it's a homogenous group in need of better representation and better leaders. So . . ." I shrugged.

"I haven't heard about your dad yet. Just Scientologist mom. And you mentioned you had a sister."

"She was once arrested for stealing manhole covers."

"I like her already."

"She said the metal industry was booming. Apparently she only stole—*helped* steal—two, but she made a lot of money off them. I've tried to guilt-trip her about the innocent children who probably fell into the sewers because of her, but she has no regrets. Except getting caught."

"And so your dad . . .?"

"Trucker. He's away a lot. Which is a shame, because he's the most normal person in the family. A really great guy." I wasn't terribly interested in digging deep into my I-miss-my-dad issues right now. "Where do you see yourself in five years?"

He laughed. "Uhhh. I won't be a private investigator. I'll be a healer. Not a super spiritual, mystical healer. Just, I want to be doing something that helps people feel better. Also, I'm gonna have a juicer."

"Ambitious."

"I know, right?"

"Your question."

He stroked his chin exaggeratedly. "Do you actually like the way pain feels? Or do you just like how it feels to know you can take it?"

An impressively perceptive question, and one I'd asked myself often in my early twenties. "A little of both, I guess. I wouldn't want some random person to punch me in the face. But with someone I trust, I really like how pain feels. What about you? Do you actually like causing pain? Or do you like the control?"

"I guess it's probably similar to your situation. I don't see a random person on the street and want to punch them in the face. But when someone's, like, getting something out of the pain—I think it's such a deep connection. You know? It's a shared experience. It's not about control—I wouldn't say that."

Before I could say anything else, a woman in a corset and fairy wings came over. She had short black hair and tattoos of keys all over her shoulders. So many keys.

"Heeey, Miles."

"Hey, Girltoy."

She patted my shoulder. She was a toucher. "Long time, no see."

"You doing well?"

"Yeah, man. I just got a good dickin' in the iron maiden. Can't complain." She put up her hand for a high five. I obliged.

"Was it everything you dreamed and more?"

"I mean, it was a chamber full of dildos. So yeah." She glanced at Drix. "Who's this?"

"This is Drix. My, uh . . ."

"One of Miles's many lovers," Drix supplied.

My face heated. "Right. Um, Drix, this is Girltoy."

Girltoy checked Drix out. "You play with Miles?"

"A little." Drix gave me a quick smile. "And I hope to more often."

"Miles is insane." Girltoy rocked back and forth. "All we talk about around here is how insane Miles is. He does shit where even I'm like, 'Yeeeeaaaaahhhh, no thanks.'"

"Thank you, Girltoy." I shook my head. "By all means, scare Drix off."

"Oh. Oh, *oh*." She was still looking at Drix. "You should be scared."

Drix laughed. "Miles seems so mild-mannered by day . . ."

"One time he was letting this guy burn him with cigarettes in Chaos. Set the fire alarm off."

Drix raised his eyebrows at me.

Le sigh. "I was younger. I wasn't as self-conscious about public play. I really wanted to experience being burned."

"I haven't seen any burn scars," Drix said. "And I thought I'd looked at everything."

Seriously, could I just sink into an abyss where shame was a distant dream? "They're somewhere kind of hidden."

"I know where they are." Girltoy jostled me. "Hey, you see who's here?"

"Who?"

She nodded toward the door. "Michael Bublé."

I looked where she was indicating and felt a moment's cold recognition.

Michael Balby—aka Bublé. The DM who'd been on duty the night of Hal's death. He had faced a pretty serious inquiry into whether he could have prevented what happened, and had been absolutely devastated after that. I'd assumed he wouldn't ever come back to Riddle. But then, I'd thought the same thing about Bill Henson. "He's DM-ing?"

Girltoy nodded. "He's back in the game. And good for him, I say."

I agreed. It was hard not to be pissed at everyone involved in that disaster. GK and Kel, Riddle's owners, for letting a notoriously ignorant dom like Bill play here. Michael for not spotting that something was wrong. Hal for choosing to play with questionable partners just for the thrill of it. And even Dave, who had been here that night and had left Hal alone after they'd had an argument. But I knew Michael wasn't a bad guy, and my experience with him had always been that he was a fairly sharp DM.

"Who's Michael Bublé?" Drix asked. "Besides the 'Feeling Good' guy?"

"He's a dungeon monitor," Girltoy said. "His name's actually Michael Balby. I'm sure you heard all about Hal from Miles. But Michael was on duty that night."

Drix looked questioningly at me.

I shook my head. "It's not important." That had come out all wrong. I could feel Girltoy staring at me. "I mean, I'll explain later."

"Ohhh." Girltoy glanced between us. "Sorry. I'm always running my big mouth. Anyway, I'd better go see what the Master wants next. Good to see you, Miles. Nice meeting you, Drix."

She wandered off.

"Who's Hal?" Drix asked.

"A friend." I was surprised by an upwelling of emotion—mostly anger—that I couldn't even begin to sort through. I *really* didn't want to talk about this now. "But he's not around anymore."

We shifted into silence. "Anything you want to ask me?" I gestured around the room. "About anything going on here?"

"I do want to ask you something."

"What?"

"Who's Hal?" he repeated.

It was the first time he'd pushed me on anything, and I wasn't sure how to react. "I'm serious. This isn't the time to discuss it."

His violet gaze was steady and intense. The intensity gave way to something that looked almost like hurt. He turned away, and I felt guilty. But still angry too. I didn't need Hal ruining my fucking night.

"Hey," I said softly.

He turned back to me.

"You, um . . ." I swallowed. "You're . . . I'm sorry. I meant to tell you the other day that I really like you too. I'll get better at sharing things with you, I think. Right now, though, I just want to enjoy having you here."

He studied me for a moment. "Sorry. I'm nosy."

"Well, you are a PI."

He smiled finally, and I reached out, not sure what I intended to do. I ended up placing my hand on his thigh, which radiated warmth through the denim. I fell completely still, staring at my hand, then letting my gaze travel up his leg to his groin. To the snap of his fly.

Then I let my hand follow my gaze. I didn't look at his face—just watched his thighs tense slightly and listened to the way his breath faltered. *It's easier. It's easier if it's sex, if it's the bucket list. If I let myself like him too much—if I like him enough to tell him about Hal . . .*

It'll end up hurting in a way I can't deal with when I have to let him go.

I stroked the bulge in his jeans. His breath hitched, and his hips lifted. The music paused between tracks, and in that moment of relative quiet, he whispered, "Could I blow you?"

My hand stilled. "Here?"

"Yeah." One side of his mouth quirked up. "What, are you shy? 'Cause I just met a woman who watched you get your secret cigarette burns in this club."

"My exhibitionist tendencies have atrophied in recent years."

"So you *didn't* like me watching Bowser staple your cock?"

I mock glared at him. "I didn't say that."

He straightened, pushing against my hand. "So what if I blow you? And what if I, um, hurt you? In a way no one can see?"

I was intrigued. I let him lead me out of the lounge. He paused for just a second in front of Tranquility, and then moved on to Refinement. As though he could feel my resistance to going into Tranquility. He really did pay attention to body language, I realized. To . . . energy, I guess.

Another couple was in Refinement—a man tying his partner to one of the suspension frames. I did my best to ignore them.

Drix and I went to the back corner, beside the spanking bench. He got on his knees. Folded that incredibly lanky frame and knelt there gazing up at me.

He looked ethereal. Like he was waiting for some holy office to be conferred upon him. I was jittery with nerves, but I calmed as I reached down and touched the top of his head. Lightly—my fingertips barely skimmed his hair. But he bowed his head, and I got a full-body shiver.

Keeping his head bowed, he undid my fly and pulled my khakis and boxers down past my hips. My cock sprang up, and he curled his hand around it gently. Stroked it for a moment. His thumb paused on the PA scar, just as Bowser's had. He glanced up at me with a slight smile.

I smiled back, a little embarrassed. "Long time ago. It made me piss weird."

He nodded without speaking. Then leaned forward and took me in his mouth.

My eyes fell shut. I moaned softly as his lips slid up my shaft. Up and then down again, taking me deeper each time. He moaned, and the vibrations traveled up through me, making me gasp. He gripped the base in one hand and used his lips to pull on the head. I sighed, forgetting about the other couple as I relaxed into the sensation.

And then I felt it.

The point of one filed tooth running slowly—*so* slowly—up my dick. My body went rigid. When he reached the ridge under the head, he pushed the tooth in a little deeper. I winced, releasing a breath. Placed my hands on Drix's shoulders, as though to force him back. But I didn't. I could feel him smile around my cock. Then he dragged his tooth down again. It felt like the skin of my cock was being split. I licked my lips, my hands still braced on his shoulders.

When he reached the base, he dug the point in again. "Ah—" I stopped the sound before it became a full-blown cry.

He went back to sucking.

I let go of him. Looked down at his long gold ponytail. Just resting there between his shoulders. I stroked it. He gave the softest whimper as I continued to comb through it. I stroked his scalp with my other hand. He stopped sucking for a moment to sigh. The blast of warm breath around my cock almost did me in.

I wound his ponytail around my hand. Gave it a light tug. This time I got a deep moan from him—a sound that went straight to my balls.

I tugged harder. He scraped my dick with his fang.

We went back and forth like that, punishing each other for the pain we caused. I'd pull his hair, and he'd use his teeth. He'd go back to sucking me, and I'd go back to petting him.

He ran his tongue around the head of my cock, and stopped with it right on top of one of the swollen, tender spots where I'd been stapled. His tongue retreated, and a sharp tooth replaced it, digging into the injured flesh. I gripped his ponytail, shaking with the pain. Then his tongue brushed my slit—gentle, soothing—while his tooth continued to push into the sore spot under the head.

My brain didn't know what to make of the jumbled signals, and I tried to breathe but ended up laughing.

Drix released me, calmly bobbing up and down my cock.

I saw the other couple watching us, and I didn't give a fuck.

"You're so good," I whispered to Drix, wrapping his hair tighter around my hand. "So good, Drix."

"Hmm-mmm," he replied, and the light buzz sent me over the edge. I came in his mouth, and he swallowed with my cock still deep in his throat.

When I pulled out, he grinned up at me. "Yeah? Good?"

I didn't know what to say. My whole body felt weak.

So I went to my knees in front of him. Cupped the back of his head and guided him forward until his face was inches from mine.

I didn't kiss him. I leaned my forehead against his, and smelled my cum on his breath and made light circles between his shoulder blades with my fingertips.

He closed his eyes and tilted his head to brush his lips against mine. And we stayed like that for a long time, caught in a mutual surrender.

CHAPTER
TEN

onday, I got an email from Cheryl with links to the profiles of four birth mothers who were willing to adopt to a single man. I almost opened them immediately.

Thought about it.

I texted my friends and asked if we could all meet at Dave and Gould's once everyone was off work.

We congregated in Gould's room that evening, because he had a desktop with a huge monitor. And I took them through the profiles Cheryl had sent me.

The first few minutes were strange, having them all gathered around while I looked. I couldn't focus as well on the profiles because I was so focused on my friends' reactions. But eventually, it became exciting and terrifying and fun all at once.

"My God, this is worse than Petfinder," Dave said as we read the profile of a baby girl seven months along whose mother had suffered brain damage during the pregnancy and wouldn't be able to care for the child once she was born.

Kamen sighed. "Yeah, Miles. I think you should adopt them all."

"Oh my God, *this one*." Dave stopped on Zac, a five-year-old with an absolutely stunning smile. Cheryl had included a note to me in the email:

Normally Beacon Center doesn't place older children, but we've agreed to handle Zac's adoption as a favor to an old friend who died with no other relatives. I realize you want to adopt a newborn, but just checking to see if you have any interest in an older child. Zac's with a foster mother right now. Very sweet kid.

"I thought you were getting a baby," Kamen said.

"Most likely." I studied Zac's pictures. He went to kindergarten in Oakdale. He loved picture books, especially *Le Petit Prince*, which he could read in French and English.

I'd taken French in college, apparently desperate to make myself seem even more pretentious than I already was. I'd read *Le Petit Prince* for the first time then, and had been surprised that a picture book could move me so much. "But I'm open."

"I don't know how you could choose," Gould murmured.

I didn't answer. I'd stopped on the next profile. A baby boy. Five months along. He already had a name: James Aidan. I'd never really thought about how naming worked when an adoption was arranged prebirth.

"You like that one?" Kamen leaned over my shoulder.

"I do."

"Even though he's not born yet?"

I nodded.

"I'll bet he's going to be the most awesome baby ever," Kamen said. "I'll bet he's a total ninja."

"Is that some term I don't know, or . . ."

"No, I mean I'll bet he'll grow up to be a ninja."

I scrolled through the birth mother's information. "That is the dream."

"Hey, you can look at waiting families?" Dave pointed to the site's sidebar.

"Yes."

"Do you have a profile on there?"

I plead the fifth.

The Beacon Center's website had always intimidated me because of the waiting families section. How many nights had I stayed up, clicking through the profiles and comparing myself to the other potential parents? Despite Cheryl's reassurance that the Beacon Center was committed to working with nontraditional families, the waiting families were overwhelmingly straight. And white. And into skiing.

Ted and Marissa and their dog, Porky, at the state park. Lisa and Bill at a ski lodge in Maine. Gary and Bev on a mission in South America. Taylor and Ben with the three children they'd already adopted, posing in front of Mount Rushmore, making the same serious faces as the presidents.

And then there was me. No partner, no dog, no exotic locales.

Just Miles.

Dave took the mouse and started clicking. He scrolled through the Derek-and-Melissas and Cathy-and-Dans. "Wow. These people all look supernormal and friendly. Does everyone own a dog? Oh my god, this couple has a pool with a waterslide. I want to live with them."

Eventually he came to my profile.

"Found it!"

"You really don't have to look at that," I told them.

But it was too late. They were all reading.

"Aw," Dave said. "You've been growing your business for three years and now you're ready to start the family you've always wanted."

Kamen frowned. "What's *Masterpiece*?"

Dave patted his shoulder. "Don't worry about it, buddy. Not in your wheelhouse."

"This makes you seem like the best guy ever." Kamen glanced over at me. "Everyone's gonna want you to father their abandoned children."

They got to my pictures.

Dave gasped. "Oh dear God."

I looked away, embarrassed. Forced myself to look back at the screen. "I know they're not great."

"Miles . . ." Dave double-clicked on the thumbnail of me leaning faux-casually against my Toyota Corolla. Full-sized, it was even worse. "What is this, an ad for Toyota's Grandparents' Day Sales Event?" He moved to one of me in a navy cardigan behind the A2A counter, giving a wide-eyed, semi-Satanic smile.

There came a chorus of verbalized cringes.

"I don't take good pictures," I said defensively.

"We're gonna fix this," Dave promised. "We're gonna get you to pose with a dog."

"I don't have a dog."

"It doesn't matter. Everyone on here has animal pictures. We'll find you a dog."

"Maybe kittens," Gould suggested.

"I mean, if we could find a foal . . ." Kamen said.

Dave glanced at him. "You think foal over kittens?"

"Yeah, 'cause kittens are common. We should put him with a baby horse so he'll stand out."

Dave nodded. "D would approve of that."

Dave's hard-ass partner had a bewildering soft spot for horses.

I grabbed the mouse and X-ed out of the photo browser. "Can we just focus on what's important right now? Obviously, some birth mothers like me even though I didn't pose with a foal. So let's talk about what child I'm going to adopt."

"You want James?" Gould asked.

I kept thinking about Zac's picture. That smile. But I'd been set on adopting a baby. I didn't know how to deal with the issues an older kid in foster care might come with, and I wanted a kid who would imprint on me. Did that make me horrible?

"Yeah," I said. "I think I'll ask Cheryl about James."

Kamen was on his phone beside me, typing.

"What are you doing?" I asked him.

"Downloading Photoshop and looking for foals."

Dave leaned over. "Let me see the foals."

This. This group was what my child was going to be exposed to.

I watched Kamen and Dave hunch over the tiny screen. Shook my head and smiled in spite of myself.

I supposed I'd just have to deal.

I called Cheryl Tuesday morning to discuss James. I also mentioned that I was interested in Zac, but after talking about it for a while, we mutually decided I'd go with James as my first choice, since I'd been preparing for a newborn.

Two days later, Cheryl called back to say that Britney, the birth mother, wanted a phone conference with me. So we arranged one for the following Tuesday, and I set about practicing my conversation with an imaginary Britney, who in my mind was polite, kind, a little lost. Devastated about giving up her child, but happy that he was going to a good home.

As the days went by, I stopped thinking generically—*my future son, the kid I adopt*—and started thinking about *James*. What he'd look like. What foods he'd enjoy. Where he'd go to school. I shared James's profile with my mother and sister, who were outlandishly excited. My mother asked again about the nursery, but I was too happy to be offended. I told her I'd send her some of my ideas.

On Thursday, I got a message from Healthvana that Drix had shared his test results with me. He'd gotten tested two days ago. Totally clean. I spent the first three hours of my shift that morning thinking about his bare cock up my ass.

A mother came into A2A with her two children, ages eight and seven. They were picking up shirts for the girl's little league baseball team. I got the same flash of panic I did every time children came into the store—as though the whole world was watching my interactions with kids to determine whether I was good enough to be a father. I greeted both children, trying not to sound either too patronizing or too stuffy. The eight-year-old boy ignored me, running to a rack of clearance shirts and shifting through them at warp speed. *Click, click, click* went the hangers.

The girl smiled at me and told me her baseball team got Hawaiian Punch after every game.

"That's cool." I'd never even been able to pull off the *word* cool. "Do you like the red or the blue better?"

She thought for a moment, swaying. Then she grinned slowly and said, "Red!"

The mom smiled at me and held her daughter's hand. "I've been campaigning for actual fruit juice, but . . ."

"But who wants fruit juice when you could have Hawaiian Punch?" I said.

God, what was I going to do if all my kid wanted to eat and drink was sugar? What if he went over to friends' houses where the parents allowed unlimited Hawaiian Punch? Was I going to be one of those parents whose kid showed up at every birthday party and sleepover and school function with a note that said, *I am only allowed one cookie and one glass of juice?*

I helped the mother carry the box of shirts to the car. She and the girl thanked me. The boy picked his nose and wiped it on his shirt.

Maybe I should adopt a girl?

I went back inside and put Jason up front for a while so I could escape to the stockroom and have a mild panic attack about parenthood. While I was breathing in through my nose and out through my mouth, my phone buzzed.

Drix.

I answered, still breathing raggedly. "Hey."

"How's it going?"

"Pretty good."

"You sound winded."

"I'm in the stockroom. It's hot back here."

We talked for a little bit about my day and his day. He seemed to sense I wasn't quite right, but I couldn't tell him what I was panicking about because he was my bucket-list buddy and nothing more.

Then he brought up the oral indiscretions we'd engaged in at Riddle the other night, and suddenly my mind was firmly off parenthood.

"That was . . . yeah," I said. "That was a—a really good time."

"You know what I like?" he said.

"What?"

"When you get all stammery, and you're, like, trying to hold on to your I'm-in-control persona, but it's not quite working."

My throat was suddenly dry. "Oh?"

"Yeah. It makes me want to just fluster you completely. Fuck you until you don't know which way's up. Until you can't use words to try to protect yourself." His voice had taken on this *tone* that was very low and soft and amused.

Well, um . . . "That's . . ."

"See how fun this is? And if you were here right now, this is where I'd start licking down your neck. Because you like that."

I gripped the edge of the crate I was sitting on. My balls tightened. "You can't . . . know that."

"I've *seen* how much you like it."

I didn't say anything. I took the phone away from my ear to wipe the grease off the screen.

After a moment, he continued. "When I got to your shoulder, I'd let you feel my teeth—just a little. Just enough so you don't know what's coming next. If I'm gonna make you bleed or make you shiver."

I did shiver, even though it was hot as fuck in the stockroom. Or was that just me?

"Then I'd take your shirt off. Slowly. Because I fucking love every muscle in your back. And I'd lick you again—all the way up your spine—just to see those muscles move as you try to hold still."

I had to get back to work. "I'm . . ."

"Miles?"

"Y-yeah?" *Fuck.*

"I'd make you take your pants off for me. Make you stand there waiting. I'd touch you everywhere—your neck. Your nipples. The insides of your thighs."

Without meaning to, I brushed my fly with my fingers.

"I'd slide my hand down the back of your underwear. Squeeze that tight ass . . ."

My breathing roughened, and I moved my hand tentatively over the bulge in my slacks.

"Pull you against me and feel how hard you are . . ." When he spoke again, his voice was hoarse. "You hard, Miles?"

He wasn't fucking around. This was turning him on too. "Yes," I whispered.

"In the *store*?" He sounded mock incredulous. "Miles . . . what if someone walks in?"

My worst fear, and, apparently, a very compelling fantasy, because my cock pushed against my underwear. I made a small sound, frustration and arousal. I stood, the phone between my ear and shoulder, and walked to the wall. Punched it lightly as I hunched over and rubbed the front of my pants with my other hand. I had to stop. *Had to.* This was totally inappropriate. "Sh-shit."

"You want me to keep going?"

"No." A less than halfhearted refusal.

A pause. "So you don't want me to take your underwear off? And bend you over a stack of boxes, and—"

"Drix!" My hand made furious circles around my groin. My eyes were squeezed shut.

"What are you doing?" he asked softly.

"I'm . . . I'm . . ."

"Are you jerking off?"

I opened my eyes. Shadows and light popped in front of me. "No."

Another pause. "I wanna hear you come."

"I can't. I'm in public."

"Who's with you?"

I glanced around, my legs trembling. "Denise and Byron."

"Do they like to watch?"

"They're the security cameras. So yes."

A soft snort. "It's your store. You telling me you don't know where to go so that the cameras won't see you?"

I'd already done it. Picked the wall and the angle where the cameras wouldn't catch me. I had a brief fantasy of the whole store watching. Jason and Claire and the delivery truck drivers and customers and cameras . . . all watching Drix hurt me. Humiliate me. "I have to work."

"Then hurry up. Because you know what I want to do next?"

If he told me, there was a very good chance I would ejaculate on the spot. "What?" I let the word out on the softest breath— so soft I almost hoped he wouldn't hear, wouldn't think I was encouraging this.

"Make you spread your legs."

"Gnnhhm," I choked out, rubbing harder.

"Put my hand over your balls."

Shit.

"Twist them, like I did the other day."

A harsh breath escaped me.

"You gonna come for me, Miles?"

I clenched my hand in an effort not to stick it down the front of my pants. "No," I whispered.

"No? Not even if I kneel behind you? Rub the backs of your thighs and tell you your hole looks so fucking tight and perfect that I want to stick my tongue in it?"

No.

"Pull your cheeks apart and start running my tongue up and down your crack?"

Yes. Fuck. Don't. Please.

"But I never lick your hole. I just keep going up and down . . . up and down . . . but I keep skipping the one place you *really* want to feel it."

Beacon Center. My future as a nice, normal dad with no dirty secrets. "Drix . . ."

"Touch your cock," he said softly. "It's okay."

I wanted to. So fucking badly. I hadn't been rimmed since I was twenty-four. I was going to fall apart, over goddamn *phone sex*. I was sucking in shuddering breaths, bracing myself against the wall, rocking my hips against nothing but air.

I straightened so quickly my head spun. "It's really not." I took my hand away from my crotch. "I can't do this here."

For a second he was silent, and I was afraid I'd disappointed him. Then he said, "When's your lunch break?"

"Um, now?" My voice cracked. And it wasn't going to be a lunch break so much as a trip to the bathroom to get acquainted with some cold water.

"I'm gonna pick you up and then fuck you in my car," he said cheerfully. "It'll be fun."

"Wait—"

He'd already hung up.

Ten minutes later, I waddled out into the parking lot, trying to shield my erection. I got into his SUV and he drove us to the back parking lot of a drugstore.

I eyed him in disbelief. "Here? There are people."

He shut off the ignition. "Tinted windows."

"They're tinted, not boarded up. People will know we're . . ."

He grinned at me. "Lucky them." He reached over me and took a bottle of lube out of the glove box. Tossed it into the back.

"I can't."

"Miles." He shook his head almost pityingly, glancing at my crotch. "Look what's going on down there. What you *can't* do is go back to work like that."

I stared at him. At the perfect line of his jaw, at those startling violet eyes. At the blue veins in his throat and temples.

Then I ripped my seat belt off and dove at him with a ferocity fueled by loneliness and shame and *want*. He caught me and pulled me into his lap and kissed me until I was shaking. Until my lips were swollen and sore from his teeth. Until I was rubbing myself against any part of him I could reach, and each breath I took snapped like a twig, and the front of my underwear was as wet as if I'd already come.

He undid my fly. "Get in the back," he whispered. "All the way."

I crawled between the seats. He caught me in the middle and pulled my pants off. Made me crawl half-naked over the very back seat and into the cargo area. He stripped awkwardly, long limbs hitting the walls of the bed.

"Is this why you have an SUV?" I asked. "Because it's the only thing with a back big enough for you to fuck in?"

"Ha-ha."

I shrugged out of my cardigan, and he unbuttoned the shirt I wore underneath, then yanked it off. I leaned against the side wall and lifted my hips as he slowly removed my boxers.

He did many of the things he'd promised over the phone. Licking. The licking was a big one. My neck, my chest, and then the V of my groin. Gave my cock a brief flick with his tongue before he started kissing me. I didn't realize how loudly I was moaning until he came up for air.

"That's so fucking hot," he said. "The way you sound."

I was panting. "Will you . . . Will . . . you . . . t-talk dirty?"

"Mmm." He slowly leaned forward and pressed his lips to the crook of my shoulder. A series of soft, delicate kisses. Stroked my balls with the pads of two fingers until I was whimpering again.

"Everyone can hear you," he whispered. He ducked to kiss me again. "Everyone walking by. They can hear you moaning for my cock."

I arched my back. *Yes.* "Dirtier."

He laughed softly—that single noise somehow lewder than anything he could say. He twisted my nipple. A spark of pain shot through me, and he leaned close to my ear. His breath was warm and ragged, and then he said, voice low, "I wanna wipe my fucking face on your hole."

Oh fuck. I almost laughed. But also I almost came.

He bit down on my ear. I hissed. He pulled, licked. Grabbed my cock and yanked it, drawing a strangled yelp from me. He worked his thumb around the ridge, then slapped the shaft back and forth. "I wanna get my tongue so far in there, you feel it in your gut."

"Ah-ah-ahhhh . . ." My head pressed against the tinted window, and I squirmed.

"Suck on your balls until they're *raw*." He flicked my sac.

"Oh God. Oh *shit*."

"So what are you waiting for?" he demanded. "Roll over. Spread your fucking legs and get your ass in the air so I can eat you out."

He pulled me up and spun me, shoving me down on all fours. Before I had a chance to suggest I freshen up with one of the sanitizing wipes in my cardigan pocket, he'd forced my head and shoulders down and buried his face between my cheeks.

And I mean he got *in there*.

None of the slow teasing he'd threatened over the phone. He inhaled with a moan like this was the greatest fucking thing in the world. And then he jammed his tongue into me. I gripped the bar below the backseat, my face chafing against the carpet. Then I shifted from knee to knee, my ass tensing as heat flooded my cock and my balls drew up and I choked on a cry.

He had one arm wrapped around my left thigh, the other holding my right cheek spread. He flexed his tongue back and forth inside me, alternating wet pressure on either side of my channel.

"Oh no," I whispered. "Oh God, please . . ."

I'd forgotten how good this felt. How filthy and hopelessly animalistic. He dug his nail in just below my tailbone, and I instinctively pushed my ass back against his face. I wanted him to keep talking to me, but I didn't want him to stop rimming.

He withdrew his tongue—slowly, so I had time to regret losing it—and then lapped at my hole. He worked until the skin around it was raw, and I was almost in tears. He pulled my balls gently to one side. "*Now* I see your cigarette burns," he whispered. And then he licked them. Traced each one with his tongue before releasing my balls and focusing once more on my hole.

His nose bumped the inflamed flesh, and then his lips. He started *sucking* on the rim, until I could actually feel it swelling. Until he was able to dig his teeth into it just a little.

I cried out, punching the floor. He alternated: one thrust inside with his tongue, one nip on the outside. Thrust. Bite. Thrust. Bite.

I raised my head and keened, rocking back and forth.

He paused to catch his breath.

"Don't stop," I begged. "Don't stop. Don't stop, please, Drix . . ."

"What do you want?" he asked.

"To come. Please make me come. Please."

He grabbed my ass and dug his nails in. "You have no *idea* how hot it is when you beg."

I twisted my hips, pushing my ass higher, not caring who saw.

"I *am* gonna make you come. But not like this."

I froze. "How?" I whispered.

"You wanna know?"

"Tell me. Make it filthy. So fucking filthy."

He slapped my thigh. I yelped. He did it again. Then pulled my cheeks apart and spit in my crack. "I'm gonna throw you on your back, bitch. Bite your throat while I fuck you."

I shuddered over and over. "Okay. Okay, okay, okay."

He lifted me and slammed me onto my back. The breath whooshed out of me, and I had no time to recover before his teeth closed on my throat.

I was kicking. I might have been kicking *him*. I wasn't sure. All I knew was that he was raking my cock with his nails, increasing his bite pressure until I choked and whimpered like a . . . like a dog.

He raised his head. My neck throbbed. "What are you, Miles?"

"Whore slut toy hole dog . . . fucking . . . fucking bitch . . ." I chanted.

"Oh God." He stroked my cheek, gazing down at me with a smile that was half-gentle, half-cruel. "You've wanted this a long time, haven't you?"

I nodded frantically, grabbing his hand on an impulse and squeezing hard.

He looked surprised for a second. Then tender. He dragged one finger down my throat and pressed my Adam's apple. "You wanna tell me what to do? Or you want me to take what I need?"

I shut my eyes as he pressed harder. "Take . . . take it . . ."

He swept his hand up and down my chest. "You absolute *slut*."

"Oh...*fuck*." A dribble of pre-cum tickled my shaft, pooled in the hair at the base.

He grabbed my balls and yanked.

"Ah!" I caught my breath, held it, opening my eyes to look into his.

"Spread your legs." He smacked my balls three times in rapid succession, never breaking eye contact.

I tipped my head back and let out a silent scream. Sweat dripped down my chest, and my muscles flexed. My breath came out in rough, frantic yelps as I spread my legs.

"More."

I couldn't without hitting the back of the seat.

"I said *more*." He never raised his voice, but it took on a dark, seductive tone that tugged something deep in my stomach. He reached over and pulled a lever on the seat closest to my head, pushing the seat-back down. Then he grabbed my left leg and flung it over the top of the folded seat, making sure my ankle was hooked around the seat that was still upright. My legs were spread so wide it hurt, and my cock dripped on my belly, my balls heavy and purple.

"What would people see if they looked through this window right now?" he asked softly, running his fingers down the creases between my thighs and my groin. He placed both thumbs against my balls and pushed down like he meant to pop them.

I didn't want to think about it. *Please be seriously tinted. Like, Mafia-getaway-vehicle tinted.*

"Miles? What would they see?"

"Mebeingaslut," I whispered.

He sighed like that turned him on as much as it did me. He pinched my sac between his thumbnails. "I ought to open up the hatch and let people take turns in your ass."

I lifted my head. "I *beg* your pardon?"

He looked alarmed. "Too much?"

I thought about it for a second. Then shook my head. "Keep going."

"But I'm *not* gonna do that," he amended, sliding his hands up my ribs. "Because you're mine. And I'm gonna bury my cock so far in your hot goddamn ass, you won't be able to speak. You'll be goddamn *impaled*, Miles. But I'm not gonna stop fucking you until you say my name. So you're gonna be in a . . . a . . ."

"Quandary?" I supplied.

He grinned. Then slapped my face. I gasped, moving my mouth in circles as I tried to process the sting. It hadn't been a hard slap, but it made my cock throb over and over—a strange, frustrating sensation, like I was coming hard, but without any of the attendant relief.

"Yeah," he said. "A quandary." He stroked my smarting cheek. So gently, and he murmured while he was doing it—no words, just a reassuring sound that made my chest tighten and my breath catch. I closed my eyes, leaning into that touch.

He grabbed the lube, popped the cap, held it about two feet above me and just started squirting. It dripped through my pubic hair and down the sides of my thighs and into my crack. He pulled my cheeks farther apart and drizzled it directly into my hole.

"Jesus, what are you . . .?"

He didn't stop until the entire bottle was emptied, my groin and ass were a mess, and the carpet of the trunk was absolutely soaked.

"I do have to go back to work, you know."

"Shh." He tried to hoist my legs over his shoulders. I grunted. I was not as flexible as I had been even a couple of years ago, so he sort of helped me stretch for a few seconds and then slowly eased my legs up into position. Ran his cock through my lubed-up crack and then pushed his way into me. I was so slick and so ready to be fucked that I barely felt the burn. He pinned my arms on either side of my head. Held my gaze as he drew his hips back slowly. He smiled.

And then he rammed me.

His thighs collided with my ass, creating a spray of lube that flecked both our stomachs.

I held my breath for a second, then let it all out in a sound of pure relief. "Ohhhhhhhhh."

I rocked my hips, trying to get him in deeper.

He rubbed my lube-drenched cock with one hand and thrust again. I moaned and sighed, my head falling back.

He did it three more times. I crossed my ankles between his shoulders, and when he stopped I used my legs to tug myself against him, trying to fuck myself on his cock. My sweaty back was raw from rubbing against the carpet. My throat was dry and my balls had pulled so tight one good twist would send me over the edge.

Drix looked at me again with tenderness and wonder. "You'd do anything I said right now, wouldn't you?"

My next breath really was a sob. "Yes."

"Give me one good reason I should let you come." His tone was wicked.

I tried to think of a reason that didn't involve *me*. That wasn't *Because I want to. Because I need to.* I tried to think of a way *he* would benefit from me coming, but my thoughts were scrambled, and nothing in the world was as real or immediate as my need for him to thrust again.

He stroked my throat with his lube-slick hand. "Just tell me," he whispered.

"Because I . . . I need it." I could barely hear my own voice.

He shifted slightly, and the reminder of his bare cock inside me—ready to hurt me or claim me or make me come—was too much.

"I need it," I said again. "Please, please, pleasepleaseplease. No one ever does this for me. I don't *let* anyone do this."

His fingers on my throat were so gentle. He gave me one small thrust, almost like a nudge of encouragement. "Keep going."

"I don't know what to say."

"Show me how dirty *you* can be."

I writhed, letting out a frustrated breath. I was stuck here on the very edge, and would be until I surrendered. "Your cock feels good. It's so big, and I want you to hurt me with it. I want you to fuck me. Make me come. I could come just looking at you, if you let me. Just give me . . ."

"Give you what?"

I fell still, looking up at him. "Give me permission."

He drew a slight, quivering breath. "I'm going to hurt you," he whispered.

I nodded. "*Please.*"

He drew his hips back. And then . . .

His palm connected with the right side of my face at the same time his cock drove into me, lifting my lower body off the floor. With his other hand, he punched me in the abs, the blow carefully placed but painful nonetheless.

He pulled out while I was still dazed. Shrugged my legs off his shoulders. "Turn around. Hands and knees."

Was he *kidding*? I couldn't budge.

Somehow, clumsily, I got back on all fours. He took me from behind, one long arm curled around my waist, his hand braced on the window. I bucked back against him, letting out a stream of curses and pleas. It felt so good. To be fucked, yes, but mostly to *let go*. My stomach ached where he'd hit me, my cheek stung, and lube streamed down my legs.

He clawed at my back, grabbing my hips, slapping my thighs. He reached around and gripped my cock. I came with a shout, streaking the wall. He groaned and pulled me harder onto his cock, grinding my ass against his groin until I felt him come deep inside me.

We both collapsed, our harsh breathing filling the SUV.

"Miles?" He sat up.

I hunched there on the floor of the hatch, his cum trickling out of me, too shattered to think or move.

"Come here," he said.

He pulled me to him. I stiffened for a second but didn't fight. He kissed my stinging cheek, and then my mouth, gently. His knuckles brushed my stomach where he'd punched me, and I flinched but pressed closer to him.

"You okay?" he whispered.

I nodded, my lips still on his. I realized I was shaking. "Thank you," I whispered. "Thank you."

He rubbed my back. After a moment, I pulled away and glanced down. My skin was soaked in sweat and lube, and I smelled like I'd been fucked. I didn't know what time it was, but I was probably long overdue at the shop.

"I can't . . . How am I going to . . .?"

Drix reached for his pants. Took his phone from the pocket. Swiped and clicked for a moment, then put it to his ear. I could hear it ringing.

"Hi," Drix said politely, a few seconds later. "This is Miles's friend Drix. I picked Miles up for lunch, and I think he ate something that didn't agree with him. He's not looking too good, so I'm gonna take him home." He paused. "Yeah. Uh, Ruby Tuesday's." His gaze flicked over to me, then he focused on the call again. "Salad bars—I know, right? I'll let him know. Thank you." He hung up.

I laughed weakly. "You are crazy."

"I lied."

"No shit."

He ran a thumb over my cheek again. "I said you didn't look too good. But you look amazing."

"Shut up."

He placed his hand on my stomach. I wasn't sure what he was doing, but then he drove the heel of his hand hard into my lower abdomen, forcing out a humiliatingly loud burst of gas and a ridiculous amount of lube and cum.

I sat there gasping for a moment, feeling the rug dampen beneath me. "You're a dick."

"And you," he said almost jubilantly, "made a huge mess. And got fucked in public. And the world didn't end."

We were going to have a hell of a time cleaning this up.

He helped me over the backseat and onto the floor between the middle seats. "You can ride right here," he said. "So you can stay naked."

"If we get pulled over . . ."

"I'll be careful."

So he drove to his place with me curled on the floor, still leaking cum and lube onto the carpet, and nothing in the world I could do about it.

I walked bowlegged for two days, and that is not an exaggeration. Jason asked if I was walking that way because I was still sick. Every time he saw me, he cringed like he thought I was going to spew everywhere.

I was sore as hell, and I loved it. Yet, what I remembered more vividly than the fucking was how Drix had kept me in bed for the rest of the evening, kissing me, lying next to me, bringing me food. Every time I'd tried to answer work emails on my phone, he'd flipped me onto my stomach and started rubbing my back until I drifted. All told, I must have slept about five hours. *During the day.*

Around six, he had filled the tub with hot water and let me soak off the rest of the lube. I'd thought there was no way I could manage any more sex, and yet once I got back into bed, my dick hardened again, and pretty soon he was licking my ass—biting my cheeks and thighs and then finally fucking me with his tongue until I gave up all pretense of dignity and humped the bed until I came. I'd reached around behind me and groped for his cock. Batted at it blindly in an exhausted haze, stopping as soon as I felt his cum streak my back. It was the sloppiest of handjobs, but he didn't hold it against me.

"You are amazing," I told him.

"Sorry I'm not a real dom. Then I'd be perfect, huh?"

"Listen. What you did in the car? About sixty times more dominant than most guys I've played with."

"Really?"

"I mean, a lot of guys put on a big act. But with you, it's like you're naturally the filthiest fucker in the world."

"Aww!" He rubbed his hands together like a supervillain. "I really do kind of feel like that's true, though."

"Yeah?"

"The reason I first was kinda drawn to the Dark Ravens is that they encourage you to connect with others using your body. Through sex or massage or dance or whatever. And I just . . . I *care* about the guys I have sex with. I don't want to do it with people I don't care about. But it's tough because sometimes I feel like I want more than other people want. You know? Like, I wanna use my teeth and I wanna knock shit over and I wanna talk dirty—but not if the guy's not really into it."

"Wow."

"I just love that you're into it. I mean, it really just blows my damn mind."

I felt a spike of guilt. He *was* amazing. Too amazing to get stuck being some guy's bucket-list fuck buddy. "I need to tell you something."

He looked wary.

I explained the situation. Beacon Center. My imminent exit from the world of BDSM. My pain-slut bucket list. "I don't want it to seem like I'm using you. But I'm kind of using you."

He nodded. "Well, I can't say I don't like being used this way." He paused. "And I'm just throwing this out there—I like kids. And they usually like me."

Of course they did. Hendrix Seger, the cuddly vampire PI.

But no.

Absolutely no.

When I became a father, I wanted my entire focus to be on that. No relationship drama. I didn't even want to *think* about sex for at least the first six months.

"Maybe I should have been honest with you from the beginning, but I thought this would just be sex. Except now I like you. I mean, I always liked you."

"Okay."

"I want you to know this adoption isn't a plan I'm going to put on hold just because I met somebody."

Drix grinned again. "You think you've met somebody?"

I didn't know how to answer. "Yes, well," I said, a bit snappishly.

"Hey." Drix caught my wrist. My blood went hot at that touch, my balls tensed, and I didn't know what the *fuck* to do about it. Drix gazed down at me. "This can be whatever you want it to be. If you want me to get lost once your kid arrives, that's what I'll do. But in the meantime, I'd really like to help with this bucket list."

That wouldn't work. Because what if I kept liking him more and more? Chances were he'd write me off as exhausting long before James got here. But what if he didn't? What if he grew more emotionally invested, and then I had this . . . mess in my life, and all of my parenting plans fell to pieces? It wasn't fair to either of us to keep going like this.

Yet I couldn't make myself say it. I felt strange—*ill*, almost—when I thought about telling him I didn't want to see him anymore.

And so I closed my eyes, let go, and said, instead: "I would love that."

He grinned. Sprawled beside me. "Just curious—why do you have to give up sex when you become a dad?"

"Not give up sex. But give up . . . sex that's loud and dangerous and involves me hurting for days afterward. I'm ready to be a little tamer."

He nodded. "Your call."

And with those two words, he officially became a better dom than any I'd had before.

Which, naturally, scared the shit out of me.

CHAPTER ELEVEN

"Spring is in the air," Dave announced, dumping Italian dressing all over his sub. "The renaissance faire is in full swing. The town crier was running through Red Oaks Plaza in a jingle hat handing out fliers."

Gould nodded. "Flowers are happening."

"God, yes." Dave tucked a renegade tomato back into the sandwich. "And everywhere I look, robins are having sex."

Kamen looked up from his meatball sub. "I used to mace robins."

"What?"

"Yeah, my mom would leave her key ring out, and she had mace on it. So I'd take it and try to mace robins. And squirrels."

"Why does this not surprise me?" Gould said.

Dave turned to me. "Miles? You excited for spring?"

"Uh. Yeah."

"You don't look happy. Are you unhappy for the same reason I'm unhappy?"

"Why are you unhappy?" I took a bite of my sandwich. "The ren faire and the robins?"

Dave handed me his phone, which was open to Riddle's twelve-page New Member waiver. "Look at what GK and Kel put into Riddle's club policy."

"Oh for fuck's sake," Gould said. "We're eating. We don't need to talk about that now."

I glanced back at the screen. We'd all signed one of these contracts when we'd joined—liability, discretion, house rules, etc. But there was now an addendum that stated:

On the Handling of Disputes Between Members

I understand that Riddle bears no responsibility for mediating disputes between members. Therefore if I have a disagreement with another member that results in either (a) discourteous behavior on either of our parts; or (b) any legal requirement that one of us stay away from the other, I realize that both of us may be banned from the premises and/or suspended from membership. I understand that such ban or suspension can be done without any regard to fault.

Please understand that the bringing of open drama into Riddle is both unwelcome and may result in the suspension of all involved parties.

"Do you see what they're doing?" Dave demanded.

I tapped the phone screen to keep it lit. "I imagine that having Bill reinstated as a member has resulted in some tension among other members. So maybe they're trying to reduce the 'drama.'"

"They're saying, 'If you have a problem at our club—i.e., if you get assaulted—don't come to us.'"

I kept reading. "But then it says, 'If a dispute involves uncivil behavior, please feel free to call our abuse hotline and get in touch with an advocate.' So, see? They're not just telling people to shut up if they get hurt."

"I still don't like it. 'Open drama?' What does that mean? That means they don't want to get caught in a he said/she said, or a he said/he said, or she said/she said. Even if insert-pronoun-of-your-choice said, 'I got raped.'"

Gould put down his sandwich. "I have plenty of contact with GK and Kel, and trust me, they're not trying to silence victims."

"Yes, we all know you have plenty of *contact* with them." There was an edge to Dave's tone.

Gould had started playing with GK and Kel a few months back. And as far as I knew, he still met with them on occasion. I didn't *dislike* GK and Kel. But in addition to reinstating Bill, they'd also asked me to participate in a roundtable discussion on race and kink a few months ago. Which wasn't inherently awful, except that I had no interest in being their black correspondent, or to find myself explaining to people why it was okay for me to be black and get whipped by white guys.

I handed the phone back to Dave. "I don't know. It doesn't necessarily refer to abuse or assault."

"The first thing you thought when you read it is that it's GK and Kel covering their asses."

I shrugged.

Dave went on, "And what did they tell me, back when I started the Subs Club? That I was starting drama. A witch hunt. By trying to keep people safe."

Kamen looked up. "Dude, maybe we should talk to them."

Dave ignored him. "This is why I think the Hymen College thing is good. If the Subs Club builds its résumé as an advocacy group, we can become kind of an alternative to the dungeon scene in this city. You know? Like, right now the community *is* basically Riddle."

"And Cobalt," Kamen said.

"Cobalt is where dreams go to die. But if *we* started doing more events—hosting events, I mean—presenting ourselves as, like, 'You don't need to go to a dungeon to be involved in the community . . .'"

I picked up a napkin and wiped my mouth. "Where the hell would we host events?"

"We should talk to some of the fringe groups. You know Finger Bang, that all-girl group uptown? They host workshops and parties and stuff, and they're not affiliated with Riddle or Cobalt. We could ask them how they organize their activities."

Kamen scratched his neck. "I thought, like, the whole point was that we were working together with Riddle now. To get them to be better about safety and stuff?"

"Yeah, buddy." Dave nibbled the lettuce that was falling out of the bottom of his sandwich. "But if GK and Kel are gonna keep making it impossible, then we're gonna have to strike out on our own. Except now we've got Gould in bed with them. Literally."

Gould, who had remained silent through all of this, looked sincerely irritated. "Would you lay off them?"

"If they don't want *uncivil* behavior in their club, they shouldn't let murderers in!" Dave shot back.

Gould's face was red. "The addendum is mostly about the people who are being shitty to Bill, okay? There's been some drama at the club because of that, so all GK and Kel are saying is that we've got to be adults and get along as best we can."

"I don't get you. *You* are the one who had to go beat the shit out of Bill because you couldn't stand the fact that he went free. He has a fucking *restraining* order against you."

It was easy to forget that ultra-quiet Gould had, after the trial, tracked Bill down and worked him over. Even now when I looked at Gould, I couldn't imagine it.

Dave raged on, "Now what, GK and Kel get you off a couple of times and suddenly you're like, 'Oh, maybe Bill's not so bad . . .'"

"That is *not* what I'm saying!"

"Guys," Kamen said firmly.

I debated stepping in, but this looked like it was going to boil over no matter what. So I let it happen.

Gould went on, "I hate Bill, and I don't think he ever should have been allowed back into Riddle. But he *was*. And I respect that GK and Kel are in a tough position."

Dave shook his head. "That makes no sense."

Dave loved Gould. I mean *adored* him. Dave and Kamen had known each other since high school and hadn't met Gould until after college. And yet it was Dave and Gould who gave the impression of having known each other the longest. But the depth of their friendship led to frequent disputes between the two of them.

"You don't have any idea what they've been through!" Gould snapped.

"What *they've* been through? Hal was a liability to them, not their fucking *friend*!"

"And what on God's glorious Earth," asked a deep, slow monotone behind us, "is going on?"

We all turned toward the kitchen doorway at once, like meerkats.

D stood there in all his mountain-man glory. Rugged, bestubbled, and wearing hiking pants and a long-sleeved burgundy polo that hugged his paunch. Hands on his hips, not a crew-cut hair out of place, his crystal-blue eyes falling on each of us in turn.

"Hi, D." I tried for a *Nothing to see here* tone, but failed.

He leaned against the doorframe. "I knocked. But then I heard yelling. And the front door was unlocked. So I let myself in to investigate."

I shook my head. "I keep warning them about that door."

"Really?" D entered the kitchen and went to Dave, who was staring at the table. D slung an arm around his shoulders and pulled him against his hip. "We might have to discuss that."

Dave rolled his eyes, then glanced up at D. "This neighborhood is charming."

"*And* full of crack dealers," I added.

"Charming crack dealers."

D bent to kiss the top of Dave's head. "So why did I hear yelling?"

"Submissives-only business," Dave muttered.

Gould was suddenly very interested in something out the window.

D cleared his throat and announced, to the room: "There is, nearby, a festival of miscreants and clowns. I am distraught by its ambience, but this place is selling ostrich legs masquerading as turkey legs. It is meat the size of a human head. I have the day off and was wondering if any of you would like to accompany me to this festival. Our mission would be to get the meat and get out as quickly as possible."

"You talking about the renaissance faire, man?" Kamen asked.

D nodded, closing his eyes briefly. "We may be speaking of one and the same event."

D had little patience for anything that involved frivolity, unnecessary noise, and people in nonfunctional hats. He did, however, love meat. He was a strange match for loquacious, artistic Dave, but they seemed to get along well. I could not for the life of me picture D at a renaissance faire, and part of me wanted to go just to see his face when some wench tried to sell him mead.

"Totally in!" Kamen said.

"I'm not really in the mood for meat." Dave leaned against D. "But I'll go."

D looked at me.

"Oh no," I said. "I have . . . work." Actually, I had to attend a gathering of vampyres because I was too cowardly to tell the man I was sleeping with that we needed to stop being a part of each other's lives. But nobody needed to know that.

He turned to Gould, who shook his head. "Busy. Thanks, though."

D studied Gould and Dave, as though he knew something was wrong but couldn't figure out what.

Dave stood, casting a last glance at Gould before hurrying into his bedroom to get ready.

The coven met in some woman named Cathy's house. I didn't know what I'd been expecting—a Gothic mansion with buttresses and spires, lit by torchlight and filled with the screams of the damned? But it was just Cathy's place, and Cathy had a kitchen full of cross-stitched platitudes and a cappuccino maker.

She served us hot dogs.

I talked to Archimedes Wendell, the coven's oldest member. He explained to me that he was four thousand one hundred and fifteen years old and had been around when the pyramids were gleaming white. He had a tattoo on his shoulder of a raven eating a Bible. He went by Archie.

"You doing all right?" Drix asked me.

I nodded. "Absolutely."

"It's going to get a little weirder. But I think you'll like the weird part."

I spent the rest of the meal watching Drix. The way he interacted with the others. He had that same vibrant, gentle-but-arresting energy I remembered from the day he'd taken the sunflower picture. I noticed too how often he touched other people. He'd warned me they were a tactile group, but it was still amazing to me. Hands on one another's shoulders, the sharing of food and drink. Hugs and kisses for greetings and good-byes.

It reminded me of how bewildered I'd been at first by my friends' easy physical intimacy.

But the most noteworthy element was how at home Drix seemed here.

I wished, for just a moment, that I had some way of making Drix feel at home with me. That I could offer him this level of intimacy and openness.

No, I reminded myself. *Don't even wish it.*

I was going to tell him it was over. Not tonight, because I knew how much he enjoyed the coven meetings, and I didn't want to ruin his night. But tomorrow, absolutely.

Then he'll think I'm ending it because I don't approve of his vampyrism. Better wait a few days.

Okay, a few days. And I'd try not to sleep with him between now and then.

After dinner, Cathy stood. "It's time to see to the initiation of our newest member."

For a second I was afraid that *I* was the newest member. That Drix had, unbeknownst to me, volunteered me for initiation into the coven. I had opened my mouth to protest that I was merely a black swan, when a young man at the end of the table rose. He was as pale as Drix, with black hair and Harry Potter glasses. Black skinny jeans and a black flowing pirate shirt.

He walked with Cathy through a door and down a flight of steps to the basement. After a moment, the rest of the Dark Ravens stood and followed. I kept close to Drix. The silence that had descended over the group was eerie.

In the spacious center of the basement, the young man knelt on a folded towel. He didn't look afraid.

"What's happening?" I whispered to Drix.

Drix put an arm around me. "He's going to be whipped."

Oh.

"Tonight," Cathy said, "Peter offers his blood in order to join the ranks of the Dark Ravens."

"It's symbolic," Drix told me in a low voice. "We won't really make him bleed unless that's what he wants. But everyone in the Dark Ravens is brought forth into wakefulness with a small amount of pain."

"It really does seem like a cult," I whispered.

"So does all your kneeling and bowing and 'Yes, Sir; no, Sir.'" He shot me a grin.

I lifted my chin, mock-haughtily. "I do *not* say 'Sir.'"

"I've noticed." He ran a hand over my shoulder.

I can't end this.

Cathy continued, "Peter agrees to uphold the tenets of the Dark Ravens. Respect all. Do harm to none. Share the experience of being alive. Of having a body that hungers for connection. A mind that lusts for knowledge. A spirit that thrives on energy."

Peter bowed his head.

Drix leaned close to me once more. "It *is* a cult. The difference is, it's for fun. We're not actually brainwashing anybody."

I was surprised when Cathy called Drix forward.

I noticed, for the first time, that Drix carried a black single-tail whip, braided leather, about three feet long. The popper was leather and tapered to a point.

Drix stood behind Peter, one hand on his nape. Cathy knelt in front of Peter and unbuttoned his shirt, sliding it down his shoulders so the fabric draped his lower back and pinned his arms, but left him exposed from midback upward.

He looks like Harry Potter. I can't watch Drix beat Harry f-ing Potter.

Drix whispered something to Peter, and Peter nodded.

Drix took his position. There was a swish and a crack as Drix delivered a throw across Peter's shoulders. Peter quivered but didn't make a sound.

Another crack.

Peter tipped his head forward.

The whip struck again, lower and a bit harder. Peter gave a soft cry.

Drix's technique was good. After a couple of sidearm lashes, he moved to knotting. These were softer, forward throws, and while Peter gasped at each, he seemed to be relaxing into the rhythm. Drix whipped down his back, easing the strength of the throws as he went lower. Soon Peter was crying out with nearly every lash, unable to hold back the sounds.

It was erotic, and absolutely beautiful. The welts Drix left were pink and would fade quickly, except for a couple of darker ones across the shoulders. Peter's sides were heaving, and his skin glistened with sweat.

It was over quickly. Drix dropped the whip.

"Stand," he said kindly.

He helped Peter up and embraced him, mindful of the welts. Peter buried his face in Drix's shoulder in a way that made me feel longing and envious.

"Welcome," I heard Drix say.

The others came forward to welcome Peter. I hung back, but caught Drix's eye.

Well done.

He found his way over to me. Put his hand in mine. I didn't pull away. "Are we creepy?" he whispered.

"I've seen creepier."

"Want me to whip you, someday?"

I can't let you.

"If you have to ask that question . . ."

He squeezed my hand and looked around the basement. "Miles, you're, like, the only person I've ever met that I felt comfortable showing this to."

That hurt as deeply as grief. Struck some place in me that hadn't been touched by anything else but Hal's death—except this time, I didn't even understand what I was losing. Safety. Closeness. Adventure. A friend. No number or combination of words was enough to describe how it felt to let go of a future I'd never know because I couldn't risk living it.

CHAPTER
TWELVE

My phone rang on Tuesday. Restricted number. *Britney.*

My heart raced. I'd been anxious since the night of *Harry Potter and the Blood Rites of the Dark Ravens.* Privately—irrationally—I feared that Beacon Center spies were planted everywhere, snapping my picture as I went to vampyre gatherings and Subs Club meetings, and then reporting back to Cheryl. I was half-afraid Britney was calling to say there was no way she'd ever give James to me.

"Miles Loucks." I answered the phone in the same clipped, professional tone I used at A2A. Winced at the sound of myself.

"Um . . . Miles? This is Britney Herbert." The voice was low. Some combination of tired and disoriented and over it, like she'd fallen asleep in class and then been called on.

"Hi, yes. Britney."

"Cheryl said you wanted to talk to me." She pronounced the name "Shurl" and glossed over the middle consonants of her words. *This is Brihh-ny. You wannid to talk to me.*

"Yes, I . . ." *don't know where to start.* "I wanted to introduce myself. And see if you feel I'd be a good candidate to adopt James."

A pause. Some staticky fumbling. A long breath. "Shurl says you got good scores on everything."

"Well." I walked into the kitchen and fumbled around, opening cabinets even though I wasn't looking for anything. "I've been working closely with Beacon Center to become the best candidate possible. I . . ." *Just tell the truth.* "I've been looking forward for a long time to becoming a father. I think I could be a very good one to James."

"You got money?"

"I'm sorry?"

"You got money?"

"Oh. Not . . . a lot, but enough to support a child. Enough to give James everything he needs. And to have a college trust."

More static. "That's good."

I tried not to make assumptions about her based on her voice. But I worried suddenly that she wasn't very bright, and that James wouldn't be very bright. That maybe I should have waited and had a biological child.

Nonsense. Any child can be educated. I'll be taking James out of an environment that won't allow him to reach his full potential.

Or I'm an asshole, and I'll make him into an asshole.

We talked a bit about her pregnancy, which was apparently going well, except that she puked whenever she ate citrus and could smell farts "from, like, twenty miles away."

At the end of the conversation, she said, "I'm gonna tell Shurl I want you to have James."

I had to sit down and wait to make sure my voice was steady before I spoke again. "Wow. That's . . . I really would like to adopt James. I'm really grateful you're—you considered me."

"Well, you seem like you'd be real good to him. You can come to the hospital if you want when I'm due. It's June twenty-fifth. You can see him when he's born."

"Of course. I'd like that." I was trying to wrap my mind around how . . . detached she sounded? Was that the right word? I mean, how could you tell a stranger you'd talked to on the phone for twenty minutes that you wanted him to take your child? How could the Beacon Center send me profiles of children and say, *Would you like one of these?* I mean, every Christmas, I sent Mom links to, say, three different pairs of shoes I thought she might like. *Do any of these suit you?*

The adoption process had been incredibly difficult and complicated on the paperwork end. But the parts that seemed like they *should* be complicated—like actually obtaining the child—were treated so simply.

"His name's James Aidan, after my cousin," she said. "He died in Iraq."

"I'm so sorry," I told her.

"It's okay." There was a crinkling sound on the other end, like she was opening a bag of chips. "I think you'll be a real good father."

I hung up feeling strange. Like I wanted to believe her that I would be a good father. Like maybe things from here on would be simple and . . . okay. I'd find the right crib, and I'd be the right kind of father, and I'd miss Drix, but I'd survive missing him.

And everything would go according to plan.

I went to the window and looked out at my manicured, swing-set-less backyard.

Just because you don't expect something doesn't make it a disaster.

I couldn't remember, for a second, where I'd heard those words.

My dad.

My dad, who'd quit his office job when I was eight to go drive trucks.

I recalled the day I'd quit my cubicle job to open A2A. I'd spent a year getting the business plan ready. Six months refitting the building. And even after all that, I almost couldn't turn in my resignation to Cubicleland. I had visions of my store sinking within months. Of having everyone know I was a failure. I drafted the resignation over and over. I recited each new draft in my sleep. I woke from dreams I couldn't remember, but that always left me feeling like I'd done something horribly wrong.

Eventually I'd gone to my boss and handed her the letter. She'd read it and congratulated me. And then I'd gone out into the world and done something that wasn't safe, wasn't easy.

I looked down at my folded arms. Realized I was shaking.

But I'd lost Hal. Just over a year after A2A opened.

I knew there wasn't a connection. Rationally, I knew it. And yet some nights I still looked in the bathroom mirror after I was done brushing my teeth, and I wondered—if I'd stayed at my old job, would Hal still be alive? Had I pulled a thread that unraveled some small section of the world? And if so, was there a way I could put things back together? Or at least avoid doing it again?

I closed my eyes.

If I stayed safe, maybe I could keep others safe. Perhaps security was contagious—like how I sometimes grew more relaxed around Drix simply because *he* was peaceful.

"You give yourself too much credit, Miles," my mother had said, the day I'd told her I wanted to adopt and then had immediately confessed my fear that something bad would happen just because I *wanted* this.

I didn't understand how that worked. How I could believe myself the center of the universe—some careless puppeteer who destroyed nations by thinking a dirty thought, or enjoyed moments of beauty through his own sheer worthiness to witness them—and still feel like I would never, ever be enough.

I opened my eyes.

So why not be brave now?

If it's all a crapshoot anyway, why not hold on to Drix and see where this goes?

No business plan. No dossier.

Just teeth and skin and breath and sweat, and his hand in mine.

Drix was at my house, trying unsuccessfully to help me unload the dishwasher. He didn't know where anything except cups went, so it was mostly him taking things out of the dishwasher and handing them to me to put away. I'd told him about the call from Britney, and he'd been good about helping me sort through my conflicting feelings and my fears about the adoption.

Maybe this was why Dave was always encouraging me to *talk* to him and the others. Because it helped.

I knew Drix and Bowser had met a couple of times recently, and I was dying to know how that was going. "So you and Bowser . . ." I couldn't find a way to initiate this conversation with any sort of finesse. "Are you getting along?"

I caught his smile before he said, "Oh yeah."

"Yeah?"

He handed me a whisk. "We've been working on some stuff."

"What kind of stuff?"

Drix bent to kiss me. "You'll see."

"Mmm." I whacked his shoulder lightly with the whisk. "Soon, I hope."

He turned away and reached into the dishwasher again. "Who's Hal?"

I tensed.

He faced me again, silverware in his hand. "You never told me who Hal was. You said you'd tell me later. But you didn't."

"Oh, uh . . ." I leaned against the counter, trying to figure out how to tell this story to Drix. I had a short version for people not involved in the BDSM scene. And most people who *were* in the local scene, I didn't have to tell. They already knew. "Hal was my friend. Part of my group of friends."

He waited.

I made sure I could keep my voice neutral before I continued. "Hal was at Riddle one night, doing a scene with a dom who had a reputation for being careless. The dom left Hal tied up on the bench in the Tranquility room. Hal had a rope around his neck. The—the rope, um, twisted. And—it—" I stopped for a moment. "It strangled Hal."

Drix gazed at me, something deeper than sympathy in his eyes. As though he understood every bad thing that could possibly happen to a person in this world, and felt others' pain like it was his own. "I'm so sorry."

I shook my head. "A lot of people blame themselves for it. That DM, Michael. And Cinnamon, this woman we know—she was in the room with Hal when it happened, but didn't realize he was in trouble. And, uh, GK and Kel. Riddle's owners. They took it hard.

"I guess the worst part is that Bill Henson, the dom—nothing happened to him. He was put on trial and found innocent. And the way the media reacted . . . you could look at comments on any news article and see that most people blamed Hal, or blamed BDSM in general."

"That must have been awful."

"Even I blamed Hal, a little. I was just never as close to him as the others were. He was always the kind of guy who stole the spotlight. You know? Every conversation had to be about him and some crazy idea he'd had, and people . . . *followed* him. Imitated him. Wanted him around all the time. And I never understood why. He took risks, and he . . . he never thought anything through." My heart thudded. I'd never said this to anyone, ever. "I sound really selfish, don't I?"

Drix smiled ruefully. "It's really okay."

My exhale was shaky. "I did care about him, though. And I don't think it's fair that Bill gets to . . . whatever."

"Make coffee in the morning and listen to the radio on his commute and binge-watch Netflix?"

"Exactly."

He put an arm around me—not a long embrace, just a squeeze. As though he wasn't sure if I'd be receptive to it.

"Thank you," he said. "For telling me."

We finished with the dishes and played a game of Scrabble, which helped the evening regain some sense of normality. By the time we got upstairs, we were both eager for pursuits more carnal than triple-word scores.

"I want to do something for you," I told him once we were naked in bed. "*To* you—kind of. Something that will hurt me."

"I'm listening."

"You might think it's weird."

"Are we not past that?"

"Do you do any bottoming stuff?"

He smiled. "A little. It's been a while."

"So my idea involves a . . ." I got up and fetched my gear bag. Removed a thick, hollow butt plug. "A pig hole."

"A pig hole?" He sat up.

I handed it to him. The tip was fairly narrow, but the flared part was about two inches in diameter. He stared at the hollow tube inside. "What goes in here?"

"Well, anything you want, really. Fingers. Crop handle. My dick." I tried to say it casually, but he looked up.

"Your dick fits in here? I'd think the plug's too small."

"Aw, that's flattering. Yes. It's a tight squeeze, but I'll have lots of lube." I didn't tell him yet what I'd be using as lube.

"So you wanna fuck me with this thing in?"

"Yes. Only if you're up for it."

He held the pig hole up to his eye like a spyglass and peered at me through it. He really would get along well with Kamen.

He lowered the plug and tilted his head, studying me. A tiny smile played on his lips. "What are you going to do?"

"How much do you trust me?"

I watched the light shift in his eyes, catching the violet contacts.

"I trust you," he said calmly.

That gave me a rush, hearing him say that. His soft voice, the determination in his gaze.

"I'm not, um . . ." He sighed. "I need to take anal stuff a little slow sometimes."

"Of course."

I reached out and stroked his long hair. Let the tips of my fingers graze his cheek. He closed his eyes, and I could have owned heaven in that moment. I slid my hand down his chest, my thumb catching on his nipple. He didn't open his eyes, but he shuddered slightly and sucked his stomach in. I did it again. His nipple started to harden, and I rubbed a rough circle around it. He inhaled, raising his arms above his head, palms out.

I shoved him back against the headboard and pinned him there, kissing him. He opened his mouth to let my tongue in, and I found the sharp ends of his canines, pressing harder with my tongue until I tasted blood. His eyes flew open, and I wondered if he was tasting it too.

I had to force myself to pull away. Otherwise I'd have been lost, I'd have been crazy, I'd have sucked and kissed and bitten him until I came just from the sounds he was making.

I tried to steady my breathing. "Hands and knees."

He gazed at me for a second, then got into position.

I smoothed my palm over his back and then pushed his shoulders lightly, guiding him forward. His pale, narrow back dipped, and I ran my fingers in zigzags over his skin until he shivered. Then I played with his ass for a few minutes, stroking it until he was shifting to try to meet my hand. Reached under him to give his cock a couple of pumps.

I picked up the pig hole and showed it to him. His breath snagged, and I kept rubbing his shoulders. After a moment, he bowed his head, relaxing visibly. I opened the lube and smeared it all over the outside of the plug.

I brushed my slick fingers over his hole, then pushed them gently inside. He was tight; I was surprised at how tight. I thrust gently a few times, getting him used to the sensation, feeling him loosen as his breath came faster. Then I withdrew my fingers and stuck them into the plug's hollow center. Lined up the tip of the plug and slowly pushed.

The tapered part went in fairly easily, but the wider it got, the more trouble Drix had. Eventually he twisted away.

"Sorry," he muttered. "I don't know why I can't . . ."

"It's okay." I glanced down at the plug. Noticed what the problem might be. I patted his ass, not sure how to say this without embarrassing him. "I think there's a little, uh, resistance in there."

"Oh God." He clasped his hands together and set his forehead on them like he was praying. "That's gross. Sorry."

"No worries." I stroked his thigh lightly with my fingertips. Leaned to kiss his shoulder. "I have a shower shot nozzle. Depends on how bad you want to do this."

He stretched out and rolled over. My gaze immediately went to his dick, which was so hard it curved over his belly. He half smiled. "So, I think I get what that means. But I, um, don't bottom a lot, and I've never, like . . . cleaned out."

His cheeks were slightly red. I felt an unexpected rush of protectiveness toward him. A total sadist, apprehensive about douching. Very cute.

I smiled. "No problem. It's simple. You wanna shower with me?"

He stared at me for a long moment, then nodded shyly.

We headed to the bathroom. I turned on the shower and let it heat up while I doused the shower shot nozzle with some rubbing alcohol. I caught Drix glancing at the nozzle a couple of times with a forced casualness.

"Get in," I told him, giving him a quick kiss.

He had to duck into the shower to avoid hitting his head on the curtain rod. I watched his lean muscles bunch as he climbed in. This was going to be fun.

And it really was. I spent so much time making out with him and soaping him up that by the time we got to the part where I attached the nozzle and helped him guide it in, he was completely relaxed. I pulled back the curtain so he could step out and get on the toilet, and then drew the curtain again so he had some privacy. When he was done, he climbed back into the shower with me, and I had to get quite stern with him to thwart his plan for a mutual handjob.

I shut the water off and handed him a towel.

I watched him squeeze his long hair dry. "What?" he asked when he caught me staring.

"Nothing. I just like your hair. I don't know if I've ever said that."

He grinned and stepped out of the tub, offering an arm to steady me as I followed, then looking down at the puddles on the tile. "Sorry, I pretty much flooded this place when I got out before."

"It's fine." It really was. More and more, I was loving the sort of messes we made together.

I might unravel more of the world by letting him go than I would by letting myself need him.

Back in the bedroom, I sat cross-legged on the bed. He tried to get back on all fours, but I had him lie down instead. Spent a long time rubbing his back, until the water evaporated from his skin. After a while, he shifted and curled next to me, his head in my lap.

I went tense, but with wonder more than anything.

He really was incredibly sweet. And open, and trusting, and just . . . beautiful.

I combed through his damp hair with my fingers.

"That feels good," he murmured.

When I was done with his hair, I moved to his shoulders, tracing circles and then random patterns. He started wiggling. Finally he rolled so he could look up at me.

"I'm so hard," he whispered, showing me. He was certainly not exaggerating. "You *make* me so hard."

I smiled. He had just said what he was feeling, in a way I was rarely able to. And he was equally at home talking dirty or talking sweet. He was a lot like my friends, who hugged, curled up together, said "I love you" at the end of our phone conversations . . . It was a skill I hadn't learned, that level of candidness, that boundless affection. Sitting here with his head in my lap, seeing that complete trust, I could suddenly understand why Bowser had commented on my dislike of aftercare.

I'd always assumed that any sort of neediness on my part would be unattractive and inconvenient to a top. I wanted my partners to admire my high pain threshold *and* my resilience. You could do a quick, hard, dirty scene with me, and I wouldn't cry on your shoulder afterward. Wouldn't need to sleep over or use your shower. I'd just get up and be on my way.

But this was wonderful. I'd helped Drix do something he'd never done before, and now he was completely at ease with me, completely . . .

Mine.

I felt somewhat unsteady as I looked around my room. Thought about Drix in this house with me. With my son and me.

Stupid. Stupid, stupid. How long had we known each other? A few weeks? The other day I'd been ready to break up with him, and now suddenly I wanted him to be my . . .

Stupid.

I brought myself back to reality. Drix and I were alone together, and this seemed like a safe place to try something new. I let my fingertips graze his cock. Watched his thighs flex in response. "You're gorgeous," I said. "And did anyone ever tell you you're very sweet?"

His smile held a hint of sadness. "I did date someone who used to say that. But he kind of ultimately decided he'd rather have a bodybuilder than 'sweet.'"

"What an idiot." I traced the line of dark-blond hair that led from his navel to his groin.

Drix swallowed. "Well, thanks." He contracted his stomach with a small gasp as I traced the path again. "We didn't date very long. I never, uh, told him about the Dark Ravens. Just pretended I was going out with friends when I went to meetings."

"Oh?"

"I mean, usually that's not a first-date revelation for me. Just, with you, because of the kink thing, I thought it'd be okay to tell you."

I felt a sharp, terrible guilt. "I am so sorry."

"No, no. I didn't mean you should feel bad. I totally get why it's weird for an almost-thirty-year-old to pretend to be a vampire."

I slid my hand over to capture one of his. "I'm glad you have the Dark Ravens."

"Thanks. They're really good. I mean, just in terms of learning to take care of people and trust one another with our bodies and our hearts. I feel like . . . my family's pretty touchy-feely, but nothing like the coven."

"The Dark Ravens sound a lot like my friends." I rubbed Drix's hip with my other hand. "They're very affectionate. And for me, it's strange, because my parents weren't big huggers or touchers. I didn't feel unloved or anything, but I think I'd like to be a different sort of parent to my son."

He nodded. "That's good. People need a lot of contact."

"I guess so."

After a while he said, "Are we gonna try the thing you want to do?"

We tried again with Drix on all fours. I added more lube, spent more time stretching him with my fingers. Guided the plug in slowly, letting him get used to it. He finally pushed back with a grunt, and it slid in.

I kissed his shoulder. "Very nice."

He twisted as he accepted the pressure, the burn. "Mmm." The sound was mostly lust, but perhaps a tiny bit of distress.

"Come on," I whispered. "You want to feel me hurt, don't you?"

His damp hair had parted, and it slipped to either side of his neck as he ducked his head. "Yes."

"It's all right." I lifted his hair and smoothed it all to one side. He laughed softly and squirmed. I ran my fingers along the edge of his ear. "You would not *believe* what this looks like."

"Is it . . . What's it look like?"

No way was this the same dirty-talker who'd fucked me in his car. He sounded uncertain.

I took several long moments to stare at his ass and think about my answer. I'd had pig holes used on me a few times, but only once had I seen someone else wearing one. An older guy I'd scened with a few times in college.

Seeing it in Drix was beyond what I was prepared for. His hole was spread wide around the silicone tube, and I could actually see inside him. It felt wrong and filthy and cruel. And gorgeous. I shouldn't be able to see that far into someone's body. I stuck my fingers inside him again and just looked. At my fingers buried deep. At the way the plug held him open for me.

"God," I whispered.

"You like it?" he asked.

"Mm-hmm."

"Can you see, like, *in* me?" His voice trembled slightly.

"Yeah. You're wide open."

He shivered. That undid me. That just crept the fuck up and kidnapped my ability to reason. "Feels weird." His laugh was higher pitched than usual. He *was* nervous.

I dragged my finger along the bones of his spine. "Bad weird?"

He shook his head.

I went back to the gear bag. Grabbed the vial of cinnamon oil.

When I turned again, he was watching me, cheek pillowed on his arms, grinning. His ass still high in the air. I grinned back. "This is sexy, right?"

"Totally."

A grave, hungry expression replaced his smile. "What're you gonna do to me?" he whispered.

I opened the vial. "Gonna fuck you."

He looked confused as I poured some oil onto my fingers. I walked around behind him and slicked the inside of the plug with a very thin layer, careful not to let the oil dribble down past the silicone. I didn't want him to feel the burn—only me. The oil I used was diluted with water-based lube—I had no interest in second-degree burns—but it was potent nonetheless, and my fingers were already starting to prickle.

When I was done, I went to the bathroom to wipe the oil off my hand. The smell was strong. Made me feel even dirtier, that fucking Yankee Candle smell, and the knowledge of what I was about to do. I returned to the bedroom.

Drix was exactly where I'd left him. His spine stood out in sharp relief. He had his face pressed into the comforter now, but I saw his body tense slightly as I approached.

I got on the bed behind him. Knelt and positioned my cock at the pig hole's entrance. Took a deep breath. This was going to hurt like fuck.

Slowly, I pushed my bare cock into the silicone channel. It took a couple of seconds for the burn to start, and even then, it wasn't too bad. But then some oil smeared across my slit. I jerked, groaning, fighting a wave of nausea. Drix stayed perfectly still, breathing hard.

The oil coated the length of my shaft, seeping into the skin, burning me all over. The pressure was building in my balls, and the sight of Drix's back muscles contracting and releasing was just fucking gorgeous.

I kept thrusting, sheathing myself to the balls each time, and the oil kept burning my cock. Bile rose in my throat, and I reached under Drix to grab him. Drix moaned, pushing into my hand.

"Does it hurt?" he asked.

"Ohhhhh, yeah."

"Use me," he whispered. "Take all the pain you need."

I pushed in again, and the fire came in waves, building and then easing for a second, only to build again. I groaned, stroking his dick.

I rubbed my balls with my free hand, trying to get the pleasure to outweigh the agony. Not a chance. My thighs were starting to tingle. I used short, sharp strokes, letting the sight of my cock buried inside him increase my desire. I let go and I came. The burning eased a bit as the oil was flushed out of my slit. A few more strokes, and he came too.

I pulled out. Carefully removed the plug.

Drix sank down onto the bed. "Never done that before."

I stretched out beside him. "Me either." I winced. "Still burning."

He stared at me. Stroked my cheek with his thumb. "Can you stay like this? All night?"

I nodded. "For you? Yeah." Wasn't like I could wash my dick without making the burn worse. Milk or olive oil would help with the heat, but would increase the mess. So yes, I would stay here. Just like this.

For him.

He wrapped his arms around me. "I want you to feel it all night."

"Okay," I whispered. I settled against him, concentrating on the pulse of the burn. It lessened as the minutes passed, but every now and then I had to push my groin against him in an effort to get some relief, some distraction from the pain. Each time, he kissed me and ran a hand over my hair. But he let me keep suffering.

CHAPTER
THIRTEEN

Two weeks later, I had a confirmation from Cheryl that my adoption of James would move forward, pending a visit to my workplace at the end of the month. I also had an email from Ellie Graham, head of the Kinky Students Society at Hymland College, thanking me for agreeing to be a guest speaker.

Since I had never agreed to any such thing, I headed to Dave and Gould's after work.

The front door was, of course, unlocked. I could hear voices in the kitchen, but when I got there it was only Dave, reading a comic. His phone was on speaker beside him, Kamen's voice on the other end.

"Yeah? You like that?" There was a wet, smacking sound. "I know you looooove listening to me chew. I know it gets you hard." More smacking.

"What the hell?" I said.

Dave looked up. "Voice mail from Kamen."

"Yeahhhhhhhhh." A slight scraping sound. "That was a little fork-on-teeth action for yah."

All I could do was gape.

"Mmmm, Dave loves to listen to me chew. It's what he pays me the big bucks for. Chewy-chewy-chewy . . ." Kamen paused. "Hey, do you think when Miles gets a baby, he'll design little T-shirts for it? And maybe—"

Dave hit End hastily and glanced up at me again. "Sorry. We really can't stop talking about the you-being-a-dad thing."

I pulled a chair out and sat. "What the *hell* is with the chewing?"

"Inside joke. We pretend sometimes that I'm a billionaire with eccentric fetishes, and he's the hooker I hire to fulfill them."

"I see." It wasn't even close to the strangest thing I'd heard from either of them, so I let it go. I folded my hands and leaned forward. "Listen. I know you did not put my name on the list to talk to that college group."

He shut the comic and stared pleadingly at me. "Miiiiiiles. It's the Subs Club. You're one of the founders."

"I am also under observation and attempting to extricate myself from the world of BDSM. So no, I will not be talking to a group of college kids about butt plugs."

"It's gonna be no cameras allowed."

"That's not the point."

"You really think the adoption agency's gonna find out? Or care?"

"You're the one who was appalled that I was even considering becoming a father, given my proclivities. Don't you think a vanilla caseworker might share those concerns if she did find out?"

"But it sucks that you won't be there. You're the one who knows the most."

He certainly knew how to appeal to my profound arrogance. "The answer is no. Take my name off the list."

Dave sighed. "Fine."

"Thank you."

"I'm just excited about taking the Subs Club to the next level."

"Mmm. You sure the club needs to go public? We're still in the doghouse with half the community after the review blog."

"But SC members are totally the right people to give this talk, since we're all safety conscious and stuff. Can you imagine if your college'd had a kinky group?"

My college had been a small private school with a building called the Briggs-Hawthorne Library of Rarities. So no, I could not imagine there being an extracurricular group known as the Kinky Students Society. "It would have been cool," I admitted. I went to the fridge for some juice.

"I want to go further with this group. Do, like, community outreach and stuff."

"What, like building houses?"

"No. Just giving BDSM—real BDSM, not *50 Shades of Bullshit*—a presence in society."

"Awesome. Do it. I just can't help."

"Fine." Dave leaned back and ran a finger along the stalk of an aloe plant on the windowsill. "Ricky texted. He was at Cobalt last night, and this black woman and white guy were doing a Ferguson-themed scene."

"And you think this is especially relevant to me because . . ."

"*No.* I told Kamen too. Like, white guy as cop, black woman as protestor. People were *pissed.*"

"I'd imagine."

"Doesn't that bother you?"

I shrugged. "We saw those Nazis at Cobalt a few months ago. It's just role-play."

Dave sighed. "But it's so insensitive."

"If kink had to look PC, there'd be no female subs with male doms, ever."

"Where's your dad when I need him to back me up?"

"Driving to Washington."

"When's his next break?"

I shrugged. "He doesn't always come home on his breaks." I drained my juice. "Is Gould here?"

Dave snapped off the end of the aloe stalk and rubbed the gel on his hand. "In his room."

"You guys made up?"

"Pretty much."

That sounded less than enthusiastic.

Dave stood. "I have to head out and meet D. But I'll tell Ellie you're not coming. And you're welcome to stay here as long as you like."

I decided to take him up on the offer and entered his room to use his computer for work emails. I heard him leave, and a little while later, I heard Gould's door open.

I got up and peered through the doorway. Saw Gould at the kitchen table, eating some cereal and staring out the window.

I stepped into the kitchen. "Hi."

Gould barely glanced at me. "Oh. Hey."

He didn't say anything else.

Dave often acted as though Gould's silence was evidence of some secret shaman within. Personally, I didn't see the appeal of spending significant amounts of time with someone who couldn't carry on a conversation. But I *did* love Gould, no matter how vexing I sometimes found him. Same as I loved all of them.

Same as I'd loved Hal.

"Something wrong?"

Gould took another bite. Chewed and swallowed. "Dave's being a real ass about the stuff with GK and Kel and Riddle."

"It's a tough situation." I'd never been good at comfort.

"Whatever. I don't want to get involved with the club politics. I just like *them*."

"So keep seeing them."

"I really am trying to move on from everything." Gould sounded slightly defensive. "From Hal, I mean. I know nobody thinks I'm doing a good job, but . . ."

For a second, I could see what appealed to Dave about Gould. He did have a very kind face. Looked just a bit fragile.

One of the first times I'd hung out with him, he'd been with Hal. The two of them were half-drunk, laughing madly in some bar, lost in their private world. And because I hadn't really known Gould without Hal, I'd assumed Gould was *like* Hal—intense and capricious and hard to be close with. It wasn't until he and Hal broke up that I saw this quieter, gentler Gould. And even then, I'd thought it was some sort of extended sulk brought on by the breakup.

I was the one who'd introduced Dave and Kamen to Gould, since I'd seen Gould at a couple of munches. But Dave had become closer friends with him long before I had. I'd heard secondhand from Dave how much Gould worried about things like his weight, his family, his job. How hard a time he had finding doms who didn't mind his silence. I'd only realized over the last year how unanchored Gould could be without people around to keep him grounded. He seemed like someone who'd just float off on a breeze.

"I think you're doing well."

He put his spoon down. "Dave says I've been acting weird since he and D got together."

So this was about more than Riddle. "*Have* you been acting weird?"

Gould gave me that quiet, stoic look that made him appear to have witnessed untold horrors throughout all his young life and borne the pain without protest. "I don't know. It's like, I really, really want him to be happy. But it's hard not having him around as much."

I nodded. I'd always suspected Gould enjoyed Dave's crush on him. When Gould and Hal had been together, I'd sometimes seen him flirting with Hal directly in front of Dave, as though he wanted Dave to see. I didn't think for a moment Gould had been consciously trying to hurt Dave. But he did have some self-esteem issues, and I think he enjoyed both having a boyfriend and knowing that his best friend was a little bit in love with him.

Now Hal was gone, and Dave had a steady partner. It couldn't be easy.

"I think it's my fault, sometimes." Gould's leg was jouncing under the table. "What happened to Hal."

I gaped. "*What?*"

"If I hadn't broken up with him, he wouldn't have played with Bill that night."

"You'd broken up over a *year* before he played with Bill."

"But if we'd stayed together . . . I just wonder."

"Are you kidding?" A look at his face told me he wasn't. "You think you should have stayed with someone who was making you unhappy just so—"

"He didn't make me unhappy." The tone was savage. Unexpected and un-Gould.

"He did, though. Toward the end."

"He didn't . . . make me . . . unhappy," Gould repeated.

"All right, fine. Yes. It was a perfect love. Real *Titanic* stuff."

He glared at me for a few seconds, then turned away, snorting. "Can you imagine him sketching me while I was wearing nothing but a giant blue diamond?"

I'd been braced for an argument, but I grinned. "As I recall, Hal couldn't draw anything but penises."

"And rabbits. He was surprisingly good at rabbits. I still have this . . . I don't know, we were at some restaurant, and he stole a pack of crayons from the basket for kids and drew all these rabbits on the placemat. And I kept it."

I nodded. "I remember how you and he used to talk all the time. For hours. I didn't believe Dave when he told me you were shy, because I'd seen you with Hal."

Gould didn't answer. Just stared out the window with a tiny smile on his face.

Gould, I realized suddenly, was maybe our best link to Hal. He held all these memories the rest of us didn't know about. He was familiar, I imagined, with Hal's deepest fears.

His darkest secret—the one I hadn't read.

"Are you scared?" Gould asked after a moment. "About having a kid?"

"No," I lied. "I feel incredibly ready to do this."

A long silence.

And then I couldn't sustain it. "That's a lie. I'm scared every day."

"Me too. And I'm not doing anything nearly as scary as what you're doing."

"If GK and Kel are making you happy, keep playing with them. Dave's just bossy."

Gould tensed. "Dave's bossy because he loves us."

Like brothers, those two. Each was the only one allowed to insult the other. Then I remembered I was pretty sure they used to be jerk-off buddies, back before Gould and Hal officially got together, and I scrapped the brothers comparison.

"Sure. But he's still bossy as fuck."

Gould shrugged. "I don't mind. I don't know what I'd do without any of you."

You shouldn't have had to learn. Shouldn't have had to learn what to do without Hal.

"It wasn't your fault," I told him. "Not even a little bit."

But he finished his cereal like I wasn't even there.

My mother showed up one evening in a U-Haul cargo van with a man I didn't know.

I stood in the doorway for a moment, staring at the van without letting her in. "Uh, hi."

She wiped her hands on the sides of her bright-purple dress. "I got you a crib."

"What?"

"I got you a *crib*." She bit off each word. "It's an old one, like we used to have for you."

The man was coming up the drive with an old drop-side crib.

"Mom. They say that kind of crib is dangerous for babies."

"Who's they?"

"I don't know. But *they* banned them several years ago."

She pushed me aside and entered the house. Drew me deeper into the hall while the man came in with the crib. "Upstairs," she said to him. "First room when you get to the top."

"I don't—"

"It oughtta be the *second* room." She headed toward the kitchen. "Why you wouldn't put your baby's nursery beside your room is beyond me."

I followed her. "We've been over this. The front room gets the most natural light; it's *bigger*, because the kid *is* going to grow; and the middle room is my office. It always has been."

She wiped her face with a handkerchief as she approached my fridge. "You're not gonna hear him if he cries."

"*Baby monitors*, Mom."

She tucked the handkerchief away and opened the fridge. "You have nothing in here any human would want to drink."

I sighed. "Just drink water."

"Do you actually drink Nature's Choice *prune* juice?"

To regulate my bowel movements and facilitate anal intercourse? Yes.

She pulled out the bottle. Stared at it. "Nobody enjoys this. Your son's going to drink this?" She held it up.

"I don't know, Mom. He's still negative three months old, so it's hard to say what he'll like."

She shook her head and put the bottle back. Let the fridge fall shut. "O-kay. I'm going to have water."

She used my ice machine to fill a glass to the brim with ice cubes, then added a small amount of water and chugged it. I watched her, not sure what to think or say. Antagonizing me had always been her game. But she had a way of hurting me so slowly and so calmly, all the while pretending she just had her teeth bared in play. I heard her friend creaking around upstairs.

"You know, you might want to ask before you bring cribs into my home. Especially death-trap cribs."

"It's a *gift*. Cribs are expensive." She set her glass, still full of ice cubes, in the sink. "I had to search a long time to find one like we had for you."

"Because they don't *make them anymore*."

She took her handkerchief out again and dabbed around her mouth. "You never died."

"Sometimes I wish I had."

I caught a glimpse of a smile before she hid it.

"Besides." She placed a hand slowly on her hip, cocked the hip, and locked eyes with me. "You've hardly done anything to prepare for your baby."

I was so angry I couldn't speak for a second. "Haven't *done anything* to prepare?" I stepped toward her. "You have no idea. I don't need a crib because I've already bought one." It was a lie. I still hadn't found anything perfect, and I was running out of time.

The man's footsteps creaked on the stairs again. "Wait in the truck," my mother called to him.

I listened to him leave. "Do you treat everyone like your personal servant?"

She narrowed her eyes. "Do you treat everyone like they're wasting your valuable time caring about you?"

I shook my head. "I'm worried that you're not going to respect my choices as a parent. And that it's going to be confusing to James."

"You are my *son*. I am proud of *all* that you are. But that does *not* mean you know how to raise a child."

"Well, I'm tired of you meddling. And if you can't show me you're responsible—that you'll listen to me—then James isn't going to be spending much time with you."

She *stared* at me. Just stared.

"I have offered to *help* you raise this baby," she said coldly, still enunciating each word. "You are not going to know what to do on your own."

I was furious. And terrified that she was right. "I'll figure it out!" I all but shouted.

"You know who else didn't prepare? Your father. Waited for life to happen to him and then took off when he didn't like the way it happened." She wasn't playing. At all. I saw her jaw tremble slightly.

I stared right back at her. "Leave," I said. "Right now. Leave."

"I am *trying* to h—"

"*Leave.*"

She left, moving slowly. When she was gone, I felt villainous, confused, and utterly alone. Too alone to even want to call Drix.

CHAPTER
FOURTEEN

I was at work, thinking about James and the crib and how to make up with my mother, when a man walked in. He had long, thin limbs and a round middle, like a spider. Black hair and mustache. Wild brows. Paper in hand. He wore what appeared to be a wrestling singlet under a pair of denim high waters and an unbuttoned short-sleeved plaid shirt. Chest hair curled out from under the spandex.

"Can I help you, sir?" I asked.

He slid the paper toward me. "You got a scanner?"

"Yes, we do."

"Okay. Okay, I filled out a thingie online. For the shirts I want. I did the words. But I didn't have the, uh, the art? My son drew the art, so I wanted to, uh, scan it and add it to my order form."

I unfolded the paper. Inside was a rough pen drawing of a smiling tooth holding a toothbrush. "Fantastic." I got on the computer. "I'll pull your order up, if you'll just give me the last name . . ."

"Branson. It's Bobby Branson."

I clicked through the recent orders and found Branson. There was a note on it from Jason: *Holding for graphic*. "I have it right here, Mr. Branson."

I opened the order. A hundred shirts. The text was to read: *Bobby's Discount Dentist. Your teeth are safe in our hands.*

My God. It was Kamen's dentist. In the flesh. I glanced at his exposed, hairy chest. In so much flesh.

"So can you . . .?" He scratched his chest. "Can you put the art on the shirt and then put the words in a circle around it?"

I had him show me what he wanted on a diagram. I promised him we would scan the tooth drawing and send him the proof for approval. As he was getting ready to leave, I said, "Mr. Branson?"

He was partway to the door. He turned.

"Could I . . . make a suggestion?" I took a deep breath as he stared at me. "Grammatically, 'Bobby's Discount Dentist' doesn't make sense. It's not the dentist who's discounted, it's the services."

He just stared.

"Even if you put an apostrophe *s* after 'dentist'—so it's like, short for 'dentist's services'—it would sound a bit odd, but it would be technically correct. But it would be better if you could say something like, 'Bobby's Discount Dental Care.'"

More staring. Finally he said, "That's just the way I say it, man. Relax."

It occurred to me with no small amount of chagrin that I might have just lost A2A a large order.

The customer is always right in theory. But the customer is not always right grammatically.

As a teenager, I'd worked as a cashier at a couple of different shops before moving on to do some gofering at my mother's office. The cashier jobs had been menial—so simple I'd worried constantly about humiliating myself by screwing up at a task a monkey could have completed. I could still remember how I'd felt about the people I'd worked with. Like it wasn't even worth finding them unlikable or obnoxious, because I was destined for something better. My tenure would be short, and my intelligence ensured that one day I'd end up working with people who were emotionally and intellectually rewarding to be around.

But now I wasn't so sure. I still felt like the smartest guy in a lot of rooms. But I didn't feel special. I didn't feel untouchable. Mostly I just felt afraid.

Drix came over that night, and against my better judgment, I told him about my mother and the crib.

"Has she always been like this?"

"Sort of. Yeah. Even before my dad changed his job." I paused. "I think she's disappointed in how mundane her marital problems are. At least her divorced friends have good stories. They caught their husbands with the nanny, or they hit the hard-drinking bastard with a frying pan and left, or *they* got caught with the nanny . . ."

Drix snorted.

"But my mom? She just has to live each day knowing her husband chose a job where he wouldn't see her very often."

"Do you think he loves her?"

I hesitated. "Yes."

He nodded.

"But she was cruel to him. Not just when she drank. That's just how she is—she prizes honesty—or what she thinks is honesty—over people's feelings. She sees the world the way she wants to see it."

"I know some people like that."

"And that's what I'm afraid of. What if my kid's difficult, and so I don't . . . treat him well? What if that's in my nature or something?"

Drix watched me for a long moment. He looked sort of confused and sad. "How does someone so smart, so . . . *accomplished* have so little self-confidence?"

That hurt and felt good. Baffled me and made perfect sense. "I do. Ask my friends. I have an enormous amount of self-confidence. I'm insufferable. I think I can do anything."

"No." He shook his head slowly. "You don't. You expect yourself to be able to do anything. And then when you—I don't know, think you've failed—you torture yourself."

I couldn't even look at him. Yes, I was hard on myself when I failed, but wasn't that just a sympathy ploy, or something? A diversion from the truth: that I believed I was superior to most people? Harbored more knowledge, expressed myself more articulately, contributed more to society . . . What if hating myself when I failed was just me covering up what a complete narcissist I was?

But I *did* hate myself when I failed. Sometimes deeply, and sometimes in a casual way, as though I'd experienced the feeling so many times I only paid lip service to it now.

I finally forced my gaze back to his. "Is that some of your vampyric, psycho-spiritual analysis? You want to play therapist with me?" It had started as a joke, but my tone was getting sharper.

I couldn't tell whether he looked stung or amused.

So I kept going. "You want to promise me you have the patience for my shit and then leave me when the going gets tough?"

Where the *fuck* had that come from?

He had that gentle, pitying look again. "Is that what someone did to you?"

For a second, I wanted to slap him. Then I ran a hand anxiously over my thigh, smoothing a small fold in my pant leg. Forced myself to calm down. "No," I admitted. "I've never given anyone the chance to."

"So what are you worried about?"

"Everything," I said firmly. "You have no idea what you're getting into with me."

"Tell me."

"I make these lists . . . I can't even explain it to you. I can't make decisions. I mean, I *do* make them. But it takes forever. There were these two cribs, and— Oh fuck it, I don't even know why I'm trying to tell you this. I don't care if you leave me." I was speaking too quickly. "That came out wrong. You're free to do whatever you want. I'm not . . . clingy. I don't . . . do that."

"Do what?"

"Try to guilt people into staying with me. I do quite well on my own."

"Do you want a massage?" he asked quietly.

"That hardly seems like an appropriate response."

"Do you want one, or don't you?"

"I don't relax during massages. If anything, gentle contact makes me more tense than pain."

"Will you let me try?"

"All right. I just wanted to warn you."

"Miles." He sounded irritated. *Drix* sounded irritated. "I don't need to read your warning labels, okay? Just let me figure out where the danger is on my own."

I sat there for a moment, stunned. "Fine."

"I could try a light hypnotic trance if you want. To relax you. I need the practice."

"I can't be hypnotized. Three county-fair magicians have tried."

He grinned and scooted closer to me, waving his finger in front of my face.

"You're getting sleepy."

"It's not working."

"Shhh. When you awake . . ." He nudged me. "Close your eyes."

I fought an exasperated smile and obliged. How did he do this? Divert my anger so effortlessly?

"When you awake, you will want to kiss me." His voice was low.

I laughed in spite of myself. "Okay. Can I awake now?"

"I'm not done. You will want to kiss me. And when I snap my fingers, you will do it. And it will be the most epic kiss that two people have ever shared. No pressure."

"Okay."

"So. Wake up."

I opened my eyes and kissed him.

I didn't think about spit or teeth or tongues, I just lost myself in the connection. I let the gentle movement of his lips sink me deeper, deeper, until I felt as if I really were asleep. Dreaming a dream more fantastic and vivid than real life. I was in a beautiful darkness, and every small movement he made passed through my skin like a signal. Every beat of his heart was echoed by mine.

"I'm not going to leave you," he whispered.

Exactly what I'm afraid of.

But I wasn't afraid of that anymore. Not really.

I had made a good choice. I had done the right thing.

The Subs Club finally met with our superfan, Ryan W, at a bar called Pitch. Ryan was quite possibly the shortest man I had ever seen. If he and Drix had stood side by side, Ryan would have looked like a child. His voice was high and loud, but oddly charming, and he had a touch of a Napoleon complex.

We all had a beer—Dave had several—played two games of pool, and then decided to head over to Dave and Gould's for more drinks. I was already tired, but the evening was a pleasant break from thinking about my mother and Cheryl and Britney and what an ass I'd been to Bobby the discount dentist, so I decided it wouldn't hurt to go back to Dave's and get drunker.

I drove Dave's car, since he was already notably intoxicated. Ryan followed us in his car. At the duplex, Gould and Kamen got out. I told Dave to stay put, that I'd come around to his side and help him. "Isn't this amazing?" Dave said to me as I offered him my arm to steady himself.

"What?"

"He's nice. Ryan's nice. And the five of us out tonight, it was almost like . . ."

I froze. It was nothing like having Hal. Ryan was a completely different person, and it hadn't occurred to me for a moment that he was filling some empty space by playing pool with us. "Don't let Gould hear you say that," I muttered.

Dave grinned. "Nooooo. I'm not telling Gould. Gould thinks there's no more Hals. No one like Hal for a million miles. Miles." He laughed. "Miles."

"Come on. Get out."

"Miles." Dave's voice was so sharp I jumped. His expression was serious now. "I'm not saying Ryan's Hal. 'M just saying tonight is fun."

We each had another beer around the dining room table, except for Dave, who opted for water, and Gould, who was out of his gluten-free brand. We discussed the Subs Club, and Ryan told us he enjoyed being a member and admired what we were trying to do. I'd seen an article that Ryan had submitted to the site a couple of weeks ago, but I couldn't remember what it had been about. I didn't remember being particularly impressed.

Kamen played a couple of songs. Ryan watched him quite intently, and Kamen kept glancing up and smiling at Ryan.

Eventually Dave asked Ryan if he'd ever done a scene with this one dom we'd all played with.

Ryan shook his head. "I don't sub."

"I thought you were in the scene," I said.

"I am. But I'm a dom."

It took me a minute to register what he'd said. Once I had, I half expected him to peel off his *Mission: Impossible* mask to reveal a different face.

"You switch?" I asked.

He shook his head. "All dom, baby."

"What?" Dave slurred. "*What*? I don't . . . Mind. Blown."

"You don't believe me?" Ryan sipped his beer.

"Then why did you tell us you were a sub?" I asked.

"I never told you that."

"You said . . ."

"I applied and you let me in. Nowhere in my membership essay did I say I was a sub."

Dave shook his head. "Not cool, man. You're a spy-dom."

Ryan didn't seem particularly concerned. "Oh, now. Why so exclusive?"

"Hey," Kamen said loudly. "I think we're all missing the point."

I looked at him. "Which is?"

"Ryan can't be a dom. He's too tiny." It was hard to tell if Kamen was drunk too, or just being Kamen.

"Kamen, shut up," Gould said.

"I don't mean it, like, offensive," Kamen told Ryan. "I'm just saying most subs are bigger than you. So it'd be hard to do stuff to them."

Ryan stared at him evenly. "It hasn't been a problem so far."

Kamen grinned. "Seriously. Dave knows. Dave does all kinds of spanking stuff. And it's, like, it works for him, because D's big. So D can make him . . . be spanked." There was a bit of a dare in his tone. It almost sounded like drunken flirting.

"You don't think I could spank you?" Ryan asked. Something was going on between them that I was pretty sure the whole room could feel.

"How?" Kamen put down his guitar. "How would a guy my size even fit on your lap for a spanking?"

Ryan's face was perfectly serious. "You want to find out?"

Kamen laughed. "Uh . . ."

Ryan scooted his chair back and spread his thighs. "Come on over here and find out how a man your size can get a spanking from a man my size."

I joined Gould and Dave for a unison "Ooohhhh" as Kamen stood, still grinning, and walked to Ryan.

Dave snapped his fingers. "Hey. Hey, buddy. How drunk are you?"

Kamen turned to him. "Nah, man. I know what's up. I go willingly." He refocused on Ryan. "Where do you want me?"

Ryan nodded at Kamen's crotch. "Pants down."

"What?"

"Pants down. Right now. Or I'll make you take down your underwear too."

"Uhhh." Kamen glanced around the room. "I don't know if they wanna see . . ."

"Come on, buddy." Dave moved his water aside. "You and I had gym class together in high school. I've seen it all."

Kamen popped his fly, then shoved his pants down. "Ta-da!"

Gould raised his brows. "Don't quit your day job, Magic Mike."

"You sure about that?" Kamen whipped off his shirt.

"God, your body really is *perfect*," I admitted.

Kamen flexed his abs. Then looked down at Ryan and spread his arms. "You want to see the whole package?"

"I want you over my knees." Ryan took Kamen's wrist and tugged him forward. Kamen's eyes widened briefly, like a shark victim being pulled under, then he collapsed over Ryan's lap.

It did make an odd picture, Kamen's hulking frame piled onto Ryan's very small thighs. But Ryan showed no sign of being uncomfortable. He started spanking without any preamble. His tiny hand rose and descended so rapidly it blurred. At first Kamen just grunted. Then he went silent. We listened to the steady rise and fall of Ryan's hand, not sure what to do or think. To my embarrassment, I realized I was getting slightly turned on. I looked over at Dave, who crossed his legs, then at Gould, whose face was flushed.

After a few minutes Kamen started hissing, and it didn't sound feigned. Ryan stopped spanking abruptly. "Get in the corner." He rolled Kamen off his lap, and Kamen ended up on his knees on the floor. Ryan pointed at the corner. Kamen looked stunned, then lowered his head and shuffled to the corner, hobbled by his pants. His cock was stretching the front of his briefs, and the skin around the leg holes was bright pink.

He fidgeted.

"Hold still," Ryan barked. Kamen stopped moving.

I had always considered spanking a rather juvenile activity. But good heavens, this was a surprisingly simple and enjoyable performance.

"So your club," Ryan said conversationally. We all turned to him. "It's about things doms do wrong?"

Dave and I glanced at each other. "Uh . . . no," Dave said. "It used to be more confrontational toward doms. In some ways. But it's really just about communication."

"But what about subs?"

"What about them?"

Ryan swigged the last of his beer. "I'm just saying, if a scene goes wrong, is it always the dom's fault? Can't subs behave dangerously?"

"Of course." Dave played with his water glass, tipping it back and forth. "Though as far as I'm concerned, the doms are the ones wielding the whips and knives. They've got the keys to the cuffs. They're the ones responsible for stopping before something goes too far."

Ryan nodded. "So what turns you off in a dom?"

Dave was ready. "When a dom's an asshole. When he thinks just because he's a dom he can order me around. That he doesn't have to get to know me or earn my respect." He stared levelly at Ryan. "What turns you off in a sub?"

"Subs who don't take responsibility for knowing and setting their limits. Blind compliance. Subs who use being a sub as an excuse for really shitty behavior. Subs with no self-confidence."

"Fair enough."

Ryan leaned forward. "I'd actually like to talk to you more about expanding the Subs Club. I worked as an advocate in San Francisco for doms who accidentally overstepped a sub's boundaries in a scene, and suffered lasting guilt and trauma as a result. I wondered if your club might want to work with some local tops to hold a discussion group on what happens when both top and bottom are traumatized by a scene."

Dave's jaw tightened visibly. "Right now, we're not very interested in poor, sad tops who couldn't read the signs."

I traced the logo on my beer. When I was twenty-one, Bowser had been the first partner with whom I'd tried needle play. He'd used a combination of hypodermic needles and straight pins, and I'd started to get queasy halfway through the scene. But I hadn't wanted to admit that. Eventually, I'd gone into mild shock. I didn't remember much about it, except that when I came to, Bowser's eyes were red, like he'd been crying. He'd thought I would never want to play with him again. But I'd been totally fine. It was the first time it had *really* hit me how difficult it was to be a dom.

"It's not a terrible idea," I said. "We've already broadened our reach to include bottoms who aren't submissive. What if we made it more of a general kink club?"

"There's tons of those," Dave replied. "That's what Riddle is."

"Riddle is a dungeon that also features a small educational component."

"Can we still get sandwiches at the meetings if we're not the Subs Club?" Kamen asked from the corner.

Ryan crunched his beer can in his fist and dropped it on the table. "Excuse me." He took off his shoe—a lightweight athletic sneaker. "Kamen. Come here."

"Uh . . . me?" Kamen glanced over his shoulder.

"Yep, you, big guy."

Kamen crossed the room with his cock tenting his briefs, looking thoroughly nonplussed. Ryan put Kamen back over his lap and began smacking Kamen's ass with the shoe. Kamen bucked and whimpered, and the rubber sole left deep-red patches on his thighs. Every time the shoe descended, the pattern of the tread appeared briefly in white on Kamen's bright-pink skin. "Ow." Kamen gripped the edge of the chair. "Ow!"

"You see now?" Ryan asked softly, gazing down at Kamen. "You see how it works—me giving a spanking?"

"Yeah," Kamen managed. "I see. I really see. Ow! God, I see so much. I just want to stop seeing."

Ryan stopped, nudged Kamen to his feet, and told him to pull his pants up and go to his room.

Kamen rubbed his ass. "But I don't live here."

"You want another round?" Ryan asked.

"You can use my room," Gould said quickly.

Kamen went to Gould's room. We were all silent.

"He seems like he'd be a fun sub," Ryan said conversationally.

A moment later we heard a crash from Gould's room. "Excuse me one minute." Ryan took his shoe in hand and walked into the bedroom. A few seconds later we heard three loud smacks, and Kamen's guttural cries. Then it stopped. There was some murmuring, some laughter. Then silence.

"You think they're having sex?" Dave asked.

Gould shook his head.

Ryan came out about five minutes later. "Gentlemen," he said, in his high-pitched voice. "It was a pleasure. Thank you for having me. Your friend is fine. He's just reflecting for a few minutes."

We were all too stunned to do more than mumble good-byes. As soon as Ryan was out the door, we glanced at one another, stood, and hurried into Gould's bedroom. Kamen was kneeling by the radiator in his underwear, hands behind his head, knees spread. He didn't move as we entered.

"What are you doing?" I asked.

"Oh, I, uh, have to stay like this for ten minutes. Ryan set an alarm on my phone." Kamen peered at the windowsill where his phone lay. "Also he gave me his number."

"You don't *have* to stay like that," I pointed out.

Gould nodded. "Yeah, he's gone now."

Dave looked about ready to explode. "Who the hell does he think he is? Coming in here all, 'Oh, I'm a secret dom . . .'"

"He's a . . . spy," Gould tried, without much conviction.

Kamen sighed. "Did all of you get hard watching it?"

"No," Dave and I protested together, at the same time Gould said, "Yeah, kind of."

"It was really fucking hot," Kamen whispered.

"I know," we all said, almost in unison.

Kamen bowed his head. "I mean, he has, like, a doll-sized hand. But he hits really hard. And I *wanted* it."

"I know, buddy," Dave said.

"You guys can go back out there." Kamen sounded floaty. "I'm just gonna think about stuff. I'll be out in a little while."

We went back to the kitchen, where we sat in silence until we heard Kamen's alarm go off. A few minutes later, Kamen came out, fully dressed. The front of his pants still bulged. "Sorry," he said quietly. "I gotta go home and see about something." He headed for the door.

"His dick, I'll bet," Dave said when he was gone. "I'll bet he has to go see about his dick."

CHAPTER

FIFTEEN

The next couple of weeks passed in a haze. Home Study 2: Workplace Edition with Cheryl went smoothly. Every Thursday evening, I attended my class for adoptive parents. And each time I came home from class, my head was filled with new horrors I hadn't even imagined. Stories of adopted kids who became addicts and stabbed their parents. Adopted kids who committed suicide because however much their adoptive parents loved them, it wasn't enough to make up for being abandoned by their birth parents.

The teacher and guest speakers were friendly and positive, but they didn't bullshit us, and I became utterly convinced I was going to raise an addict or a school shooter or a manhole-cover stealer. There was a power couple in my class, the Renfers. They'd adopted three kids over the past ten years, and at first they seemed a beacon of hope. Then I learned that their first son had been hospitalized following multiple suicide attempts, and their daughter had served jail time.

But almost every night, I was with Drix. And he got me to relax. Hurt me, held me. Made me laugh. He told me anonymized versions of cases he was working on, and I told him about my classes. I was surprised that someone I'd known for so little time could feel like such a good friend.

And I worked on trying to open up. To submit.

"You're just a little clinical about it," Bowser had said.

What was I supposed to be? I wasn't some submissive stereotype, crying and broken after a scene, waiting to be put back together. Or else soaring through subspace every time I was so much as shown a flogger. I gave what I could and I took what I needed. But Drix was bringing out something different in me. He didn't ask me to relinquish my control, my body, or even my fears. He simply made me want to *share* those things.

I'd never let anyone else make decisions for me. But I started to let him do it. Simple things: what cock ring I wore, or how I was positioned, or how long a scene was going to go. I *liked* it when the choice was his.

Most nights, we didn't even get kinky. And most of the kink we'd done so far was relatively mild compared to activities I'd done in my early twenties. I told myself that was just because Drix was new to all this, but actually, I didn't miss the hard-core scenes. What was urethral torture compared to dirty talk with someone I cared about? What was branding compared to easing Drix through losing his shower-shot-nozzle virginity?

We played with Bowser a couple more times, and Drix was way more confident now. He could use an array of implements, from canes to crops to floggers, and we even tried some knife play and electro torture.

"I'm getting good, right?" he asked after one particularly brutal session.

"You're awesome," I agreed, discreetly checking the cane welts on the backs of my thighs.

"Sweet." He grinned. "Because Bowser and I are planning something big for you."

"Oh?"

"Uh-huh. It's kind of like my final exam before I graduate from kinky college. We were thinking maybe early next month?"

Well, I wasn't going to say no to that.

Drix went through a period of a couple of weeks where he seemed down. When I asked him what was wrong one night, he said again that he was unhappy with his job. "I don't want to make people's lives worse. And that's all I'm doing." He leaned back on the pillows.

"Don't you help people who need proof their partner's cheating?"

"How does that make anything better? I'm spying on one person to give another ammunition. Everything's about deception and blame and I hate it."

"Drix." I almost laughed. "That's just the way life is. People are greedy and paranoid and manipulative. Welcome to the world."

He shot me an unconvincing glare, twisting his mouth to one side. "Don't mock me. I know I sound like some fucking Disney princess. I just really want to do something I like, and that other people like."

"I felt that way for a long time before I opened A2A," I told him, shifting closer to him on the bed. "I had a nine-to-five in an office. If you don't like what you're doing now, you'll find something else."

"I guess." He paused. "Maybe I'm just freaking because I'm turning thirty soon."

"The end of the line, huh?"

He forced a smile. "The Dark Ravens have been really supportive. Like, encouraging me to find what I want to do. I love them. I love being a part of that group. But sometimes I feel so stupid."

"Why?"

"For being a grown-up and playing this game."

Him feeling stupid was probably my fault. I laced my fingers through his. Felt the warmth of his body against mine. "I like the game. Keep playing the game. Everyone needs a game."

He looked at me. "I might just quit. My job, I mean. Not the game."

A slight nervousness crept in. *Just quit? Without a solid plan?* I made a noncommittal noise.

His gaze searched mine. "You think that's an okay idea?"

He needs you now. Your support, not your judgment. Be here for him.

I hooked my chin over his shoulder, the way he sometimes did with me. "Deep breath."

He tried. I breathed with him. He smiled. "You're good at that."

"I learned from the best."

"I know I'm supposed to live in the now." His voice sounded younger, softer than usual. Almost tentative. "I know time's a meaningless construct. But . . ."

"It's okay to worry about the future." I kissed his neck. "It really is okay."

He hesitated. "I trust you."

I reached up and pushed his hair back from his face. "It really means a lot when you say that. Just so you know. I think the things you say to me matter more than all the things anyone else has ever said to me."

"I *do* mean it." His smile gradually faded. "I want to tell you something. And you can take it or leave it."

I was instantly wary. "Okay."

His fingers curled against my skin, and I heard him swallow. "I really like you. And I would gladly hang around once you have your kid. Like, I understand if you want it to be just you and your son. But I'd help out, you know? If you wanted. Even if it didn't work out between us, I'd help for as long as I was around."

I lay there, my heart going wild, my body perfectly still.

You can't mean that.

"I really want to be *useful*," he added.

I didn't know what I wanted.

Or I did, but it seemed too simple.

I wanted him. Around.

I wanted my son to have a family.

And suddenly it hit me in a way it never quite had before—my kid was *always* going to have a family. My friends were a part of this. My mother, however crazy she drove me, was part of this. My sister. My dad.

And now Drix.

If I wanted him.

And I did want him.

I hesitated. Wasn't quite sure how to say this, so I just opened my mouth and let it come out. "If you're gonna be hanging around, then you have to meet my friends."

I went to see Mom the next day. Found her weeding her garden. I apologized to her, and though I knew from experience she was unlikely to apologize to me, it still hurt a little. I crouched, reluctant to get my pants dirty, and tried to help pull a few weeds.

I told her about the classes, and she did a long, slow turn to gaze at me. She could look imperious even on her hands and knees in the dirt. "You can bet I didn't have to take any classes in order to adopt your sister. They couldn't wait for me to take her. They gave me a—"

"Dairy Queen Blizzard, I know."

She regarded me coolly. "A *coupon* for a Blizzard."

"I don't believe that for a second."

She wiped her forehead with her arm. Her wrist was covered in red marks from her rubber band. "You don't have to."

"Mom," I said after a moment. "I'm scared."

She pulled out a giant weed and tossed it aside. "I threw up twice the day we took Malina home. And it was tied for the happiest day of my life. But I still threw up. Twice."

Because Malina wasn't around, I chanced asking, "Do you ever feel differently toward me than her?"

Mom's forehead furrowed. "What? Because she's not my blood?"

"Yeah."

"You *listen* to me. About this *one* thing, at least. Love is love, kid."

"I know, but—"

"I'm not finished. Adopting someone else's kid is a leap. It is *brutal*. You don't get to learn how that baby kicks inside you. You don't get to sing to her before she's born. Your body doesn't change because she's a part of it. They just put her in your arms, a stranger, and you figure her out. But it. Is. Worth it."

I didn't understand what was happening. One minute I was fine. I was listening to my mother's advice, and I was fine. The next minute I was crying.

I wanted to beg her not to tell anyone she'd seen me like this. I wanted to go inside and be alone until it stopped.

But she held me before I could make my escape, her dirty gloves leaving smudges on my shirt. And I didn't have to ask her not to tell, because she wouldn't. She'd seen me like this a hundred times, with scraped knees and B's on my report card and torn to pieces after my first breakup and missing my dad when he took off on his first drive.

"I don't know anything," I sobbed into her shoulder. "I pretend to know everything, and I don't know anything. I'm such a *bastard*."

She patted my back. "You get it from me, hon. You get it from me. And look. I did all right. I made a lot of mistakes. But I'm a pretty smart cookie."

I tried to pull back. "I'm sorry."

"For what?" She clutched me tighter. "I did sing to you before you were born. Why're you trying to hide from me now?"

CHAPTER
SIXTEEN

After that freak-out, I got infinitely better. I mean *disconcertingly* better.

I showed up at Dave's that Friday, feeling slightly self-conscious in a new outfit I'd bought, but mostly . . . light. *Happy.* I was even dressed differently. Under my tight gray tank top, I had marks from a night with Drix, faint and still sore. I paused on the porch step, not sure whether to button my overshirt. One button, maybe? Or just leave the whole thing undone?

The door was open. I didn't even scold Dave and Gould for not locking it. Kamen was in the kitchen, making a crumb-strewn wasteland of a Fig Newtons carton and playing his guitar.

Dave was trying to roll some kind of dough out on the counter, and Gould was pulling barbecue ribs out of a slow cooker.

"Helloooo!" I called cheerfully.

Dave looked up first. "Holy crap. Mr. Rogers, did Mr. McFeely steal your sweaters?"

"Who is this new Miles?" Gould asked as I joined Kamen for a duet of "Down on Wayne Street." "This is like the scene from *Grease* where Sandy comes out in leather pants."

Dave had to shout over Kamen and me. "Yes, he appears to have good-bye-to-Sandra-Dee'd his cardigans."

"I'm just trying something new," I called back, stealing Kamen's air mic and sashaying over to serenade Dave.

Dave ducked away from me. "I'm both frightened and pleased. All right, my friend. We need to have a conference. Come into my room."

I followed him in.

Along one windowsill was a line of painted foam mannequin heads, each with a different wig. One had a shag, another a mismatched bob. Surfer-boy locks. A Mohawk. The fifth was rocking "The Rachel" from *Friends*.

"What the hell are those?" I asked.

"Those are my heads. I've been practicing for styling school." He pointed to each head in turn. "Annie, Lamonda, Percivenne, Stromboli, and Tara."

"Have you heard back from any schools yet?"

He shrugged. "One in Perrystown, but that's too far away. I'm still waiting on others. But I figured shears and I should get reacquainted in the meantime."

I glanced again at the heads. "They look beautiful."

"Thank you. Now tell me why you're giddy and wearing normal-man clothes."

"What are you talking about?" I said innocently. "I'm just enjoying spring."

"My ass. What's going on?"

I sighed. "The guy I've been playing with—the bucket-list guy?— is amazing. And we're getting serious."

Dave's eyes widened. "Oh *really*?"

"And I don't want to keep it from you. And I just want to say, Dave, that I think what you want to do with the Subs Club is cool. And I *will* do the talk at Hymen College. Because I *want to*."

He gaped. "Miles. That's awesome. I need to meet this man who's rewired your brain."

"You will meet him. Soon." I paused. "But I have to tell you something about him. And you have to promise not to taunt me."

His mouth twitched. "Agreed."

I stared at him warily for a moment.

"What? Miles, I agreed!"

I took a deep breath. "He's a vampyre."

"Excuse me?"

"With a *y*. He's part of the vampyre community."

"*What*?"

"Just get over it. Okay?"

"You're dating a vampyre."

"Yes. Calm down."

"Ohhhh, Miles. Does his skin sparkle?"

"If you mock me, I'll tell D."

"No." Dave was grinning, shaking his head. "You don't understand how this works. I only get in trouble if I'm being a real asshole. Right now I'm teasing you with affection. So much affection." He approached me, arms out. "Come on. Endless hug. Come on." He wrapped his arms around me.

"What are you doing?" I mumbled into his shirt.

"Just let me love you."

I let him love me, remaining rigid. "Can this stop now?" My voice was still muffled.

"The point of an endless hug is that it's endless," he whispered. But he let me go. Leaned back and studied me. "I can't believe you. You sly old dog."

Kamen entered with a platter of ribs balanced on one hand and a single rib in the other. The ribs all had some greenish sludge on them. "Look what Gould made! *Pork.* I asked him if God's cool with that, and he said he doesn't care."

"Did you put guac on those ribs?" I asked.

"Yesh." Kamen spoke through a mouthful of rib.

Dave was sitting perfectly still, his lips pressed together. I tried to give him a warning glare, but he was practically bouncing. "Kamen, guess what?"

"Dave," I warned.

"Please?" He looked at me. "We're all friends."

"Tell me!" Kamen said.

I sighed, which Dave took as acquiescence. "Miles is dating a vampyre."

"Cooool." Kamen snagged another rib.

"I'm serious," Dave said. "He's gone *Twilight* on us."

Kamen licked at the barbeque sauce around his mouth. "Vampires aren't real."

"Vampyre," Dave corrected. "With a *y*."

"What's the difference?"

I closed my eyes briefly. "Vampyres with *y*'s are humans who pretend to be vampires with *i*'s."

Kamen frowned at the guac that had fallen off his rib. "That's a thing?"

"Yes," Dave said. "And this vampyre is making Miles very happy, so we must respect him."

"I already respect him." Kamen held out a rib to me. "Here. Congratulatory guac rib."

I shook my head. "No, thanks." All I wanted to do was talk about Drix and my newfound happiness. "I don't even know how to describe it, you guys. I just . . . feel better when he's around. I mean, yeah, he dresses funny and has fangs. But for him, time is a meaningless construct. So he lives in the now. Except when he's worried about turning thirty."

Dave squinted at me. "Are you drunk?"

"On *life.*"

"Ohhhh boy."

"So, see, *I'm* trying to live in the now."

Dave shook his head. "When we went to see *Rent* a few years ago, you said the 'no day but today' stuff was bullshit because people need to take responsibility for their futures. But a guy who likes dressing like Dracula tells you to live in the now because time is a meaningless construct, and you think that's profound?"

"Not profound. But it's working for me right now." I snatched a guac rib from Kamen's plate. "I actually do want one of these."

"So we get to meet him soon, right?" Dave said.

"Yes. Maybe dinner here this weekend?"

"And how do we *know* he's good for you?" Dave was smirking, so I could tell he was waiting to deliver a line. "I'd like an interview with him. An interview with the vampyre, if you will."

I rolled my eyes. "Oh for Christ's sake."

Dave cackled.

I pointed at him. "*Don't* interrogate him. Remember how nervous you were bringing D over for the first time?"

A brief flare of empathy in Dave's gaze. "Miles. I just want to ask him a few questions."

"So, like, did you meet him at the club?" Kamen asked.

"No. He, uh—he's a sadist. Which is cool. But he didn't know BDSM. So . . . I've been having Bowser train him."

"Wait," Dave said, at the same time Kamen said, "What?"

Dave stared at me. "*Bowser* Bowser? From Riddle?"

"Yeah," I said impatiently.

"I thought you'd only played with Bowser, like, once."

I shook my head. "We've played quite a bit over the years."

Kamen took a long, slow bite of guac rib. "Are you serious?"

"We get along really well as play partners. And he doesn't want to be anything more than a mentor."

Dave grabbed one of the foam mannequin heads from the windowsill. Smacked me with it several times. "You never. Tell us. *Anything*!" The wig fell off.

"I know, I know." I held up my hands. "I'm telling you now."

Dave tossed the head aside. "So he and Drix top you?"

I nodded. "They work well as a pair. Like the velociraptors in *Jurassic Park*."

"Raptors are the shit," Kamen said.

I went on. "It's nice, because I'm more bottom than sub. I like telling them how to—how to hurt me."

Dave punched the air. "Miles is fucking *crushing* it! He's got two guys after him. One of whom's a vampyre."

Kamen waved a guac rib excitedly. "So this is literally *Twilight*."

"Yes! Miles is a clumsy boy in cardigans who has captured the attention of a gorgeous vampyre—" Dave looked at me. "Is he gorgeous?"

I nodded. "Oh yeah. But this is n—"

"A gorgeous vampire with a dark past. Enter the werewolf—"

"Who's actually a Viking," Kamen pointed out.

"They'll have to duke it out for his heart. Oh my God, Miles, you're going to have the best dirty secrets of any dad who's ever lived."

"Ugh, don't remind me." I put my face in my hands. "I don't *want* to have dirty secrets. I want to be a superior father."

"You will be. But you're also always gonna be a kinky fucker." Dave sat on the bed. "So what's his name?"

"Drix Seger."

Dave nodded. "Okay. Strange, but I'll take it. And what's he do for a living? Or does he suck blood full-time?"

I'd really been hoping to avoid this part. "He's a . . . private investigator."

Dave's mouth fell open. "Oh. My. G—"

"You don't have to say anything."

"I do, though."

"No. You always, *always* have the option of keeping your mouth shut."

"So he's Drix Seger: Vampyre PI."

I glanced around, as though others might be listening. "Shh."

"Say it. Say, 'My boyfriend is Drix Seger: Vampyre PI.'"

"He's not my—"

"Shut up and tell me your boyfriend's a vampyre PI."

"I can't shut up *and* say it," I pointed out.

Dave lit an imaginary cigarette. Took a drag and gazed off into the distance. "The air was muggy and stifling and stretched over the city like the roof of an Ottoman yurt. I was in my—"

I groaned. "Please stop noir-monologing."

"I was in my office, poring over my latest case—seems a shop owner I'd bumped gums with a few times had met with the business end of a wooden stake—when in walked Miss Kitty La Fey."

"David . . ."

Kamen had paused with a rib midway to his mouth. "No, I wanna hear this."

Dave continued. "Kitty was to bad news what baseball is to America. I took one look at her beautiful gams and glistening fangs and was lost in a reverie of sweat and sunshine, and . . . *Reno*."

I shook my head. "You have serious problems."

David ground his imaginary cigarette out. "He's a *vampyre*. And a private eye."

I sighed. "I know."

"And he's making you happy."

"I know."

"Let's tell Gould."

I didn't stop them as they headed into the kitchen and casually announced that I was dating a vampyre. Gould seemed genuinely pleased on my behalf.

"*And* Miles isn't really a sub!" Kamen informed Gould. "He's a *bottom* who likes to dom his tops!"

Gould mock-gasped as he put the lid back on the guac. "Kick him out of the Subs Club."

"He's a witch!" David cried. "Burn the witch!"

"You guys. I really do like being submissive. Sometimes."

"He's a switch!" David cried without missing a beat. "Burn the switch!"

Le sigh.

They all descended on me, chanting "Burn the switch!" and pretending to gnaw on me.

I fended them off. "You guys are such freaks."

"But we're awesome, right?" Dave asked.

"You're not too shabby."

"And we're gonna light Hymen College on fire with our awesome. Right?"

"Let's settle for having a civil, rational discussion."

"Fire!" Dave yelled.

I let it go.

CHAPTER
SEVENTEEN

On Saturday, I went over to Dave and Gould's an hour before Drix was due there for dinner. Dave was chopping peppers at the sink. Kamen was at the table laughing at something on his phone and waiting for it to be time to grate cheese for the chili. Gould was finishing the last of some wine that was lying around, so that we could "feel okay" about opening a new bottle when Drix arrived.

"You guys are going to be good for Drix, correct?" I asked.

No one answered.

"He's so *tall*," Kamen said for the umpteenth time. I'd shown him a picture of Drix and me, and he hadn't been able to get over Drix's stature. "I can't believe you're dating someone that tall."

I set the table. "What does his height have to do with anything?"

"It's just funny."

"Uh-huh." I gave him a gentle shove. "I think you have an unnatural fixation on people's heights. First Ryan, now Drix . . ."

Kamen looked up from his phone. "It *is* funny when people are either really tall or really short. And Drix is, like, Godzilla."

Dave glanced over at us. "That's who you think of when you think tall? Godzilla?"

"Yeah."

"Not, like, Yao Ming, or that guy from *The Raymond Carver Show* . . . No, not— Wait." Dave paused, holding a knife loosely in one hand. "Who's Raymond Carver?"

"Books," I said.

Kamen raised a hand. "I had to read a story by him in school."

"Do you mean *Everybody Loves Raymond*?" Gould asked.

"Yeah, *Everybody loves Raymond Carver.*" Dave went back to cutting. "You guys never watched that? I feel sorry for you."

Kamen narrowed his eyes. "You're lying, right? There's no show about Raymond Carver."

Dave tossed a piece of pepper at him. "Yeah, buddy. I'm lying."

"I thought so."

Dave held up a hand. "Air high five."

They air high-fived from opposite ends of the kitchen.

I joined Dave at the sink and opened a package of ground beef. "So you guys *are* gonna be nice, yes?"

"Of course," Dave said. "It's important to treat Godzilla with respect. Hand me a pan."

"I have meat hands. Do *not* refer to him as Godzilla."

Dave opened his mouth. "Wh—"

I cut him off. "Edward Cullen is not an acceptable substitute."

"What about Lestat?"

"No."

"Andre the—"

"*No.*" I walked over to him. "God, can D just . . . start a hotline or something that we can call when we need him to come cane you?"

Dave reached around me to get a pan. "That *is* an idea he's bandied about."

I grabbed him from behind. Squeezed him around the middle and lifted him up. He yelped.

"Meat hands!" he shouted.

"Just call him Drix. Okay?" I set him down.

He yanked his clothes straight, muttering to himself.

Kamen picked up his guitar. "I just got inspired."

"Kamen?" I said sharply. "I think it's time to grate the—"

Too late. Kamen sang:

"He's a vampire, and a private eye

"All rolled up in one.

"He feasts on the blood of his human slaves,

"And he found the Maltese Fa-al-connn . . ."

He smashed out a chord, doing some painful-looking headbanging.

"Vampi-ire!

"Private Eye!

"Catches criminals!

"Bleeds them dry!"

He trailed off.

"Doo doo doo da dee die die . . ."

We were all silent a moment.

Then Dave tossed the meat into a pan and asked, "Can I call him Damon Salvatore?"

They were good.

Until wine happened.

We talked about Drix's job, about Dave's efforts to style his mannequin heads' hair. About the Subs Club and the coven and James, and Kamen's secret chili ingredient—which was crushed corn chips, and not a secret at all.

Dave was on his third glass of wine when he offered Drix more rice for his chili and said, "So after you destroyed the city of Tokyo, did you—"

I rammed my elbow into his side.

"Ow!" He dropped the rice spoon.

I turned apologetically to Drix. "He thinks you're as tall as Godzilla."

Drix laughed. "I am really tall. Not gonna lie."

"I think you're awesome." Dave picked up spilled rice grains and set them on a napkin. "I just have a few questions. To make sure you're good enough for Miles."

I rolled my eyes. "Dave. Don't—"

"What? Your dad is off driving trucks, so I have to be, like, the dad with a shotgun and make sure Drix treats you right."

"You do *not* have to do that."

Drix looked at Dave. "I would be happy to hear your questions."

I swatted Drix's side. "Don't encourage him."

"Shh, Miles." Dave waved me away. "This's businessss." He focused on Drix. "Okay. Miles is a masochist. *But* . . . true or false: You're not going to *hurt* him hurt him."

"Dave—"

"Let him answer, Miles."

"True." Drix glanced at me. "I would never hurt him in a way he didn't want to be hurt."

"Okay, cool." Dave pretended to mark his answer down and then flipped the page of an invisible notepad. "Second question: Are you responsible for Miles no longer dressing like Mr. Rogers, but rather, a hipster who ate a hobo?"

"Uh . . . no," Drix said.

Dave turned to me. "And that was a *compliment,* Miles. I like the hipster-hobo stuff." Back to Drix. "The last one is the hardest of all."

"That's what she said," Kamen muttered.

Dave looked sharply at Kamen. "I do believe she mentioned that, yes." He focused on Drix.

Drix nodded. "I'm ready."

Dave paused dramatically. "Does the fog hang heavy over the city as you make your way to your third-floor office? Are you lost in a haze of memory and smoke as you contemplate the gold ring on your desk? The ring given to you by William 'Bag o' Bones' Wilkinson, on that day twelve years ago in Chelsea?"

"Uhhhh . . ." Drix turned to me for help.

I sighed. "He wants you to do a noir monologue."

"Do you know a Miss Kitty La Fey?" Dave demanded. "The dame's all business, but trouble follows her like a cat looking for cream."

Drix smiled and leaned toward Dave. "It was actually a cold, crisp day. I'd just been to the deli and had ordered a hell of a ham sandwich. On rye. I walked the city streets, recalling the days when I was just another gumshoe pounding the concrete jungle. I reached my office and had no sooner picked the lettuce from my teeth when a dame walked in I'd have known anywhere. Houndstooth coat and legs for hours."

Dave was staring at him, entranced. "Who was it?"

"Who else? Missy Van Belle."

Dave slapped the table. "Oh my God. She's got trouble written on her like—"

"Like the twenty-fourth of October," Drix finished.

Dave burst out laughing. "You're really good at that."

"It's not the first time I've been asked to monologue." He leaned back. "Now it's my turn for questions. Where did you all meet?"

"Mmm—" Dave bit into a chip. Chewed for a few seconds. "Kamen and I went to high school together. But we never really talked. I mean, it was classic jock and queer kid. Except Kamen was an incredibly nice jock, and everyone loved him."

Kamen grinned. "Awww."

Dave did an exaggerated shrug. "It's true! Kamen won prom king by a landslide, and then he broke his crown into three pieces and gave one piece to each of his opponents."

"That *never* happened," I assured Drix.

"You weren't there, Miles!" Dave said.

"Yeah," Kamen said. "I totally did that."

Dave scraped the last of the chili from his bowl. "Okay, fine, I made that part up. But Kamen really was a nice jock, and I actually never got bullied. By him or anyone. But we still ran in different circles. We graduated, and then two years later—"

"I was at a leather bar," Kamen said. "It was my first time there."

"I was there too," Dave said. "My second time. I about shat myself when I saw Kamen. We did some catching up. Then decided to go to Taco Bell, because we were twenty years old and scared shitless of all the half-naked people blowing each other in dark corners."

"I had like eight Gorditas," Kamen added.

"And I had nine. So, uh . . . I guess we started hanging out. And then a couple months later we heard about a munch—"

"—and we couldn't stop laughing at the word 'munch.'"

Dave nodded. "We met Miles there. And Miles knew *everything* about BDSM."

"So we wanted to be friends with him." Kamen smiled at me.

I remembered the two of them—twenty years old, laughing at things that weren't that funny, Dave experimenting unsuccessfully with hair product . . . I was only a couple of years older, but I'd wanted to help. Wanted to share all I knew. Wanted them to look up to me.

"We asked Miles where all the gays were," Dave went on. "Because this munch was, like, Het City. Middle-aged White Het City."

"And *I* said"—I broke in—"that I knew a guy who'd been to some of the munches. But I hadn't seen him in a while." I looked at Gould.

"Gould!" Dave said. "But we tracked him down on Fetmatch. And he knew Hal . . ."

Kamen spread his arms. "And the rest is history."

I caught Gould's bitter smile. The rest wasn't history. Not by far. The rest was messy, complicated, and had changed each of us.

Gould said, very quietly and to the floor, "Hal's fly was down."

We all turned to him.

Gould reached for his wineglass. "That's the first thing I ever said to him. 'Your fly's down.'" He drained the last of it. "We were at a synagogue potluck, and his pants were unzipped. And normally I was too quiet to say anything to a stranger, let alone anything I thought would embarrass the other person. But Hal was . . . I wanted a reason to talk to him. Seeing that little bit of his dumbass smiley-face boxers seemed like a gift from God. A reason to go up to him."

We waited to see if there was more forthcoming, but Gould busied himself pouring another glass of wine.

The rest of us went on to talk about the upcoming season of *Space Camp*, but after a moment, Gould made a small sound between a laugh and a hum. I glanced up and saw that his eyes were wet. Dave noticed at the same time and started to say something, but Gould stood abruptly and walked to his bedroom. Shut the door.

"Hold on." Dave got up and went to Gould's door. I offered Drix another glass of wine, but Drix shook his head, and neither of us could keep our eyes off Dave.

Dave knocked on Gould's door. Waited a moment, then knocked again.

Just let him go, I wanted to say. *If he doesn't want to be out here, then he doesn't want to be out here.*

But Dave would never let go of anything Gould-related. He had to protect him, as though Gould were some glass ornament that would break if you tapped it too hard.

He's a grown man, I thought suddenly, savagely. *He doesn't need you to kiss it and make it better for him.*

Which really wasn't fair, because Gould's grief was real. I was just tired of it mattering more than the rest of ours because Gould had shared some special connection with Hal.

Dave turned and saw us all watching. He went to the freezer. "Dessert time?" he asked, opening it. "We have ice cream."

An "Uhhh . . ." from Kamen was the only response he got.

Dave let the freezer fall shut and walked back to Gould's room. This time he didn't knock—just opened the door and went in, closing it behind him.

I tried to give Drix a reassuring smile. "Sorry about that. They'll be fine."

Drix nodded.

Kamen picked up his guitar. "Gould's just really sensitive about Hal."

Drix and I listened to Kamen play for a few minutes. Eventually Dave emerged from Gould's room, shutting the door softly. He came back to the table. "He's gonna stay in there a while." Dave looked at Drix. "He said to tell you it was really nice meeting you, though."

"It was nice meeting him too," Drix said.

Dave sat. "He really, really loved Hal. It's not his fault—he just gets really sad sometimes. And it's almost the two-year anniversary of Hal's death." He sounded somewhat apologetic, but mostly defensive, as though he suspected Drix of secretly condemning Gould's behavior. Which irritated me in some small way I couldn't articulate.

"Of course." Drix glanced around. "I'm sorry for your loss. All of you."

Dave nodded wearily. "Believe me. We're sorry too."

CHAPTER
EIGHTEEN

I bought baby things. All at once, in a ridiculous online spree. I bought a crib that wasn't a death trap. A dozen blankets. A mobile. Colorful nursette bottles. A bassinet.

I placed the items in the nursery as they arrived. I found it impossible not to go in there several times each day and look at the room that would belong to James. The room where I'd rock him to sleep and read him stories. The room his earliest memories would be tied to. In the closet, I'd stored the crib Mom had given me. I didn't know what to do with that. I couldn't sell it or give it away, so I left it in there. And as long as the closet door remained shut, the room was . . .

Perfect.

June twenty-fifth was only two months away. Britney shared her ultrasounds with me via Cheryl. Cheryl showed me examples of the type of pictures and letters I would be required to send Britney for the first year of James's life. I went back to wearing cardigans. I talked to my dad on the phone, and he assured me he'd be back in town for James's birth. Dave wanted to throw me a baby shower, but I said absolutely not.

I invited Drix over to see the nursery once I had everything in there. "This thing is particularly awesome," he told me, flicking the space mobile. The next time he came over, he brought gender-neutral sea-creature wall art, and I accidentally told him I loved him. I proceeded to stammer through an explanation that I hadn't meant it *that* way, and he kindly changed the subject. He told me some stories about the neighbor kids he'd babysat in his teens. Kept me relaxed with tales of babies he'd calmed and diapers he'd changed and bottles he'd warmed.

He came over nearly every day now, but it never felt intrusive. It felt completely natural to have him in my home—even when he forgot to take his giant vampire boots off at the door and tracked dirt on my rug. I got used to him trying on costumes for coven meetings and asking me which of his largely homogenous black ensembles looked better. I was indescribably grateful for his offer to help me once I became a father. But at the same time, I was terrified. What if I got used to having him around? What if James and I depended on him, and then he left? He wanted to quit his job to pursue an admirable yet nebulous goal: helping people. What if he was like my father, or like Hal? Unreliable. Given to whims.

Ridiculous. Drix isn't going to disappear.

But if I was just like my mother, then who did that make Drix?

One evening, I listened to him recount some anecdote about the Dark Ravens, and I grew inexplicably angry. How could he stand there talking about Archimedes Wendell's additions to the coven's rulebook, when in seven weeks, I was going to have a child? Did anybody but me understand how important this was? Drix could pretend to. But he wasn't going to be James's father. If the going got tough, he could leave anytime. And, stupidly, I resented him for that.

I started to pick at him. Only sometimes, and only in small ways. Just to see what he was made of. To see if he'd stick around. I wasn't proud of this, but it was like a demon took me over and forced me to nag at him. Tease him just a little too harshly. Send him on errands just to see how efficiently he executed my instructions.

Finally, he called me out on it. Very casually one night, while I was chopping vegetables and criticizing his choice to buy a broccoli crown instead of the whole head.

"You're not going to scare me off, Miles. Just so you know."

I nearly sliced my thumb off. So I was that obvious?

Que vais-je devenir?

The whole group came out to Riddle the night Bowser, Drix, and I went to try the dildo iron maiden. Even Dave, who wanted nothing to do with the place, tagged along.

The line for the iron maiden wasn't as long as it had been a couple of months ago, when I'd first brought Drix here. Drix and Bowser and I had two couples in line ahead of us. I held Drix's hand like it was a perfectly natural, adult thing to do.

BellaSade, a DM, was standing beside the chamber like the person who decides if you're tall enough to ride a roller coaster. Bella was a transplant from San Francisco, perpetually unimpressed with our city's geography, architecture, and the selection of play partners in the local scene.

Dave stared at the chamber. "This looks right up your alley, Miles."

The woman currently inside the iron maiden was thumping around and crying, while the man standing outside ordered her to "Stab yourself on the big cock. The purple one." And keep "the fat blue one" in her mouth. He whacked the side of the chamber with a stick and shouted, "Is your wet, dirty pussy sucking on the cock yet?"

"Kamen," Dave said. "Why do you keep looking around?"

Kamen shrugged. "I asked Ryan to meet me here."

"Ohhhh," Gould said. "My, my."

Suddenly a woman's voice called, "Hey, boys!"

Kamen's mouth fell open. "Oh, *shit.*"

We all turned as one.

Mrs. Pell was waving to us from a few places back in line.

"It's my mom!" Kamen ducked his head, shielding his face with his hand. "My mom's here to try the dildo iron maiden. I have to leave."

"Kamen . . ." Dave said warningly. "She's allowed to have a sex life too."

"*Don't say those words!*"

"Be good, buddy. Say hi."

Kamen turned again and waved tentatively.

Mrs. Pell held up a large, lumpy black bag, cupped her other hand to the side of her mouth, and yelled over the music, "They said it was bring your own dildos, but they didn't say how many to bring. And they mentioned there were adaptors so you could attach just about any kind, but I figured suction cup bases were probably ideal, right?"

People were starting to stare. Kamen faced us again, cheeks flushed. "My mom brought her own dildos. She's got a *bag* of dildos. I'm never gonna—never gonna be okay again."

"Shhh." Dave rubbed his back. Looked at the rest of us. "I'm gonna take him to get some water."

He and Gould shepherded Kamen out of the line and toward the dry bar.

Drix watched them leave. "What's going on?"

I squeezed his hand. "Kamen's mother is also in the scene. Occasionally they run into each other. They get along very well in the vanilla world, but Kamen has a hard time when he's forced to confront that his mother is a sexual being."

When we reached the front of the line, BellaSade gave us a bored look.

"Welcome," she said flatly. "You are aware that the dildo iron maiden is bring your own dildos?"

We held up our bag of dildos.

"And that there are no actual spikes or blades of any type allowed in the iron maiden?"

"Did somebody really try that?" Drix asked.

BellaSade nodded tiredly. She gestured to the open chamber. "As you can see, the iron maiden has steps inside so that you can impale yourself on different dildos on different levels. Any projections near the eyes or ears must be no longer than four inches and completely blunt. This is the signal hole." She indicated a large hole in the side of the iron maiden. "If you need to safe signal, use that. That—" She pointed to another large hole in the back "—is the grope hole. Please do not signal through the grope hole or grope through the signal hole."

"We wouldn't dream of it," I promised.

"Because the dildo iron maiden is in high demand, the time limit for scenes is one hour. You are responsible for wiping out the inside of the iron maiden with disinfectant when you're done." She stepped back. "Have fun and enjoy the dildo iron maiden."

"All right." I turned to Bowser and Drix. "Let's mount our phalluses."

"If I had a dime . . ." Drix opened the bag, and together we decked the iron maiden with dildos.

We placed a large VixSkin dildo right about where my ass would be on the lowest level. A thicker ejaculating dildo even with my mouth, with the pump outside so Bowser and Drix could control it.

We'd filled it with a faux cum called Nut Butter, which, according to the package, smelled and felt just like the real thing. We situated a vibrating phallus right around where my groin would be. The rest of the dildos we placed in various holes without much rhyme or reason.

Drix handed me the lube. Gave me a quick kiss, right there in front of everyone. I could feel Bowser watching. "Get on in."

I climbed into the chamber, the tips of the dildos brushing against me. Bowser shut the door with a very Mario "Here we go!"

There was a click as the doors latched.

It was . . . dark. And it smelled like disinfectant. Every time I moved even an inch, a dildo jabbed me somewhere. I undressed and left my clothes on the floor. Climbed onto the first step. The ejaculating dildo poked my face. The VixSkin cock rubbed against the backs of my thighs.

"Miles?" Drix's voice came through the grope hole.

"Yeah?"

"You doing okay?"

"Yep."

"Awesome. Get your ass lubed, and then back it up onto the VixSkin, okay?"

Before I could open the lube, another voice drifted through the signal hole in the side of the iron maiden.

"Miiiiiles," Dave whispered. "We don't want to disturb your headspace. We just want you to know how impressed we are."

Then Kamen's voice: "Yeah, dude. You are a strong, confident man, and you are *inside* that iron maiden."

"Could you guys get the fuck out of here?" I said. "I'm trying to do sex things."

Some laughter, and Gould's voice reached me next: "Whatever you do, don't signal through the grope hole."

I heard Kamen dissolve into laughter again.

"And we look forward to a full report later," Dave said.

Slowly I stuck my arm out the signal hole and lifted my middle finger. There was more snickering, and then they were gone.

The dildo iron maiden was . . . not a disappointment, exactly. But being in a public place, even if I couldn't see the public, felt odd. Knowing there was a line waiting for me to finish, and being able to hear Skrillex pumping in through the speakers—it was all a bit much. Bowser and Drix took turns groping me through the hole and ordering me to stand on this step or that step and mount the corresponding dildo. They had brought the human cattle prod, which they put to good use—though they made me signal after each shock, which also took me out of the scene.

They tried a little dirty talk, but it was hard for me to hear them, and—I thought—tough for them not to be able to see my reactions.

Eventually I was fucking myself on the VixSkin dick while I sucked on the ejaculating dildo. Drix zapped my ass with the wand, making me clench like crazy around the VixSkin, and I came with Bowser pumping Nut Butter down my throat.

I swallowed the last of the Nut Butter, still surprised by how relatively boring the whole scene had been.

When they let me out, we took our dildos and put them in a bag for cleaning. Wiped down the iron maiden. Headed to the bar.

Dave was there, but I wasn't sure where the others were. I saw Kamen disappear into Refinement with a very short companion who could only have been Ryan. And eventually I spotted Gould by the door, talking to Kel. As I watched, Kel leaned forward and kissed Gould's forehead tenderly.

I turned to Drix, but he was talking to Dave. So I slid over to the stool beside Bowser.

He nodded in the direction of Chaos. "Iron maiden not as exciting as you'd hoped?"

I always forgot how well he could read me. "Could have been better. But thanks for trying it with me."

He nodded and sipped his soda.

"I hope you don't think I'm using you," I said after a moment.

"This is what I like to do, Miles. I like to mentor. You're a lot of fun, but you're not my only sub. So don't worry."

Wow. Okay. Message received.

I couldn't help giving him a wicked smile. "But you've always wanted to see me actually submit."

He shrugged, but I caught a hint of an answering smile. "Wishful thinkin', I guess."

"Why don't you make me? You and Drix? Why don't we do a scene where you force me to take whatever you want?"

"I don't really want to take it. I want you to give it."

What did it mean to give versus letting it be taken? Didn't I get up on Bowser's table and spread my legs when he told me to? Didn't I let him stick needles in my balls and staples in my dick? But part of me understood. I wanted to stop being the know-it-all. Wanted to let myself cry in front of a partner—not just because I was in pain, but because what we were doing meant something to me. I wanted to be shown what I *didn't* know.

"I'm not really sure what you mean," I confessed. "Maybe I've never given that to anyone."

"It's all right." Bowser set his cup down. Nodded toward Drix. "I think you do give it to him. Because he's the right person to have it."

CHAPTER
NINETEEN

A week later, both of them stood on my doorstep for Drix's graduation scene.

My whole body warmed when I let them in. I noticed the black bag in Bowser's hand, and the single-tail whip tucked in Drix's belt, and I smiled. "Is this my surprise?"

Drix smiled back. "Yes. We want to kidnap you and take you back to our lair."

"No, please. Anything but your lair." I stepped forward to kiss him.

"Ah, ah." He placed a hand on my chest. "I didn't give you permission to touch me."

I laughed, a little confused. "Ooh. Big scary dom."

Bowser handed me a folder. "We've put together a dossier of things we might do to you tonight. You don't get to choose *what* we do. But you do get to tell us if any of these things aren't okay."

I took the folder. I'd never seen the two of them like this before. Both so commanding. I didn't think being forced was somehow closer to "real" submission than anything I'd done so far. But I wanted to experience having the control stripped from me, of having both of them call the shots.

"We'll give you a few moments to look that over." Drix clasped his hands behind his back. "And then you're ours."

My stomach twisted. I opened the folder and read through the typed list of activities. I raised my brows at a few of them, but the more I read, the harder my cock got. By the time I looked up at them, I was squirming.

"Anything you can't handle?" Drix asked. "Otherwise you're our slave until dawn."

I smirked. "Is that when you have to get back in your coffin?"

Drix glanced at Bowser. "Did you hear that?"

Bowser nodded. "I heard it."

"Come here, Miles." Drix said it so softly, but the tone was absolutely terrifying.

I stepped forward warily, my breathing rough.

Drix reached out and touched the hollow at the base of my throat. Stroked it until I swallowed.

Fucker ripped my cardigan off. Buttons popping, the whole nine yards. He stripped me quickly, efficiently, until I stood naked in front of them.

Drix stepped behind me. Wrapped the lash around my neck and pulled gently, until my ear was close enough that he could bite it. One of his fangs pricked the cartilage. I leaned back with my head against his chest, and an involuntary whimper escaped me. He tugged the lash, sliding his other hand down my stomach and splaying it just above my groin. "You liked watching me whip Peter that night at the gathering. Didn't you?"

I nodded. The lash tightened.

"Did you imagine it was you?"

"Yes."

"Did you think about me whipping you in front of all those people?"

"Oh God . . ."

"Kneel," he whispered. "Kneel at my feet."

I didn't move. He slipped his pinkie down slightly so that it brushed the top of my pubic hair.

"I said kneel, Miles." His breath was hot in my ear. He moved his pinkie farther down to graze the base of my cock. Inhaled, then nuzzled my temple. "I'm going to whip you. And you're going to love every fucking *second* of it."

My stomach tightened and released, and I struggled to stay upright. "Make me," I forced out. "Make me kneel."

He laughed softly and licked down the side of my neck. When he reached my shoulder, I got a warning scrape of his teeth, and then he plunged them into my skin. I gasped. He twisted the lash so it dug into my neck. With his free hand, he made a fist around my shaft and my balls. He twisted sharply and bit harder, until I felt the skin break.

The pain turned everything white. The lash fell away from my throat as I slid to my knees. He knelt with me, keeping me close to him. He put his finger to the throbbing spot on my shoulder and pressed. I choked back a cry, my head falling forward. He removed his finger and showed it to me. The tip was slick with blood.

With his other hand he caught my chin. "Much better," he whispered.

I glanced to the side and caught Bowser's eye. He looked back at me hungrily.

Drix moved fast, slugging me in the abdomen. It knocked the wind out of me. Bowser stepped forward and shoved my shoulders down. Placed his shoe on the side of my head, forcing my cheek against the carpet. I remained there, breathing hard, my ass in the air, my stomach throbbing. I was caught between terror and arousal. Drix's boots came into my line of vision. I swallowed convulsively as I stared at the spikes on the heels. The lash of the whip brushed the floor in front of me.

The tread of Bowser's shoe was pushing hard into my temple. I tried to move my head out from under his foot, but no luck.

Drix slid the lash closer to my lips.

He shoved the toe of his boot under my cheek, so that my head was clamped between his foot and Bowser's. I grunted. He pulled it out again and angled it, bringing one of the curved heel spikes closer and closer until it touched my lower lip. I stopped breathing. He used the spike to push my lip downward. "Lick," he ordered.

I licked the spike, pressing my tongue against the point.

"Mmm, he's a good little pain slut," Bowser said.

My shoulders were starting to ache. Drix withdrew his boot and drove the toe into my stomach. I struggled to inhale. "Keep him in place. I want to whip him."

Bowser increased the pressure on my head, and Drix moved around behind me. "His cock's already hard," Drix said conversationally. "Miles?" He nudged my thigh with the toe of his boot. "Hold your balls out of the way."

I reached slowly between my legs, supporting my weight on my shoulders. Took my cock and balls in my hand and pulled them forward.

Crack.

The lash fell so hard and so fast that I jumped. The pointed leather tongue left a slash of fire across my left thigh. I swiped my thumb over the head of my dick, pushing pre-cum down the shaft. The whip cracked again, and pain ripped across both cheeks. Drix wasn't holding back the way he had at the Dark Ravens meeting—these were full-force blows.

"Spread your legs," Drix ordered.

Shaking with the effort of controlling the pain, I moved my legs farther apart. The next blow landed before I was done, the lash catching the inside of my left cheek, just below my asshole. I bit my tongue and stifled a cry.

I heard the jingle of a belt buckle. Bowser lifted his boot from my head. Grabbed me by the shoulders and pulled me up onto my knees. He undid his fly and yanked his dick out. Pressed my face into his groin until his cock touched the back of my throat, making me gag. His pubic hair rubbed the tip of my nose raw as he thrust into my mouth over and over.

The whip cracked again. Then again. Tears streamed from my eyes, but I forced myself to keep my ass out. Another lash, and my skin felt dangerously close to splitting.

Drix placed his hand on my back. Stroked gently for a moment while I struggled to catch my breath around Bowser's cock. Then he stepped back and threw sidearm again, catching me diagonally across both cheeks.

I heaved, releasing Bowser's dick and going down to all fours. Bowser moaned, rubbing my scalp roughly with one hand.

"Kneel up," Drix said softly.

I rose slightly, straightening my back and bracing my hands on Bowser's thighs as he went back to fucking my face. Drix threw the whip so that the tip of the lash struck my left shoulder. I tensed, gulping, and the movement of my throat sent Bowser over the edge. He came hard just as Drix dealt a matching blow to my right shoulder.

Bowser withdrew. I swallowed.

PAIN SLUT

Drix ran the whip down my back. I felt hyperalert, my mind working frantically to process the pain and to anticipate what might come next.

His fingertips moved in light circles over my nape, and I slowly calmed.

Bowser had made his way unsteadily toward the gear bag. "We brought something to decorate your cock." He held up a cock cage. Stainless steel, three bands. The middle band had six sharp points that could be screwed progressively tighter. And at the top of the cage was a urethral plug.

I moaned, wishing I could beg for mercy even as my cock swelled at the thought of more pain.

"And look what I made." Drix held up black leather gloves. The palm sides glittered with tiny spikes.

Bowser sent Drix into the kitchen for some ice, and they held the cubes against my balls until my erection wilted.

Drix put on a vampire glove and pulled a small vial from the bag. Cinnamon oil.

Drix took the cock cage from Bowser, dipped the urethra plug into the diluted oil, then snapped his fingers and beckoned me over. I crawled to him. Knelt up, spread my legs. I was still breathing hard. He stroked my cheek for a moment with the gloved hand. The tiny needles scraped my skin, made me sigh with pleasure. He got on the floor in front of me, opened the cage, and set my cock inside it. I yelped, jerking. The metal was *freezing*.

Drix flashed his pointed teeth. "We kept it in a cooler on the way here. Little chilly, huh?"

"You bastard. I think you should—"

"Uh-uh-uhhhh. You're not in charge tonight, Miles." He scratched my scalp gently with the glove until I moaned. He hooked two fingers of his bare hand around my lower lip and ran them back and forth along the edges of my teeth. "Are you?" He took his fingers away and kissed me softly.

"No," I whispered as he fastened the cage around my cock.

I don't have a choice.

It felt fucking amazing.

The cold metal made me shiver. I winced as the spikes in the central band dug into my shaft. Held my breath as the tip of the plug pressed against the slit. "Get ready," Drix warned.

He began to push the plug into my cock.

There was a sharp pain, then an ache that went on and on as the plug was forced down my urethra. The cinnamon oil started to burn.

And burn.

I grabbed his wrist, breathing through my teeth.

I'd done chemical play with almost everything in the book: gingerroot, ginger extract, peppermint oil, toothpaste, seven varieties of hot sauce, radishes, hot pepper soap plugs, you name it. The only thing that burned worse than cinnamon oil was Spicy Sam's Wowza! Ghost Pepper Sauce (Now with twenty percent more Wowza). I squirmed, arching my back in an effort to take my mind off the pain. I had to piss, had to come, had to escape . . .

Bowser knelt beside us and screwed the cock cage's spikes tighter and tighter. I opened my mouth and squeezed my eyes shut. Bowser tightened each spike until it dug into my shaft. At first the pain was too big to process, and then slowly I began to feel the gut-wrenching sting of each individual spike.

"Get up," Bowser said with a hearty slap to my ass.

I couldn't see anything through the tears. My stomach churned, the back of my throat ached. I tried to climb to my feet, but stumbled.

Drix caught me.

I exhaled in a shuddering whoosh. He held me tight against him. The glove's points scratched my sweat-drenched skin, and I clung to him, letting out harsh, wet breaths as the cinnamon oil continued to sear the inside of my dick. My sobs didn't even sound like me. I flexed my legs, trying to press them together. I was vaguely aware of Drix murmuring something, but my hips were jerking involuntarily, my shoulders tense and my throat tight, and I couldn't pay attention.

"Miles," I heard him whisper. "Miles, it's okay."

Drix passed the ungloved hand down my back and around, and then slowly gripped my balls. He squeezed. I clenched my hands into fists, still holding him. He brushed his lips over my nape and then sank his teeth into the soft skin there. My cock tried to harden again as his teeth pricked me. But as it rose, the spikes plunged into the shaft, and I gripped Drix with all my strength. The burn from the oil and the pain of the spikes eclipsed every other thought. I was almost relieved when he pulled me down onto my stomach over his lap.

I couldn't tell what he was doing, but after a moment he rubbed a slick finger over my hole. Then pushed it inside. The burn started a second later. His finger was coated in oil. He added a second finger and spread the oil inside me, thrusting until it felt like he was fucking me with fire. I choked and panted. This was what I needed. What I had needed my whole fucking life. To hurt for someone I loved.

Drix shifted me over his lap and smacked my ass with his bare hand. Did it again.

Oh hell no.

"What do you think?" I could hear the amusement in Drix's voice. "Too juvenile?"

I couldn't answer. Drix kept swatting me, and then he stopped and dragged his gloved hand over the smarting skin. The points caught on the welts from the whip. He grabbed my left leg and bent it back, using the glove against the sole of my foot.

I grasped his thigh, tensing.

"I don't think he likes being spanked," Drix said innocently to Bowser.

No. No, he does not.

"Hmm," Bowser said.

"You want to try?" Drix asked. He stood, dragging me with him, and all but threw me onto Bowser, who bent me over his hip. His huge hand rose and fell with a speed and strength I wouldn't have thought possible.

I tried to stay still and take it, but almost every part of me hurt, and I was making muffled sounds of pain long before he was done. When Bowser let me go, I sank to my knees, head bowed, waiting for the worst to pass.

They gave me a minute, and then Drix called my name softly. I looked up. Tried to focus. Drix had taken off the glove and was holding something. Thin silver chain . . . talon clamps. I groaned, and Drix laughed. "Come on over here, Miles."

I crawled to him once more. Hesitated only a second before setting my chin on his knee and gazing up at him. He appeared surprised for a moment, and then his eyes filled with wonder, and he stroked my scalp. I closed my eyes. Kept them closed as he pinched my left nipple, rolling it until it was stiff and aching. Then the five sharp conductors sprang shut around it, and I hissed and clutched his leg to keep from pulling away. The talon clamps never got easier to take. The sensation they produced was constant, unrelenting. If it had been a sound, it would have been high-pitched, unbearable. Nails on a chalkboard.

He put the second one on mercifully quickly. I could feel every individual conductor digging in. If I tried to concentrate on the pain on one side, the pain on the other side became even sharper until it pulled my focus.

I opened my eyes, listening to the broken rhythm of my own breath. Drix stared back at me, his expression kind. He leaned forward and kissed my forehead, and that was nearly what destroyed me. The softness of his lips, the love in that gesture. I steadied my breathing and tipped my chin up to kiss him on the lips, my heartbeat echoing through my entire body.

This is for you. For you.

He picked up another set of talon clamps. I winced as he fixed them to my balls, but I didn't cry out. I was slipping into a place where the pain all blended together. Where nothing really mattered but Drix. But every time I started to slip, something pulled me back: the burn in my dick. The talons digging into my nipples, my balls. The welts on my ass.

He and Bowser helped me to my feet. They put Drix's long coat on me and tied it shut, but they made me leave my clothes. They gathered the gear bag and ushered me outside, to Drix's SUV. Opened the door and indicated one of the middle seats.

There was something on the seat. A wooden board with upside-down bottle caps glued to it. Bowser pulled my coat up in the back so that I had to sit bare-assed on the bottle caps. I refused to so much as flinch, but it hurt like hell, all those rough metal edges cutting into my welts. Drix put my seat belt on.

They made me keep my coat open. Drix drove, and Bowser sat next to me and grabbed my balls. Twisted them, pushed at them with his thumb, jarring the talon clamps. The cock cage's teeth dug so deep into my swelling shaft that I started to cry. The burn from the oil dulled as new sources of pain competed for my attention. He used the genital whip on my balls and nipples, right at the base of the talon clamps, and I could see Drix's mouth in the rearview mirror, smiling as he listened to me sob.

At red lights, he'd reach back and play with me too, and all I could do was sit there on the bottle caps with my legs spread and take it. I forced myself to look up so Drix could see my tears. When I did, Bowser gave my balls another lash with the whip, and I let out a strangled scream, my gaze never leaving Drix's. Bowser put aside the whip and wrapped an arm around me, stroking and shushing me. But still playing gently with my cock and balls.

This was it. This was fucking trouble. If we got pulled over, I'd bite my cyanide capsule.

When we reached Bowser's house, they dragged me inside and upstairs. Not to the doctor's office, but to a spare bedroom I'd only seen once, several years ago. There was a double bed in one corner, covered in towels, and there were pulleys and hooks in the ceiling and walls. Several oddly shaped pieces of furniture had been set throughout the room. They led me around by the chains of the talon clamps, making me scream again as they pulled in different directions. Then they were all over me, grabbing my caged cock, slapping my ass, my thighs. Punching my chest and stomach, making the urethral plug shift and sting inside me.

I felt disoriented until Drix started kissing me. Then my whole body seemed to gravitate toward him. My bare skin pressed against the fabric of his black shirt, his tight jeans. I rubbed my cock against his groin, ignoring the pain of the clamps and the cage.

He whimpered into my mouth, but then pushed me gently away and led me to the bed. "I have a surprise," he whispered.

I could hear Bowser across the room, setting up.

Drix opened the cupboard under the nightstand and held something up. "Look at this."

I could only stare.

He had a scold's bridle. Not just some cheap tin imitation of a scold's bridle, but one that actually looked like it belonged in a torture museum.

The metal framework almost resembled a royal crown, and the muzzle had a bit plate that went into the mouth. The bit plate was spiked. "Oh my God," I whispered.

He set it on the night table, grinning. "We thought you'd like it."

I put the tip of my finger against one of the spikes. It was blunted, but still sharp enough to send a shiver through me.

"They won't actually cut if you try to talk." Drix put his hand on top of mine and pushed my finger harder against the spike. I gasped and tensed, my balls pulling tight. "But it'll hurt like hell."

"Put it on," I said impatiently.

Drix reached out and stroked my cheek. Ran his fingers down to the corner of my mouth. "So demanding," he murmured. "Better get it out of your system now."

I sighed and opened my mouth. He put his finger inside, and I sucked on it until he moaned softly, shifting. I placed a hand on the front of his pants and rubbed the bulge there. Scraped my teeth along his finger and sucked harder. "Oh . . ." he whispered.

I flicked my tongue against his fingertip.

"You're distracting me," he said, slapping my cheek lightly with his other hand.

I let go of his finger. Gazed at him.

"Open up." He was soft-voiced. Steady.

I obeyed. The heavy cage went over my head, and Drix eased the curb plate into my mouth. My chest tightened with panic as I felt the spikes. I wasn't sure where to put my tongue to avoid them. Drix proceeded slowly, though, and rubbed the back of my neck for a moment before locking the bridle in place. I moved my head slightly, just to test the weight, but held my tongue still. I glanced up at Drix, who smiled back at me. "Looks good," he said. "Stand up."

He led me over to Bowser, who was sterilizing an anal hook. I watched him through the bridle, my heart pounding. Saliva was starting to drip from the corners of my mouth.

"You know what this means?" Drix asked in my ear. "Means we can do anything we want to you. And you can't scream."

I would have come if the cage hadn't been around my cock, I was pretty damn sure. I drew ragged breaths around the plate, shaking with adrenaline.

Bowser handed Drix the anal hook. "There's bigger balls over there." He nodded at the medical stand.

"That's *definitely* what she said." Drix grinned and walked over to the tray. I watched as he confidently unscrewed the steel ball on the hook and replaced it with a much larger one.

My cock tried to rise.

"We both have shears." Bowser showed me his. "You signal if you want us to cut the rope. Show me the signal to stop."

I held up two fingers.

"What's the signal if you need to stop for a minute and talk to us?"

I held up one finger.

They tied me with my ankles chained to rings in the floor, my arms bound above my head with leather cuffs and rope. Drix hummed softly as he worked, which made me laugh. The sound was muffled by the bridle, but Drix heard it and grinned at me.

I shifted, flexing my arms to feel the resistance from the ropes. I kept doing that, partly for the thrill the pain gave me, and partly to keep my mind off what they were about to do.

They rigged the anal hook to a pulley in the ceiling. But instead of putting the hook up my ass right away, they placed it around my neck. Then they hoisted me onto my toes. Fear flashed through me, and I loved it. They'd adjusted it so none of my weight was actually supported by my neck—the wrist cuffs were keeping me on the balls of my feet. And yet the feel of that metal hook around my throat, the illusion that if I broke position I'd choke myself, gave me a massive adrenaline rush. I squirmed, exhaling against the metal plate in my mouth, dipping my head to make the hook press against my windpipe, and watching my drool puddle on the floor.

Drix took the cock cage off. I sighed with relief and then yelped a second later as the blood rushed back to the spots where the spikes had been pressing, and the cinnamon oil seemed to burn with renewed strength now that the plug was out. He rubbed my shaft gently, and I started to lose myself in the pleasure of the sensation. Bowser's fingers slid along my welted shoulders, and I struggled not to come. I concentrated on the weight of the cage around my head, the sharpness of the spikes against my tongue.

Eventually they both stepped back.

I heard something swish behind me. A cane. Then another swish a few feet away.

They both had canes.

Drix tapped my ass with his—Delrin, fairly thick—and I bowed my head.

The cane whooshed and cracked sharply across both cheeks. I bit back a groan and went as far up on my toes as I could manage, my muscles tensing and releasing. Another thwack, and I jumped, moaning.

The next time I felt the cane, it was against my shoulders. Two warning taps, then a swish, followed by an acid burn that bled into my throat, made my stomach clench and my eyes sting. I panted helplessly, hauling on the ropes just to give myself another sensation to concentrate on.

Bowser tapped me with a much thinner rattan cane, just under my arm. Then he gave me a sharp stroke across the armpit. I hissed, jerking in my bonds. Drix's cane fell again on my ass, and Bowser worked on my upper arms and shoulders. Drix even pulled my cheeks apart and smacked my hole three times with the Delrin tip. I gripped the ropes that bound my wrists, trembling furiously as my hole spasmed.

The blows came fast, and I was never sure what to expect. Drix's strokes were heavy and even; Bowser's were done with more of a wrist flick, the cane's tip often landing before the rest of it. But they didn't alternate consistently, and the unpredictability of who was going to hit me next and where forced me to stay present. To experience, fully, everything they did.

And yet I found that it was possible, to an extent, to choose my focus. I concentrated on Drix's movements. On sensing where he was in relation to me. Recognizing the sound of his cane, the unique style of his blows. I could feel him learning me—playing me like an instrument to produce the sounds he wanted, the jerks and shudders. I was peripherally aware of Bowser and the pain he caused—the way it supplemented, harmonized with what Drix was doing. But I was suffering because of Drix. *For* Drix. And I knew he knew it.

By the time they were done, my entire back and ass were raw, and I could feel blood trickling down my thighs. But it was breaking the connection with Drix that left me stunned, disoriented. Cold and anxious. They untied me, and Drix led me over to the bed. I walked so close to him that I tripped. He bent me over gently and cleaned the broken skin while Bowser set up for the next part of the scene.

"You all right?" Drix asked.

I nodded. Mumbled, spreading my legs to show him my swollen cock.

Drix laughed, making a loose fist around my shaft, then squeezing the base until my breath caught. "Not yet."

Bowser pulled the bench to the center of the room. It looked like a piece of exercise equipment—metal frame, and a black plastic surface angled downward. At the bottom was a footrest.

Drix helped me climb onto the bench, while Bowser sorted through the rope. I winced as my thighs made contact with the plastic. Everywhere Drix touched me my skin was hot and the sting made me shudder and gasp. I felt beyond human. Beyond speech, beyond pleasure and pain both. My body was just chemical reactions. But at the heart of that tangle of chemistry was a reckless gratitude toward Drix. Toward both of them.

I reached out and grabbed his hand. He squeezed me hard. "Signal?" he asked.

I held up two fingers.

"Good deal." He leaned down and ran his lips over my ear. Nipped the lobe, jabbing a fang into the flesh.

I moaned and laughed, my head lolling.

"Bend," Drix said quietly.

I bent at the waist. My ass stuck over the top of the bench, and the skin stretched tight, pulling on the welts. And as I leaned farther forward, the position only got more humiliating—my cheeks parted, leaving my hole completely exposed. But I reached down toward my feet until I was effectively folded in half, my chin touching my kneecaps. Bowser came over and tied me into place, winding the rope around my arms, legs, and the bench. Drix kept a hand on my shoulder, rubbing the sweaty skin between my welts.

Drix's breath was warm in my ear again. "Do you know how bad you're gonna hurt when I'm done with you?" He whispered the words—crooned them, really—like they were an endearment.

I whimpered, running my tongue along the spikes of the bridle plate, wishing those points were Drix's teeth.

Drix knelt next to me. "Oh, shhh, shhhh." Now his reassurance sounded almost like a taunt. That voice. He knew how to do such fucking *worthwhile* things with that voice.

"Here," Bowser said behind me. Drix stepped back. A second later the steel ball of the anal hook pressed against my swollen hole. There was nothing I could do, no way to escape as Drix gouged me with that hook, forcing the large ball into my ass and then pushing the hook in deeper, deeper, until the ball rubbed over my prostate and I jerked.

The thing about anal hooks wasn't the size or even the length. It was the bizarre angle, the unyieldingness of the steel, the pressure that seemed everywhere at once—on my prostate, my bladder, and somewhere deeper, almost in my gut. "Don't come," Bowser reminded me.

Fuck.

Bowser tied the hook to the back of my bridle. Now I had no choice but to keep my head lifted, or I'd pull the hook even deeper into me, increase that terrible pressure.

I love you, I wanted to tell Drix. *I love this. Love being yours.*

Something metal touched my back.

A blade.

The point dug gently into my shoulder, and my cock twitched against my belly.

A second later, the blade trailed down my back. I moaned, my heart going so fast that the unnatural speed of it increased my panic. Bowser was the one holding the knife, I was fairly sure.

He placed it against my throat, and I went perfectly still, my balls aching.

"See, he likes that," Bowser said to Drix. "His eyes go black, and he shakes just a little . . ." Right on cue, I trembled. Bowser pushed the flat of the knife harder against my throat. "But he loves it."

I gasped and flexed my fingers, trying not to come.

A small cut between my shoulder blades. The slightest thread of blood, running toward my neck. Then the swipe of an alcohol pad, a brief sting, and Bowser's hand steadying me as I continued to shake.

Drix's fingers traced circles on the small of my back. "Fuck yourself," he said quietly. "With the hook."

I bobbed my head, pulling the hook deeper into my ass. Drix knelt beside the bench. He reached between my torso and thighs and yanked my cock out to the side. I whimpered and kept nodding. His mouth closed around the head, and he sucked, lapping the slit with his tongue and humming gently. Sweat poured off me as I continued to move my head, the hook rubbing against my prostate. The blade of the knife swept lightly through the slickness in the small of my back.

Then Drix dug one fang into the slit of my dick, and I came. The sort of orgasm I'd never even dreamed of—a fit of hysterical pleasure, an absolute detonation of my senses.

I laughed for about five minutes when it was over. Kept snickering as they undid the ropes and removed the bridle. They slid the hook gently out of my ass. They never let me feel alone—one was always touching me, whispering words I was beyond understanding. Drix lifted me off the bench and carried me to the bed. Wiped my face with a tissue and rubbed the marks the bridle had left.

"We're not quite done." His voice was gentle. He waited, as though expecting me to protest. When I didn't, he stood and left me there on the bed.

I panted, suddenly afraid again. Now that I wasn't aroused, I hurt in a way that was so shocking, so constant, that it made me feel fragile and sick. Unprepared to defend myself against whatever came next, but also unsure how to pick myself up, how to take care of the damage that had been done. I wanted to lie here until the sensation subsided. I'd never seen pain as an enemy before. It was always something I sought, always something I couldn't get enough of. My ability to absorb it, to find it inadequate, to triumph over it, had long been a source of pride.

I opened my mouth to safeword. No fucking more of this. But I'd never safeworded before, and I didn't want to now.

I closed my eyes. Inhaled slowly. *You can take it. It always fades. It won't kill you.*

It was supposed to be Drix's choice, not mine. I *wanted* it to be his choice.

I heard Drix rooting around in the gear bag, and my heartbeat went weak. My eyes prickled, and I fought a rising panic.

No. This needs to be my choice. I just don't know how to make it.

Maybe crying would help. I saw guys cry in videos—*really* cry, not just dry sob the way I sometimes did when the pain overwhelmed me. I'd always felt smug and superior, knowing I'd never need that intense emotional release. If I could get them to stop without actually *asking*, then I didn't have to make the decision. I could tell them later that I was fine, that they shouldn't have stopped.

I felt so fucking *frustrated*, so fucking lost.

Talk to him. You know the drill. If you're having trouble, talk *about it.*

Out of the corner of my eye, I saw Drix return with a small wooden paddle. I buried my face in my arms and gripped the bedspread. A wooden paddle wouldn't have been a big fucking deal at all, except that it would be on top of the damage from the cane. Drix sat on the edge of the bed. Placed a hand between my shoulders. I flinched.

"Are you okay?"

"I want to stop." The words came so easily, I wasn't sure at first I'd really said them.

But Drix put the paddle down and pulled me up into a hug. "Okay," he murmured against my neck. I was too exhausted to resist the comfort. And I had no desire to resist it. I pressed against him, hugging him back. He seemed completely unfazed by the blood on my legs and shoulders. Bowser came in a moment later.

I tried to get up.

"Miles," Drix said in my ear. "It's okay. It's okay now. Lie down."

I did as he said, my body softening under his touch. I clutched at his sleeve, and he leaned in for a kiss.

"You're amazing," he whispered over and over. "I mean it. You are."

Bowser watched us for a moment, then left quietly. I heard water running in the bathroom as I lay with Drix, listening to his heartbeat.

Eventually he carried me into the bathroom and set me in the tub. The water was warm and up to my neck and felt more luxurious than anything I'd experienced up to that point in my life. My welts stung, but only for a minute. Drix wet a cloth and washed me. I could see a little blood in the water. Could feel the places where the skin was broken. I sat limp, my eyelids nearly too heavy to hold open.

"You look beautiful," Drix whispered. "All bruised like that."

I snorted.

"I mean it."

"You . . ." I struggled to get the words out. "*Thank* you. Both. For . . . doing this for me."

"What do you think?" Bowser asked me. "Does Drix pass?"

I smiled, letting my eyes fall shut. "Yes."

Bowser knelt by the tub. "Then I now pronounce you dom and sub. You don't need me anymore."

"Shut up." I cracked an eye open. "I'll still see you around."

He placed a hand gently, briefly on the back of my neck, and smiled. "Maybe so."

I wasn't sure what exactly happened after that. I remember waking in the night in the guest bed, curled against Drix. Everything ached. I could smell antibiotic cream and felt gauze taped to a few spots on my shoulders and thighs. Could hear Bowser snoring down the hall in the master bedroom. I watched Drix sleep for several minutes. I was so content, so relaxed. I wriggled closer to him, and his arm tightened around me.

"You okay?" he whispered.

I kissed his cheek and drifted back to sleep.

CHAPTER
TWENTY

T he next day, at home, I stared at my naked body in the mirror. At my bruises, my welts, my swollen lips. At all these things I'd craved for years. That I thought were part of an identity that made me truly unique. An identity I'd celebrated and advocated for and educated people about. But right now, I didn't feel proud at all. I felt sick.

I'd been fine when Drix had dropped me off. A little tired and depressed, but that was understandable after a night of intense play. He'd asked about a hundred times if I was all right, and I'd thought I was being honest when I said yes.

But now that I was alone, everything seemed strange.

I ripped the gauze pads off my shoulders and ass and studied the deeper wounds, the ones that were dark with dried blood.

The problem with the BDSM community was that in an effort to rebrand itself after centuries of bad press—to prove that its participants were mentally stable, fun-loving, communicative, "just like everyone else"—we'd failed to take into account what I'd once told David. That the kinky world was comprised of people. And a lot of people are fucked up.

It was definitely not normal to want to be hurt as much as I wanted to be hurt. I looked in the mirror, and I saw a sickness, and I saw all the ways that sickness might be transferred to my son through me, and I wanted to die. Or just . . . to never have been born. Or to have been born vanilla. Maybe that was less melodramatic.

But I wanted to be melodramatic. I wanted to scream and break the mirror. Was there anything I could do to make these bruises heal faster so I could be clean, start again?

"We need more non–self-loathing masochists," Kel had told me the night I'd gotten my cigarette burns at Riddle.

Well too fucking bad. Sometimes I did loathe myself, because I was human, and I wasn't going to pretend to have some cornucopia of self-esteem just so I could be a shiny ambassador for the BDSM world.

How my friends thought I could do the Hymland College talk was beyond me. The last thing young adults needed was my influence. I'd been those college kids once. Throwing around terms like "sex positive" and "RACK" and "safe space." I'd believed so thoroughly that I could do good work as a queer masochist. That I could be a role model.

But I had loved last night so much.

I touched a bruise on my chest. Definitely time to go for the full melodrama. Drix had called my bruises beautiful. Which gave me this unbelievable peace and pride. Made me feel like someone extraordinary.

But *why* did he think I looked beautiful when I was hurt? Was it only because I liked it? Or would he like it even better if I was unwilling? Helpless? Sadism and masochism *were* disorders. Years ago, I'd read all kinds of shit about it. Treatment. Reconditioning. Helping people like me lead "normal" lives. One site I'd visited had said that sexual masochism usually impaired an individual's ability to function. Was that true? How did I know the difference between sexual fantasies—which I had *frequently*—and an obsession that impaired my ability to function?

I pressed another bruise. I needed to talk.

And I knew who I needed to talk to.

"So," I said. "I've called this emergency meeting of the Subs Club because I'm having an identity crisis."

I sat with Gould beside me and faced Dave and Kamen across the table. The table was covered with pink-white petals from a bouquet of shedding flowers in a vase. I focused on the petals and forced myself to speak.

Kamen was tuning his guitar. Gould was skewering petals on a toothpick. Dave was watching me.

Kamen positioned his fingers on the neck of the guitar. "We're listening, dude."

"I, um . . . did a very intense scene last night."

Gould and Kamen both looked up.

"And it was . . . good, but . . ." I really didn't know how to explain this. "Okay, better than good. Beyond reason."

"But?" Gould said.

"But I just don't see how masochism can be normal."

Dave cocked his head. "Of course it's not normal."

"What?"

"It's a diagnosable disorder. It's in the DMV-4 or whatever."

"*DSM*," Gould said.

Dave nodded. "That too."

I'd been hoping for something more along the lines of, *It's totally fine, Miles. You're a special butterfly.*

Dave continued, "Masochism's not normal. Neither is me shitting in a child's potty-chair so that my partner can get off on humiliating me. Pretty much everyone has some kind of disorder. It doesn't mean we're bad people."

Kamen nodded. "Like how Gould can't watch NBC because it's an odd number channel."

"Exactly." Dave swept his hand toward Gould. "And look how cool Gould's life is, aside from the fact that he can't watch *The Voice*. Which is probably a good thing, because the voting on that show is a travesty." He shook a fist at the heavens. "Amanda Brown . . ."

I sighed. I should have known they wouldn't take this seriously. "But I don't *want* to have a disorder. If I do my weird shit healthily and consensually, then what's the problem?"

"Exactly," Dave said gently. "Your being a masochist doesn't have to hurt anyone but you. And you like when it hurts."

"But it could hurt my child!" I snapped. I didn't even know James yet, but I felt protective of him in a way that was overwhelming, immeasurable.

Dave gave me a strange look. "Only if you, like, throw yourself in front of a bus outside of his kindergarten just for the thrill of it."

I put my head in my hands. They didn't understand. Because they were younger. Because they all had relatively mild kinks. Because their bodies didn't bear evidence for days on end of the things they wanted in the bedroom. Because they weren't about to become fathers. "I don't want him to lose any chance of being normal just because I couldn't be."

"Miles." Dave waited until I looked up. "Your kid is never gonna *be* normal. He's gonna be raised by a pain slut, a six-hundred-year-old vampyre, Lady Bracknell, your very pleasant and surprisingly normal dad—when he's around—and your sister, who, I'm sorry, is six different kinds of certifiable."

"Also there's us." Kamen glanced up from tuning his guitar. "And as a group, we've been banned from two water parks, one bar, and a dog-grooming salon."

Dave nodded again. "That kid doesn't have a fighting chance of blending in. But if you just accept that now, then you can get ready to support him through being the awesome little badass he's sure to be."

It wasn't that simple. How fucking *terrified* would I be to end up with a kid like me? To learn—even if he was of legal age and with someone he loved—that he liked being hurt? I'd never be able to relax.

"Miles," Gould said quietly. "Are you just freaking out because you had fun last night?"

"No. I'm freaking out because I'm terrified about my future and my child's future."

Dave leaned back. "What happened to living in the now because the Dark Ravens think time is a meaningless construct?"

"Fuck the Dark Ravens," I muttered.

"You know what you're gonna do, man?" Kamen came around the table, strumming his guitar. He sang:

"You're gonna go to Hymen College,
"And you're gonna tell the youth
"That being beaten is awesome,
"And that's the goddamn truth.
"And you're gonna keep getting beaten,
"Cuz that's what you like to do.
"But you're not gonna tell your kid

"Until he's old enough to . . . handle it . . ." He kept picking and humming.

Dave bobbed his head in time to the music. "You kinda lost it there at the end, buddy."

Kamen leaned down and banged out a chord in Dave's ear. "It was an artistic choice."

I smiled in spite of myself. "You guys are so weird."

"We're actually way weirder than you," Dave pointed out. "Except in bed."

"Do you spend all day thinking about being hurt?" Gould asked. "Like, how often do you think about it? Every three minutes?"

No. I spent most of my time thinking about fatherhood. My friends. My family. Whether A2A needed a new logo. What I was going to make for dinner. Really, I thought about pain very little, except when I was around Drix, who made me crave it. "I don't usually think about it that much."

"There you go."

"But sometimes I think about it a lot."

Dave shrugged. "Sometimes I spend literally a whole day thinking about a Philly cheesesteak."

"This isn't as simple as you're making it," I argued.

"It's not as complex as you're making it. If you feel mentally ill, then go to a therapist. If not, keep getting beaten by a vampyre."

"I'm not going to Hymland College," I warned. "I really do have to pull back from the public scene."

Dave raised his brows briefly. Sighed. "Fine."

"Why are you pissed at me for having legitimate concerns?"

"Sorry." He didn't sound sorry.

"You're not sorry."

He shrugged again.

Gould glanced at me with a fair amount of sympathy. "It's okay if you don't wanna do it, Miles."

"Yes." Dave shot Gould a look. "Each man must act in accordance with his traitor's heart."

Gould kicked Dave under the table. He was hiding a grin. "Hey. I didn't let you bully me into not playing with GK and Kel. I'm not gonna let you bully Miles either."

Dave got up and crossed behind Gould to throw his arms around him. "I know. You shouldn't." He planted a kiss on the top of Gould's head.

I would never understand those two. Handsy as a couple of newlyweds. As exasperated by as they were enamored of each other. I felt that familiar brush of jealousy. I'd likely never have that level of closeness with any of them. I would always be just a little bit peripheral.

"If I do it," I said slowly, "it'll be my last hurrah. My last contribution to the community."

Dave nodded. "Before you become a father with filthy secrets."

The About Me journals flashed through my mind. Gould's neat handwriting. Kamen's chicken scratch. Dave's undotted *i*'s. And Hal's journal, which I'd never opened.

I could take it out. Read his darkest secret. But I wasn't sure I wanted to know. I liked him as a mystery.

He and I had gotten high together one night, years ago. It was only the second time in my life I'd smoked, and rather than mellowing out, I'd mostly gotten irritable and desperate for the experience to be over. And then later I'd vomited off the front porch.

I kept waiting to remember something from that night, from that conversation. Something profound Hal had told me. In my imagination, he took a hit from the pipe, looked up at me, and said, like, *I'd rather be anything than a caged bird, man.* Something neither of us realized at the time was portentous, but was now imbued with a deep meaning.

But all I could actually remember him saying that night was: *"I'm so stoned,"* and *"Do you think the hobbits ever had sex with each other?"* I also remembered him telling me his parents had been high all the time when he was a kid. I'd said something about how that was sad, and he'd said, *"No, man, it was awesome. They introduced me to my dealer."*

He'd kept the conversation going, even as I'd gotten grouchier and sicker. I had experienced, that night, a little of what my friends seemed to love about Hal. His ability to make you feel like nothing in the world was too bad to handle. Like you were important to this moment, to his story—even if it was a superficial sort of importance.

I'd always thought Hal was the messiest of all of us. The least anchored and the least reliable. But maybe he had always known what he wanted: an easy life, with good friends and good drugs, and every night an adventure that was, at its core, familiar.

CHAPTER
TWENTY-ONE

"Awww, the student post office." Dave pointed. "Doesn't this make you guys miss college?"

"Not particularly." I followed the others up the giant staircase in the middle of Hymland's student center. It had been four days since my scene with Bowser and Drix, and I was still aching pretty badly. But I loved it.

"Well, Miles, you probably didn't do anything in college but study. Some of us had fun."

I gazed over the banister. Students sat in the coffee shop, or stood in line for the post office, or sprawled on the couches in the common area. Actually, college had been fun. It was just that I'd spent most of it with the sense that I was waiting for my life to begin. And now these kids all seemed so *young*.

"I texted Ricky," Gould said. "To see if he was part of this group. He hasn't responded."

"Dude—" Kamen tripped on a step, then steadied himself. "Have you *seen* his updates on Fet? He's getting hot and heavy with someone."

"Wish I knew who." Dave reached the top of the stairs and glanced around. "Why doesn't he tell me these things? He used to come running to me when he got a paper cut. Like I'd think that was super kinky or something."

Gould sighed exaggeratedly. "He's growing up so fast."

I'd expected KSS to meet in a classroom, but they just congregated in the third-floor lounge, where anyone could walk by and see. I sat on a sofa next to Kamen and studied the group. Nine students: six women and three men. They all seemed comfortable with one another—they talked among themselves while Ellie greeted us.

A few more stragglers came in. Just watching the group, it wasn't too hard to pick out who was just here for the novelty of being in a kinky club and who was here because they had a genuine interest in kink.

Ellie finally called the meeting to order and made introductions.

"These guys are all part of a local group called the Subs Club," Ellie said. She turned to us. "You guys want to tell us a little about what you do?"

"Well," Dave said, "mostly we sit around and talk. But we talk about stuff that I think is really important if you're at all interested in a kinky lifestyle."

He went on to explain about the Subs Club providing a place for bottoms to talk openly about rape, assault, and abusive relationships. Listening to him speak, and seeing the connection he had with the students, I realized just how much he'd matured in the years since I'd first met him. He'd been sort of all over the place back then—his stories about kink had all involved strangers and glory holes, or getting drunk and belt-spanked by some random daddy in a leather bar.

And now here he was, talking to college kids about RACK.

All in all, the meeting went well. The students were attentive and receptive and had lots of questions. By the end, I'd shed my nerves completely. I barely noticed the other students who walked past the lounge, and I felt glad, so fucking glad, that I'd agreed to do this. These students were my heroes. They were me six years ago. And while maybe I'd grown jaded since then, Drix was bringing me back to a place where this was all new.

When the meeting was over and we were packing up, one of the women came over and introduced herself to me. "I'm Maya. I'm a freshman."

Maya had a thick cloud of black hair and high, arched brows, and she carried a kraken messenger bag.

I smiled. "Hi, Maya."

"I have a question."

"Okay."

"Um, so when they started this group, there were some people in the area protesting it. And, like, not even because it was a kinky group. I think because, like, people think we're kids. And that we shouldn't know about this stuff yet, or there's no way we can do it safely because we're too young."

"Do you feel too young?" I asked her.

"No," she said sharply, her dark eyes darting. "But I guess I don't know much of anything. Like, how do I find a partner who wants to do these things with me? I have to be twenty-one to go to dungeons. And I hate Fetmatch. It's so creepy. And then . . . how do I know if the fantasies I'm having are regular kinky fantasies, or if I'm f—messed up?"

"There are no wrong fantasies. As long as you act them out consensually and sa—"

"Yeah, I can read all that on the internet. What I want to know is what to do if I'm hard-core and I can't find anyone to be hard-core with me?"

She gazed at me almost defiantly.

"Give it some time," I told her. "I knew I was kinky when I was six. But it was sixteen more years until I could find anyone to play with."

She sighed. "I hate waiting."

"I know." I glanced at the door, where Gould, Dave, and Kamen were talking to Ellie. When I turned back, Maya was still staring at me. I recognized that expression: young Dave. Coming up to me at the munch, complaining that there was no one there he wanted to play with. Bragging that he'd already been fucked by most of the regulars at the leather bar. Looking at me like he was daring me to challenge him but, at the same time, like he wanted to beg me to help him. Guide him through this terrifying world of bruised and pierced people who whipped one another and pissed on one another and dressed in pigtails and diapers . . .

"Can I join your club?" Maya asked quietly.

"Uh . . ." She *was* eighteen.

I dug out a pen.

"I'll give you the website. And you can fill out an application." I wrote down the site for her on the back of a receipt. "Just answer the application questions as honestly as possible. We like having new people join."

She took it. "Thanks, Miles."

"You're welcome. And good luck finding what you're looking for."

She gave me a strangely intimate look. "It's funny that the four of you are guys. Because women get assaulted and abused the most. So maybe you need a female perspective at your meetings."

I was too surprised for a few seconds to answer. "That's . . . a fair point," I said finally.

"I'd like to get involved. I'm not going to be your token girl, though. Just so you know. I don't ever want to be a token girl."

She turned and walked away.

⸻ ⚞▬▬▬ ⸻

"I have an announcement," Dave said a few days later.

The rest of us looked up from the pile of Pixy Stix sugar on the table we were taking turns sucking up through the straw.

"What?" I asked.

Dave passed the straw to Kamen. "I'm giving up my membership to Riddle."

We stared at him.

"Don't all faint on me at once," he said.

"Why?" Kamen asked.

"I just don't agree with how they're doing things." He glanced at Gould. "And I don't mean anything against GK and Kel. We just don't see eye to eye."

"It's fine." Gould sounded like he meant it.

Dave nodded. "I really want to do this kink community-outreach thing. I loved what we did at Hymen. And I want to think about what Ryan said too. About maybe not limiting the Subs Club to submissives and bottoms. So I've been talking with Finger Bang, that women's group uptown. And we're gonna outreach."

"That's great," I said.

Dave gave me a tentative smile. "And we'll approach kink mainly from a queer perspective too. So we help get rid of this idea that BDSM is all straight man doms and lady subs. Because, like, what's the problem when you go to a dungeon? It's mostly straight people. So we'll host our own play parties for queers. And we'll do workshops focusing on lesbian kink, trans kink . . . kink-for-gay-men-who-are-not-leather-daddies."

"Will there still be some leather daddies?" Gould asked.

"Oh yeah. Leather daddies will be welcome. But we'll also discuss nondaddy options for gay men."

"Sweet," Gould said. "Leather daddies are important."

"So." Dave raised his arms. "I am ready to claim my destiny. To be a leader for the nonstraight kinky masses."

"All hail gay kinky Jesus!" Kamen yelled.

We all chanted for gay kinky Jesus.

Dave raised his arms higher. "I shall lead my people into the light. And then I shall be martyred on the St. Andrew's cross."

Gould and I groaned. Dave looked at us. "Too soon?"

Gould shrugged. "Well, no. It's been like two thousand years."

I nodded. "True."

"So I'm good?" Dave asked, his arms still out.

"You're good," I said.

"It's just kind of tasteless," Gould added.

Dave shrugged. "Well, it's Jesus. He'll probably forgive me."

"Quit while you're ahead," Gould suggested.

Dave dropped his arms. "Okay. Anyway, I just wanted you all to know this is my plan. And if you want to help take the Subs Club on the road, I would welcome it."

"I'm in," Kamen said.

Gould nodded. "Me too."

Dave looked at me. "Miles? You're done with all things public?"

I smiled and nodded. "Yes. Unfortunately. But I wish you luck."

Kamen sucked up the last of the powder, then blew the straw at me. "I don't know if you're allowed to have sandwiches anymore at our meetings."

I made a sad face. "Please?"

He studied me. "Aw, okay. I can't stay mad at you."

My phone buzzed. I was still laughing as I took it out.

Cheryl was calling.

I brought the phone into the living room and answered cheerfully. "Hey, Cheryl."

"Hi, Miles."

Something about her voice made my stomach drop.

"Is everything okay?"

She was silent for several long seconds. "I have some bad news."

CHAPTER
TWENTY-TWO

I sat on the couch and gripped the phone as Cheryl explained the situation.

Apparently Britney's best friend went to Hymland. This friend had been Britney's confidante when Britney had been looking for adoptive parents for James, so she had seen photos of me. And she'd recognized me as she'd walked past the lounge during the KSS meeting the other day. Had heard a little of what I was saying to the group.

"I'm afraid Britney no longer feels comfortable allowing you to adopt James," Cheryl said. "I'm so, so sorry."

There were a million things I wanted to say. I'd start with, *My private life is private.* Move on to, *There are laws against discrimination.* But instead I voiced my greatest fear: "Does the Beacon Center think I'm no longer a viable candidate to adopt?"

"No," Cheryl assured me. "We respect what you do in your private time. But this is Britney's choice. If she feels uncomfortable, there's not much we can do."

"Can I talk to her? Try to . . . explain?"

Explain what? That last week you let two men beat you until you bled? That you've tried to quit the lifestyle, but you're addicted to being hurt?

"I'm sorry, Miles. I know this is a blow for you. I can send you other profiles of children who might be a good match." She paused. "I also wondered if you still have any interest in meeting Zac?"

Zac. With his sweet smile and his love for *Le Petit Prince.* But I had two cribs in my nursery and a space mobile. Most of the parenting books I'd read were about raising an infant.

"I am," I said finally, trying not to let my voice shake. "I just . . . I'm not sure if I'd be the right father for him."

"What about a meeting with him to see how you two get along?"

"Can I get back to you on that?" My throat was dry, and I was worried I'd lose it if I stayed on the phone with her. "I'm interested. I just need a little time."

"I understand." She apologized again and said she hoped to hear from me soon.

When I hung up with her, I called Drix. He was at work and didn't answer. So I texted him. Set the phone down. I could hear the others talking loudly in the kitchen, laughing about something.

I debated slipping out the door and going home.

But then I made myself stand and go back to the kitchen to talk to them.

Against my better judgment, I went to my mother's two days later. I found her sitting at the kitchen table with a copy of *The Celestine Prophecy*. My jaw hurt from the tension I'd been carrying since Cheryl's call, and my head was starting to ache.

"You don't look so good, kid," she said.

I didn't speak for a moment. "I got some bad news."

She closed her book. "What is it?"

"I, um . . . I can't adopt James." I barely kept my voice from breaking.

She stood slowly, her hips swaying as she walked over to me, imaginary drink in hand. "Oh, Miles. Ohhhh, Miles. What happened?"

"I don't—" I couldn't figure out what to say.

She guided me into the living room, and we sat on the couch. I took several deep breaths. "I want to tell you something about me. And I understand if you're surprised or you have questions. But you're my mother, and I'd really like to be honest with you."

She clapped a hand down on mine. "Who'd you kill?"

I stared at her hand on top of mine. These moments when she seemed like my best friend were sometimes harder to handle than her moments of cruelty.

I tried to smile. "No one. Do you know about BDSM? Like . . ." What I was about to say made me die a little inside, but I wasn't sure what other reference she'd get. "Like *Fifty Shades of Grey*?"

She narrowed her eyes suspiciously. "I have a working knowledge, yes." She dabbed her forehead with her handkerchief. "You telling me you're an eccentric billionaire with girls tied up in your red room of whatever-the-hell?"

"I'm more like the girl who gets tied up."

She nodded. Put the handkerchief down. "You better grow out of it before your kid comes along."

"Excuse me?"

"Wrap it up. Get your kicks. Then cut it out. And don't come telling your poor mother the details. That's private."

"Mom. I'm . . . not going to grow out of it." I didn't tell her how much I'd been hoping I would. "I'm telling you because I want you to understand me, and I want you to understand what happened. I helped with a discussion at Hymland College. With their kink group. James's birth mom . . . her friend saw me there and told her. And now she doesn't trust me with—with James."

I could only imagine what Britney thought. *Pervert. Psycho.*

Mom stared at me. "So you explain to them you're stopping. You tell them it's not what they think."

"But I'm not stopping."

"Kid, wake up." Her voice was sharp. "You're telling me you'd give up the baby before the handcuffs?"

"No, Mom. You're not listening. *One* person wasn't okay with it. Beacon Center doesn't mind. I might be able to adopt this other boy, Zac, and—"

"Your baby," Mom repeated, her voice soft. "My little grandbaby boy."

This was going far worse than I'd anticipated. "You'll still have a grandchild. I'll still have a son. I could really use your support here."

She slammed her hand on the couch. "Of all the stupid things you've done, Miles."

I couldn't breathe. I heard a door open upstairs. Latin music blared.

Malina pounded down the steps and strode into the living room. She had long, leopard-print fake nails and a yellow crop top.

"What's going on?" she asked.

But Mom didn't look away from me. "To. The. Manor. Born." She put a space between each word. "You think you can go through life doing anything you please without consequences."

"That's not what I think."

"Mama, shut up." Malina sat on the arm of the chair across from us. "Whatever Miles did, it's not worse than shit I've done. So shut up."

Mom didn't speak to either of us. Finally she said, "My auditor's coming. I have to get ready." She got up slowly.

My anger gathered and then boiled over. "You think my heart's not fucking broken? You think I'm not devastated?"

Mom didn't answer. I rose and stormed for the door.

Malina followed. "Will someone tell me what's going on?"

I stopped and whirled. "And you can just quit with the fake accent and the fake nails," I shouted. "Good God, between the two of you it's no wonder I turned out fucked up!"

I left, slamming the door, and drove home.

When I got into my driveway, my phone was buzzing. I figured it was Mom or Malina.

But it was Mrs. Pell, Kamen's mom.

I steadied my voice and answered. "Hello?"

"Miles, honey?"

I forced myself to unclench my aching jaw. "Yeah?" I ran my finger along my jawline and stopped at a small, swollen spot.

"Have you talked to Kamen recently?" Mrs. Pell always sounded a bit like a bird to me. She had a light, scratchy voice and spoke in little staccato bursts, like she was pecking. "I just tried to call him, and the robot woman said the number was disconnected."

I rubbed the swelling. "Oh yeah, that's his new mailbox message. It's him using a voice changer to make his voice sound like the robot woman. If you keep listening, eventually he breaks in with his real voice and pretends to have a battle with the robot woman from which he emerges victorious."

Mrs. Pell sighed. "Oh, when I get my hands on him . . ."

"Yeah. He's—" A sob escaped.

"Miles? Honey?"

Oh, I so could not do this right now. "I'd better go. I have to ... to ..."

"Tell me what's wrong," she ordered.

And for whatever fucking reason, I did. Everything from my dealings with the Beacon Center to the talk at Hymland to the fact that I wasn't allowed to adopt James anymore. When I finished, she was quiet for a few seconds. Then she said, "Miles, there's nothing wrong with what you do. Don't think that for a second."

"I don't." I rubbed my eyes with my fist. "I mean sometimes. But I know, logically ... I'd just hoped my mom would be okay with it."

"It'll be all right, honey. You—"

I hung up. Closed my eyes and rested my head on the seatback. After a few minutes, I went into the house. Walked straight upstairs and flopped facedown on my bed, and let the hours pass.

Drix stood in the doorway to my bedroom. I was in my pajamas, under the covers. I'd had my phone off for two days. An empty box of cracked-pepper crisps was on the night table.

"How did you—?" I started, as he entered the room.

I'd left my front door unlocked. I'd actually left my fucking front door unlocked.

Oups, autant pour moi.

"Get up," Drix said.

"No, thank you."

"Yes. Up."

I just lay there.

"You haven't answered my calls."

I shrugged.

"When's your meeting with Zac?" he asked.

"I haven't called Cheryl yet," I told the ceiling.

A moment later, my phone appeared in front of my face. "Here."

I pushed it away. "I need to do some thinking."

"You need to call Cheryl."

"Nobody believes I can do this. Be a father." I touched the right side of my jaw, where the pain had been steadily growing over the past two days.

"Bullshit. Get up and call Cheryl."

"*You* get up and call Cheryl." My oratory skills had deserted me in this dark hour.

Drix sat on the bed and pried me up. I surprised us both by snarling and lashing out. Then briefly clinging to him. Then shoving him hard. And finally falling completely still.

"*Je suis en disgrâce,*" I said after a while.

"*Vous ne l'êtes pas,*" he replied.

"I didn't know you spoke French."

"I didn't know you were a quitter."

"You don't understand."

"Kamen told me what happened with you and your mom."

I jerked my head up. "How did he know?" I looked away. *Shit.* Mrs. Pell.

"I'm very sorry." Drix sounded sympathetic but firm. "But there's a kid who needs you."

"I know," I whispered.

He softened a little then, and touched my cheek. "It's gonna be all right. I'm not going to let you hang out here alone feeling sorry for yourself anymore."

"Can you stay here?" I asked.

"As long as you need me to."

My throat constricted. "*Ne me blesse pas ce soir,*" I said softly into his neck. I didn't care how pathetic I was.

Don't hurt me tonight.

He seemed to need a minute to work that one out. Then he tightened his arms around me. "No." He kissed my temple. "We can watch a movie, take a walk. Whatever you want. But first you have to call Cheryl."

I called Cheryl and set up the meeting for a week from Wednesday.

Drix fetched me some clothes from the closet and threw them at me. "Dress."

I dressed slowly. "What's been going on with you?" My attempt at casual communication sounded stilted even to me.

He sat on the edge of the bed and smoothed his hands over his thighs. "We're setting up a crowdfunding campaign for the coven. So we can become almost like a church—supported in part by people who want to give."

"Whoa." I pulled on my socks.

He hesitated. "My plan is to quit my job and devote more time to the Dark Ravens. I want to teach workshops that will help people communicate with their bodies and maximize their energy."

"So what, like, vampyre yoga?"

He laughed. "No. Just, like, understanding how energy flows through the body. Helping with mobility, flexibility, feeling comfortable with our bodies . . ."

"That is most certainly vampyre yoga."

"Maybe so."

I got a terrible sinking sensation. He'd seemed so on the ball. A good job, an actual house with furniture. Why? Why had I ever thought he and I could be parents, when we were both so fucking far away from grown-up? "You want to crowdfund your coven so that you can teach yoga instead of working?" I was aware I was already picking the worst way to say this.

"I'll be working. Teaching. Not just coven members, but outsiders who want to learn more about the lifestyle. Kind of like what you and your friends are doing."

"Are you sure you've thought this through?"

His expression was growing warier. "Yes, Miles. Being a PI's not cutting it, so I'm going to try focusing on what I find truly rewarding. What's the problem?"

Our lifestyles shouldn't be our lives.

That was the problem I sometimes had with the Subs Club. It asked me to think too often about a part of my identity that really shouldn't matter. My identity as a business owner, a friend, a son, a brother, a father . . . those were so much more important than my identity as a masochist. Years ago, I'd thrown myself into kink as though it were the only really important thing in the world. The only way for me to define myself. I didn't want Drix to make the same mistake with the vampyrism.

But it wasn't just that. It wasn't even mostly that. I was jealous and in awe that he could do this without a year's worth of planning. Without fear or regret or endless drafts of his resignation letter. That he was *truly* brave, truly skilled, truly kind—always and completely. Instead of faking those qualities on occasion, the way I did.

"I just don't know if it's the best idea," I told him.

He gazed at me calmly, but his body was tense. "Did I ask you if it was the best idea? Or did I tell you I'm doing it?"

"I'm only saying—"

"Why are you so afraid of being happy?" he demanded.

"We can't just do whatever feels good!" I snapped. "We need, as humans, to work to build some sort of stability, some—some measure of agreed-upon normalcy. Anarchy is not the answer."

"You think you doing BDSM or me doing vampyre yoga is *anarchy*?"

"You have a stable job. Why would you throw that away?"

"Because it's not making me happy." He said it patiently, almost condescendingly. I knew I was on dangerous ground.

I couldn't admit what was really going through my head—that his stability was important to me because I couldn't stop picturing our future together. Couldn't help wanting him to be around forever.

"Miles," he said unsteadily. "I want to be with you. I do. But you've got to get over this—this thing where you have ideas about who people should be, and you blame them if they don't fit your standards."

"No," I snapped. "*You've* got to understand. I had a *son*. I knew his name. I bought him toys and a crib, and I looked into fucking preschools even though that's years away, and I've pictured what he'll look like and what his voice will sound like . . . and now he can't be my kid."

"I understand all that. But what does that have to do with supporting me? I want to be your partner. Not just your—your nanny or whatever."

"Because I *am* going to be a father, even if it's not to James. And I need to put my kid first. If I have a partner helping me, I want him to be someone with a legitimate job. I need some stability."

He stared at me. Shook his head. "Wow. I don't even know if you hear yourself right now."

I didn't answer.

"So I'm gonna go." He rubbed his forehead with the heels of his hands. "And this is probably good-bye for a while. If not . . ." He blew out a breath. "Whatever. I need to leave now."

I stood there, still angry and confused.

And I let him go without saying good-bye.

CHAPTER
TWENTY-THREE

I kept hoping Drix would relent and contact me, give me a chance to apologize. But he didn't. The next night, Mrs. Pell showed up at Gould and Dave's while we were all hanging out.

She breezed through the front door, hugged us all, and then zeroed in on me. Her frosted blond hair hovered around her head in stiff curls, and her low-cut shirt showed the tops of her extremely large breasts. "Miles, honey," she said. "Your mom's on her way over. We're all going to have a little talk."

"Wait, what?" I stood.

"I invited her to talk to us."

"Oh God," Kamen said beside me.

I whirled on him. "Did you—"

Mrs. Pell snorted. "No, honey, Kamen had nothing to do with this."

"I really didn't," Kamen said pleadingly to me.

We heard a car pull up out front. Mrs. Pell headed for the door. "That's probably her."

The four of us followed her.

"I don't understand what's going on," I said.

Mrs. Pell glanced over her shoulder. "You three, stay here," she told the others. "Miles, come on outside."

Dave and Gould stopped in their tracks. But I could hear Kamen behind me as I followed Mrs. Pell out the door.

She walked to the edge of the porch. "I just have a thing or two I need to tell your mother."

"Please don't . . ." But Mom was getting out of her car. I thought about warning her it was a trap, but I was curious to see how this would go down.

"I'm so sorry," Kamen whispered to me.

"Mrs. Miles," Mrs. Pell called as Mom approached.

"Loucks," I corrected quietly.

Mom looked confused. "Why'd you call me here? You said Miles needed my help?"

Mrs. Pell nodded. "I'll only take a minute of your time."

Mom stood on the porch in front of us. I thought about bolting.

Mrs. Pell was swift and deadly. "Mrs. Loucks, Miles recently told you something about himself."

No. Oh, no, no, no.

She went on. "From what I understand, you weren't very supportive. So I just want you to know I'm part of the same lifestyle Miles participates in. I consider myself a decent person, and I was able to raise my son to be a gentleman. I have continued to be a good daughter to my parents and a good sister to my siblings and a good friend to the people who need me."

"Mom," Kamen said again.

She didn't break eye contact with my mother. "There's nothing wrong with the lifestyle I live. It's nothing I'll grow out of. And if that girl who got knocked up can't deal with who Miles is, then that's her problem. To withdraw your support now, at a time when Miles needs it, is *not* okay. Do you understand me?"

Kamen and I both stared.

No one talked to my mother that way. It was reasonably awesome. But I couldn't imagine that what followed would be pretty.

Mom held Mrs. Pell's gaze. "I am not failing to support Miles," she said at last, her voice low. "I merely pointed *out* to him that he may need to rethink his priorities now that he's decided to become a parent."

"It's really fine," I told Mrs. Pell. "I don't need her support."

She turned to me. "Honey. Trust me. You do."

"I'm twenty-eight. I don't need my mother's approval for everything I do."

Mrs. Pell faced Mom again. "He was *crying* when I talked to him the other day."

"Mom!" Kamen yelled. "This is totally inappropriate."

"Oh hush up, Kamen."

My mom stepped closer to Mrs. Pell. "It is not your business the way I communicate with Miles."

"It is," Mrs. Pell said. "I care about Miles. I care about all these boys."

"Miles knows that I love him. And he can handle my honesty."

"*Actually*," I said suddenly.

Everyone looked at me.

"Actually, you do make me feel bad sometimes," I told Mom.

Mom pulled out her handkerchief. Wiped her face.

"Not just about this," I went on. "But sometimes the advice you give . . . the way you say things . . . it really hurts me."

She tucked the hankie back in her pocket and studied me.

"I'm sorry," I said. "But it's true. I have done . . . everything. Everything I can think of to try to be . . . *good*, and—and successful, and . . . *prepared*. I have worked really, really hard to make this adoption happen. And I'm . . ." I hesitated. "I'm proud of what I've done, even if you aren't."

She stared for a while. Then her expression softened, and her jaw trembled slightly. "You were always so good with your sister. So sweet."

I thought about that time I'd left Malina on the way to the park. Telling her no one wanted her. Guilt flooded me so fast I felt ill. A bolt could have come down from the heavens, split me in two and left me in flames, and it would have been less than I deserved. "I don't know," I said, quietly enough that I hoped only she could hear me. "I always wish I was better."

She stepped forward, and we stood eye to eye. Then she cupped the side of my face. "You will be a *wonderful* father."

I started to pull away. Stopped.

She dropped her hand from my face and looked at Mrs. Pell. "I love my son," she said coldly. "Don't you ever act like I don't love my son."

Mrs. Pell didn't flinch. "Then don't *you* ever act like you don't love him."

Mom nodded. "I'm sorry," she said to me.

And that was pretty much it. The first time my mother had apologized to me in memory, and all I could do was stand there and gape.

She left almost immediately after.

Mrs. Pell ran her fingers through her hair. "I'd better go too." She turned to Kamen. "I brought brownies. Will you boys eat some brownies?"

"Mom," Kamen muttered. "I can't believe you got involved in Miles's private life. Like, fucked up his whole day and then brought brownies. That's weird."

She straightened her shirt. "I'm sorry, Miles. But it needed to happen."

"It's okay," I told her. "Um, thank you. And . . ." I exchanged a glance with Kamen, then looked back at her. "We will take some brownies."

I drove to the suburbs the next day to apologize to Malina. She waved it off. "*Babi.* I'm doing a lot of stupid stuff right now. I get why you don't like the accent or whatever. But you gotta find yourself in your twenties, you know?"

Apparently.

We went outside and sat on Mom's front step. She glanced at me, looking almost shy. "*Newsies* goes on tour again next year. All I need is an agent and an equity card. And to be a pretty blond white bitch."

"You need me to stand in for Crutchie while you practice?" I asked wearily.

She dug me in the ribs. Froze. "Hey. What's wrong with your mouth?"

"What do you mean?"

"One side is all puffy. And you're making a face like you're dying."

"I have some kind of tension headache or something."

"In your jaw?"

"I don't know. It's a toothache. It'll go away. Shut up."

"You're such an ass. You need to get that looked at."

I thought about my mom's words. "*You were always so good with your sister.*" Malina had been a mystery to me when Mom and Dad brought her home. I'd taken a picture of her for show-and-tell that year. Watched her grow into a wild, dark-haired little girl. She started beating me at video games. Told me I could legally change my name by sending a letter to the president. She wore wedge heels to her eighth-grade dance, then fell and broke her ankle. Drew pictures of the doctors and nurses all over her cast. They thought she was hilarious.

"I'm really, really glad we're related," I told her.

"Aw. Don't get mushy on me, *please*."

"No, but seriously. I've missed you these past few years."

She half smiled, ducking her head. "I've missed you too."

"When you're an aunt, can you fix my kid each time I screw up with him?"

"So, like, when you give him a set of china dolls for Christmas and tell him they're only to be looked at and never played with, I can give him, like, fireworks or something to make up for it?"

"No fireworks. Ever. Please."

"Do you want me to teach him to steal manhole covers? Because the metal industry—"

"Absolutely not." I slung my arm around her.

She leaned against my shoulder. "What will you do if he's a criminal? Or if he likes all those Fast and Furiouses or something?"

I shrugged. "Love him. I hope."

She elbowed me. "Of course you will. You love me."

"Tell me you don't like The Fast and the Furious?"

"Those are, like, my favorite movies, *babi*."

"Something went horribly wrong somewhere." I hugged her close. "But I do love you."

Kamen kept shooting glances at me as we moved both cribs out of the nursery and into the garage. The pain in my tooth was relentless.

"Miles," he said. "You can't wait any longer. You gotta go to a dentist. Like, *now*."

"Well, seeing as there are no dentists open at 7 p.m., I'm going to have to wait." I couldn't keep the irritability from my voice. Every time I moved my jaw, I nearly blacked out from the pain.

Kamen's gaze shifted to the side, then back to me. "You're not gonna like this."

"What?" I shoved the crib farther back against the wall.

"Bobby's has evening hours."

I turned slowly toward him and stared. "What?"

"Bobby's Discount Dentist. They're open till 9 p.m."

I shook my head. "No. I won't."

Kamen studied me for a moment, his expression unreadable. Then he cocked his head. He didn't look at all angry, but he said, "You stuffy little bastard."

I thought at first he was joking. But there was something steely in his gaze I wasn't used to seeing there. "Huh?"

"Why are you too good for everything? Huh?"

"Lay *off*, Kamen. I've had a terrible week."

He nodded. "I know, but, like, be nicer."

I gripped the rail of the crib. "So you're the latest person who's upset with me because I can't be what you want?"

"No." He was still shaking his head. "You *are* what we all want. We love you. And then you push us all away by pretending we're not the people *you* want us to be." He jabbed a finger at me. "But you *love* us. Drix, me, Dave, Gould . . . you love us. If I didn't believe that, I wouldn't be here. And that's why we all put up with your shit."

I swallowed, experiencing something dangerously close to a lump in my throat. "Kamen—"

"Don't make excuses. And don't apologize."

"Then what do you want?"

"Just be nicer, dude. That's all."

"Drix hates me," I said. "You have no idea how badly I screwed up."

"Then fucking apologize to him and don't be a dick again."

Why was that so simple for everyone else?

He pointed through the open garage door, down the driveway. "Get in my car."

I didn't budge.

He moved before I realized it. I'd had no small number of unsolicited hugs in the past few weeks, but this was by far the most physically painful. He didn't let go for a long time. Eventually I stopped trying to get away and leaned forward, my forehead on his shoulder. Brought my arms up and squeezed, as though by holding on to him, I could hold on to some part of me that was always in danger of vanishing. The part that loved people so fiercely and unconditionally that I was terrified to face it.

"Get in the car," he whispered, a lot more gently. He let me go but kept one hand on my shoulder as we walked down the driveway together.

Bobby's Discount Dentist was indeed right beside an arcade. The two buildings even had an adjoining door.

"This feels like a place no one leaves alive," I whispered.

Kamen was texting but looked up. "Do you wanna play Skee-Ball until they call you in? They give you, like, those buzzer things they have at restaurants."

"You're not helping."

But when I was led back to Bobby's actual office, I found it clean and comforting. The walls featured cheerful posters of smiling people—much different from the usual dental office artwork depicting plaque, the minutiae of a root canal, laser-whitening before-and-afters . . .

I was half-afraid that Bobby would use his drill to get revenge on me for the grammar debacle. I made Kamen come back with me. Tried to explain to him, in a whisper, why I was nervous.

He shut me down. "Dude, Miles. Bobby's a really nice guy. I'm sure he forgives you."

Everyone was forgiving me too easily. Except the one person whose forgiveness I needed most.

Why, why, *why* hadn't I just told Drix I wanted him to do whatever made him happy?

The procedure was relatively simple. I was given lidocaine, which made me not just numb, but woozy as fuck. Then came the draining of the apparently massive abscess that had formed in the back of my mouth. Followed by some kind of special rinse, which I couldn't swish around because I was so numb, so most of it just dribbled out the side.

I felt thoroughly wretched, though the pain improved pretty much instantly.

Bobby went off to get me a sucker, and when he came back into the room, Drix was with him.

I thought at first he was an illusion—some side effect of the anesthetic. But then Kamen said, "Oh, hey, Drix."

"Hey." Drix was looking at me.

"What...?" I started. But there was a wad of cotton in my mouth, and it was not helping the drool situation.

Kamen squeezed my shoulder. "I called him and told him you were here."

"You did?" I mumbled.

"Yeah. I maybe made it sound worse than it was. Like your tooth was falling out and there was blood everywhere." He shrugged and addressed Drix. "He really was hurting, though. Look how pathetic he is. Don't be mad at him."

Drix sighed. Leaned down, in front of Bobby and everyone, and kissed my head.

"You...I'm..." I searched for the words I wanted.

"I'm here," was all he said.

He helped me to the waiting room, where Bobby charged me Mexico prices.

"You go home with Drix," Kamen told me at the door. "I'll get your prescription filled if I can find anywhere that's still open."

"Tha' you," I mumbled.

He just waved me off.

I let Drix lead me to his SUV.

He shot me a mild glare as he started the car. "You do look pathetic."

"'M sorry." I leaned against the window. "For everything."

"Leave my heartstrings alone, you wretch."

He drove in silence. I tried not to drool. Finally I took the cotton out of my mouth. Not sure where to put it, I stuffed it in my pocket.

"I was not good to you," I said as we passed A2A.

"You hurt my feelings," he said. "Pretty damn bad."

"I'm sorry," I said again.

We pulled into his driveway a few minutes later.

"I'm a mess," I admitted.

"I know." Drix reached over and gently cupped the nonswollen side of my face. "I'm gonna take good care of you."

CHAPTER
TWENTY-FOUR

Z ac's foster mother, Dana, was tall and thin, with long brown hair, tired eyes, and a bright smile. We met at Mel's Sandwich Shop, and Dana bought everybody milkshakes, despite my and Drix's protests.

Zac was . . .

I didn't have words.

Huge, blinding smile. Black fuzz on his scalp. Giant brown eyes. He wore a tiny cardigan, which I appreciated. Khaki pants, and tiny blue Converse knockoffs. He wasn't very focused on me—he was more interested in watching the milkshake blender in action, and in pouring salt into his napkin. But I observed the way Dana interacted with him. How frank she was about the situation, about the fact that I was a potential adoptive parent, and that Drix was my boyfriend.

There was no sense at all that Zac had been coached to give me big orphan eyes or to be on his best behavior to impress me. When Drix took Zac up to the counter to get a drink, Dana was honest with me too. About some of the problems Zac was having with bullies at school. About the dreams Zac had about his mother—he dreamed she was still alive, and sometimes when he woke up, he had trouble distinguishing reality from the dream.

I watched Drix and Zac return with two bottles of juice. For a terrifying moment, I had the sense again that I had misjudged myself. That I was foolish for even thinking I could handle this responsibility. Zac was only five and had been through an event more traumatic than many kids could imagine. What made me think I could keep him safe from a world that was as random in its cruelties as in its kindnesses?

But all that vanished after a few minutes. I could be a difficult person: uptight, obsessive, insecure. But I loved deeply. I worked hard. And I was no stranger to grief.

I could do this.

Zac let Drix pour his juice into a plastic cup. Then he said something in a language I didn't recognize.

Dana caught my expression and smiled. "He's been learning Arabic since he was three. And he speaks some French. He wants to be a translator when he grows up."

"That is incredibly cool," I said.

Zac grinned at me and said something else in Arabic.

"He's asking how you are," Dana told me.

I smiled at Zac. "I'm great. I'm really glad to be meeting you."

Zac turned to Dana. "Where does Miles live?"

"Why don't you ask him?" Dana suggested.

Zac faced me again, squirming in his seat. "Where do you live?"

Uh . . . Does he want a street name, or a type of house, or . . .?

"I live near Brinkley Park. In a—a house."

"Do you know where . . . um . . . where, um . . ." Zac was twisting his shirt in his hand. "Where Kellan lives?"

I glanced at Dana. She nodded. "Kellan's his friend from school. They're both very into spooky stuff. Right?" She ran a hand over Zac's head.

"Spooky stuff?" Drix inquired.

Dana laughed. "They love the vampires and the werewolves and the zombies and all that. Gives me nightmares."

"Not me!" Zac turned to me. "Do you like vamp . . . vampires?"

I bit back a laugh and tried not to look at Drix. "Yeah. I do."

"Do you like zombies?"

"Uh-huh. I mean, in theory. I don't want them eating my brains."

Zac glanced at Dana again. "Can we go to Miles's house?"

She straightened his cardigan. "Today, we're just going to stick with sandwiches."

Back to me. He gazed at me a long while. I felt a warmth toward him that came easily, that didn't scare me at all. He put his finger on the table and pushed, as though the table were a giant button. "Do you think zombies eat your brains to get smarter?"

"It's very possible. I'm not sure why they eat brains. Maybe they're just hungry."

Zac laughed, as though I'd actually made a joke. Something lifted in me at the sound, and I smiled back. I felt Drix's presence beside me, peaceful and sure. If he were to take a picture of me now, I hoped I'd see a real smile. That I'd see somebody who knew he couldn't control the world, but who was starting to find a strange sort of comfort in uncertainty.

Outside, Drix and I accompanied Zac and Dana to Dana's car, and we said our good-byes. Zac hugged me. Which seemed too scary, too trusting, too much like a promise. But I hugged him back and hoped that it wouldn't be the last time.

They left, and Drix and I decided to walk to Dave and Gould's since it was just down the street. I put my hand in Drix's. Poked my back tooth with my tongue. No pain. Drix had taken good care of me.

I turned to him. "Can I use you? Not for the bucket list, but for the really scary stuff? Advice about school and bullies and not eating vegetables?"

He nudged me. "I'm not gonna be much help. I still don't eat my own vegetables. But you can use me for anything."

I closed my eyes for a moment, then made myself say what I really wanted to say. "Do you mind if I love you?"

His smile started slowly and grew. "Not at all. In fact, I'm pretty glad to hear it. Since I'm not altogether un-in-love with you myself."

"Okay." I nodded. "Okay."

He squeezed my hand harder. Until it almost hurt. "Okay?"

"Okay," I agreed. "Then I want to ask you something."

"What's that?"

I stopped walking. "Would you please be there when he comes home for the first time?"

He stopped too. I felt his gaze on me, but it was a few seconds before I managed to look at him. "You're serious?" he said quietly.

I nodded. "I want . . ." *I want Zac to get to know both of us, together. I want him to see our home.* "I want you there."

He stepped closer to me. His head tilted forward, and it reminded me of the night he'd gotten on his knees at Riddle and bowed his head. Like it really did mean everything to him to be able to *give*.

I didn't quite know what all I had that I could give in return.
But I was ready to find out.
"Then I'll be there," he said softly.
It was nice of him to say it, but he didn't have to.
I knew.

RP

Explore more of *The Subs Club* series:
riptidepublishing.com/universe/subs-club

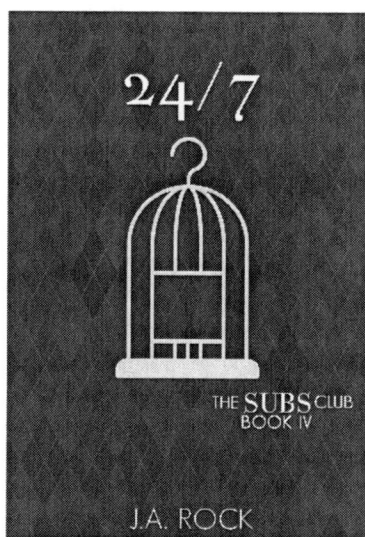

THE
SUBS
CLUB

THE SUBS CLUB
BOOK I

J.A. ROCK

MANTIES
IN A
TWIST

THE SUBS CLUB
BOOK III

J.A. ROCK

24/7

THE SUBS CLUB
BOOK IV

J.A. ROCK

Dear Reader,

Thank you for reading J.A. Rock's *Pain Slut*!

We know your time is precious and you have many, many entertainment options, so it means a lot that you've chosen to spend your time reading. We really hope you enjoyed it.

We'd be honored if you'd consider posting a review—good or bad—on sites like **Amazon, Barnes & Noble, Kobo, Goodreads, Twitter, Facebook, Tumblr,** and your blog or website. We'd also be honored if you told your friends and family about this book. Word of mouth is a book's lifeblood!

For more information on upcoming releases, author interviews, blog tours, contests, giveaways, and more, please sign up for our weekly, spam-free newsletter and visit us around the web:

Newsletter: tinyurl.com/RiptideSignup
Twitter: twitter.com/RiptideBooks
Facebook: facebook.com/RiptidePublishing
Goodreads: tinyurl.com/RiptideOnGoodreads
Tumblr: riptidepublishing.tumblr.com

Thank you so much for Reading the Rainbow!

RiptidePublishing.com

RIPTIDE
PUBLISHING

ACKNOWLEDGMENTS

Thanks as always to Del, for your patience and wisdom. To Dirk, for answering a burning question. Fred and Angie, for the last-minute French lessons. AJ, for the writing company, adoption info, and help visualizing certain . . . choreography. And to Jen, for the wine-fueled blurb assistance.

ALSO BY
J.A. ROCK

The Subs Club Series
The Subs Club
Manties in a Twist (Coming April 2016)
24/7 (Coming June 2016)

Minotaur
By His Rules
Wacky Wednesday (Wacky Wednesday #1)
The Brat-tastic Jayk Parker (Wacky Wednesday #2)
Calling the Show
Take the Long Way Home
The Grand Ballast

Playing the Fool series, with Lisa Henry
The Two Gentlemen of Altona
The Merchant of Death
Tempest

With Lisa Henry
When All the World Sleeps
The Good Boy (The Boy #1)
The Naughty Boy (The Boy #1.5)
The Boy Who Belonged (The Boy #2)
Mark Cooper Versus America (Prescott College #1)
Brandon Mills Versus the V-Card (Prescott College #2)
Another Man's Treasure

Coming Soon
The Silvers

ABOUT THE AUTHOR

J.A. Rock is the author of queer romance and suspense novels, including *By His Rules*, *Take the Long Way Home*, and, with Lisa Henry, *The Good Boy* and *When All the World Sleeps*. She holds an MFA in creative writing from the University of Alabama and a BA in theater from Case Western Reserve University. J.A. also writes queer fiction and essays under the name Jill Smith. Raised in Ohio and West Virginia, she now lives in Chicago with her dog, Professor Anne Studebaker.

Website: www.jarockauthor.com
Blog: jarockauthor.blogspot.com
Twitter: twitter.com/jarockauthor
Facebook: facebook.com/ja.rock.39

Enjoy more stories like
Pain Slut
at RiptidePublishing.com!

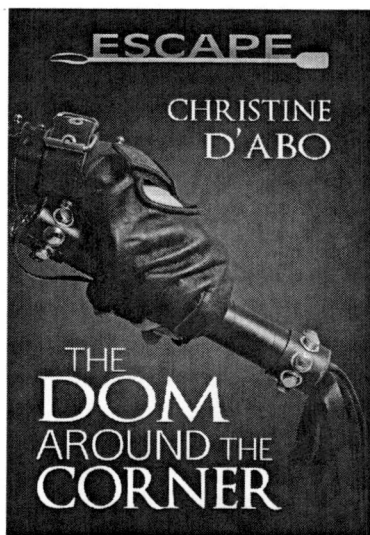

CPSIA information can be obtained at www.ICGtesting.com
Printed in the USA
LVOW10s0751210116

471647LV00004B/93/P